INVARIANT

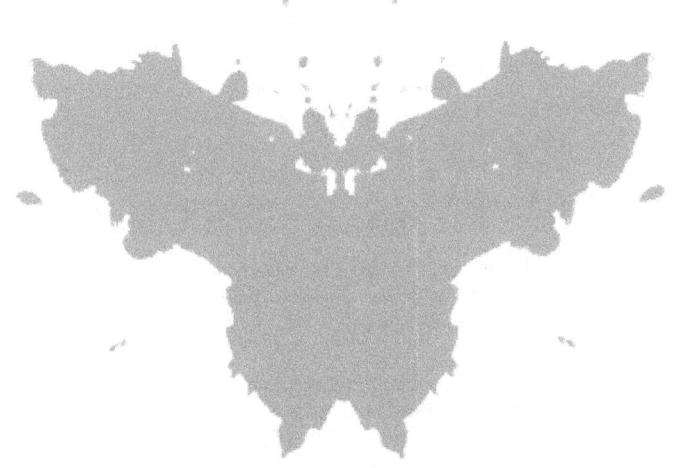

A.G. SULLIVAN

INVARIANT

ISBN: 978-1-7342443-9-7
Library of Congress Control Number: 2025909341

First Edition: May 2025

Disclaimer

Cover Design by Extended Imagery

www.invariantbook.com
www.agsullivan.info

To my family.
It's not blood that makes you family.
It's love.

BOOKS BY A.G. SULLIVAN

THE KATZENSTEIN KIDS
AND THE EYE OF HORUS

THE KATZENSTEIN KIDS
AND THE 12 MINOTAURS

TRYPOPHOBIA
A NOVEL

INVARIANT

TATTOOS & POETRY

"Love is the one thing we're capable of perceiving that transcends dimensions of time and space."
Dr. Brand, Interstellar

CONTENTS

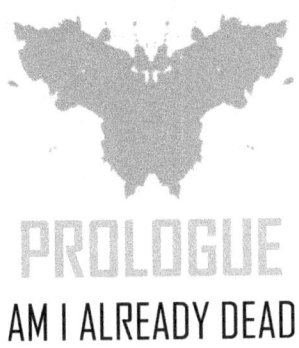

AM I ALREADY DEAD

Cold. Clean. Empty.

The hospital room could have been carved from ice. The walls, pale white, stretched endlessly, scrubbed clean and devoid of warmth, excitement, or color. There was no personality in this room, no comfort. The sterile smell of antiseptic lingered in the air, mixing with the faint, distant sound of someone crying. The soft hum of machines, the flickering lights, the quiet beep of a heart monitor—all the sounds blurred together, creating a constant noise that only emphasized how empty everything felt.

Nothing happened that wasn't by design. A bed rolling from one room to the next, a patient wandering about and getting lost on the stairs, or the inevitable and eventual flatline echoing down the halls. All were part of a meticulous plan, and central to this was a lone figure. The old man lay in the bed, his body weak and still. His eyes flickered open, then closed again, not sure of what he was seeing, or if it even mattered. His chest rose slowly with each shallow breath, and the cool air from the ceiling vents brushed against his skin, leaving him with a deep discomfort that never quite went away.

Every day felt the same. The same sounds, the same cold air, the same white walls. It was like he was stuck in a loop, unable to escape. He wondered how long he had been here. Days? Weeks? It didn't matter. Time had lost meaning.

The door opened quietly, and a nurse entered. She appeared drained from back-to-back double shifts. Heavy bags hung beneath her sunken eyes—a testament to a woman who had grown accustomed to surviving off cold coffee and stale bagels—glanced down at her tablet displaying the old man's medical records. The blinding shine of the cold lights could not compare to her sun-starved skin, and if it weren't for her crumpled scrubs, stained with blotches, she'd resemble a modern interpretation of death itself.

She didn't speak, didn't acknowledge him directly. She went about her daily tasks: checking the IV drip, adjusting the machines beside him, and scrolling through his records without a word. She never expected anything other than what she saw before her.

A dying old man.

She didn't know his history, and his name was a mystery. His was a story written in invisible ink on hidden pages inside a secret book lost somewhere in the world.

According to her, he was just a man who walked in off the street, cold and alone.

His records told her only the simple truths: blood pressure—unextraordinary; cholesterol levels—a little high. A crack appeared on her lips as they stretched wide open, releasing an unexpected yawn. She shook her head, updated his vitals, and left the room as silently as she had entered it.

To the old man, she was but the ghost of a fleeting moment. He'd spent many of those moments in the current bed, lucid. He'd blink, and the room would fill with snow; the next blink would have the walls peeling away, revealing cracks that led to dark corners—hiding places for slithering, slimy predators.

Then there was the bird, very peculiar yet also familiar. It had been there for a while now, always coming back, perched silently on his chest. Its feathers were white, almost blending with the sterile room, but its eyes were bright yellow—sharp, unblinking. They always stared at him, as if it knew something he didn't, and its beak seemed deadlier than an assassin's dagger.

At first, he thought it was just a hallucination, a trick of his tired and fading mind. But no matter how many times he blinked, the bird was still there, sitting calmly on his chest. It was real, and it was watching him. And the sharp sting of its talons was enough proof of its existence.

Once again, his eyelids fluttered open weakly, his eyes meeting the bird's piercing gaze. His lips cracked as a gasp escaped—a soft sound, hardly noticeable if not for the still air allowing it to be carried far away, breaking the unnatural silence.

"Why are you here?" he whispered, though his voice was barely audible. The bird didn't answer, of course. It never did. Its yellow eyes just continued to stare, unblinking. "Why do I dream of you?" he continued, the words spilling out from the crack in his lips and through the morphine-induced fog he was in. "There must be a meaning. Can you exist without meaning?" The bird didn't respond, not that he expected it to. Still, a simple shake of its plumage or blink of the eyes could help to ease his mind. Instead, it continued to stare, a hint of desire behind those beady pupils.

"Perhaps this time you have come for my soul," the man said, his shaky breath causing the bird's feathers to sway like charms on a wind chime. "Am I already dead?" The bird's yellow eyes brightened, as if to answer him, acknowledging his unspoken fears. The old man's thoughts drifted. It was hard to keep them together. His mind felt fractured, like pieces of a puzzle that didn't fit. *Was he already dead? Was this what it was like? Was he just waiting for something to happen?* Surely the nurse would have noticed if he were dead. She wouldn't have left him there in his bed as an empty shell no longer clinging to the cruelties of the mortal prison called life.

Suddenly, his skin crawled, a chill working its way through his veins and down his spine, its origin unknown. His blood froze, the hair on the back of his neck standing on end as his fingers gently twitched. The thin hospital sheet wrapped around his body and the controlled room temperature did nothing to ease the overbearing heaviness.

The rhythmic beep from his machine faded, drowned out by the sound of his pounding heart. Each beat reminded him of his fragility. He felt a slight relief that he was still alive, and he would rather his soul be damned than lay in that bed, awaiting death's cold hand to snatch him from the land of the living. His attempts to move were futile. He could see himself lifting his arm and waving the bird away, yet his arm did not move.

Was the bird some harbinger of judgment, bringing him these recollections to fulfill its duty as a sentinel of the afterlife?

He eyed the bird, still perched on his chest, unfazed by the man's words or slight movements. He tried moving again, arching his back to shake the bird off him; however, he didn't even move an inch. It was as if some unseen force was pushing him into the bed, keeping him in the present moment. As for the bird, it remained as unmoving as ever, with its gaze intensifying on the old man. Eye to eye, whispers escaped the old man's lips.

"I remember you now my old friend, I now know why you are here... Mr. Owl."

It was during this struggle that he saw a field opening up before him. The field had flowers with gold petals, its grass blades drenched in dew drops, and bees were buzzing in the soft, warm breeze. The lights flickered, and the field immediately faded. The scene changed, and a room, cold, dark, and damp, replaced the field. Black mold climbed up the walls of the room, and the tiled floor had cracks that seemed to spread from one end of the room to the next.

A figure appeared, a man, as tall as the ceiling and

dressed in white, and he seemed to be frowning at the old man.

No. Not frowning. Smiling.

His head was brushing against the floor as he hung upside down before the old man. He didn't possess any features besides a wide, toothy smile.

The lights flickered again, and the scene shifted back to the field. However, the golden flowers in the field seemed to pierce through the molding walls. The man moved closer, his smile fading. The mold on the walls eventually grew over the flowers; the cracked tiles seemed to rip apart the grass-covered soil. The bustling bee activity also halted. The upside-down man continued to move closer and closer, akin to darkness filling every part of the room.

Everything blurred, and thoughts raced through the old man's mind, yet the owl's gaze remained unyielding. *Were these simply the images of an unraveling mind or old forgotten memories of a life long lived?* the man wondered.

His chest tightened, as if the air in him wouldn't be able to complete the journey to his lungs. The owl remained on his chest, unmoving, yet its presence became more noticeable. Its talons began digging in deeper, it's eyes glowing brighter as it flattened his chest more and more.

As the upside-down man stood over the hospital bed, the old man could clearly see that his coat had the texture of feathers, and his nails were as black as night.

The man's mouth moved, black lips curling and stretching to form words. And then the voice came. Low. Distorted. The words barely recognizable, but still clear.

"Kill him... kill him."

The words hung in the air, heavier than any silence the old man had ever known. He felt them crawl down his spine, sending a chill through his already frozen body. The owl's eyes never left him, never blinked, never wavered. The upside-down man remained still, his grin stretching wider with every passing second.

The air grew thick, suffocating. The old man's chest tightened, his breath coming in short gasps.

"Why?" he whispered to the empty air. The question hung in the stillness, unanswered.

CHAPTER 01

JOHN DOE

Bzzzt, bzzzt, bzzzt!

David groaned as the vibration shook his bedframe, sending an empty can of Red Bull rolling off his nightstand and onto the floor. His eyelids felt like they were glued shut. Somewhere in the distance, his phone buzzed persistently, its faint glow illuminating a small patch of his otherwise dark and cluttered dorm room.

He reached blindly, his fingers brushing against the cold surface of the phone before it clattered to the ground.

"Ugh... Seriously?" he mumbled, his voice hoarse from overuse and late-night study sessions.

Bzzzt, bzzzt, bzzzt!

The buzzing continued. Reluctantly, he leaned over the edge of the bed, groping for the phone. His fingertips finally hit the cold rubber of his phone's casing, and he grabbed at it like an ape would for a banana and slammed his thumb onto the screen, putting an end to the relentless sound.

"Hello…" he mumbled through the heavy drowsiness that refused to lift. A woman's voice greeted him. It was soft but urgent, the kind of tone that instantly made him sit up straighter.

"David Bishop?" she asked.

"Yeah, who's asking?" He rubbed his eyes, still trying to shake the fog of sleep.

The woman's voice quivered. "You need to come to Mass General Hospital now. It's urgent."

He frowned, his brain struggling to process the words. He was about to respond but got cut off by the woman continuing.

"Are you there? Did you hear me?" she urged.

"Wait, what? Who are you? Why would I need to go there? Did someone—?"

"I can't explain over the phone," she interrupted, her voice growing sharper. "There's not much time! You need to come now. It's… important," the woman repeated, her voice now laced with a sense of impending dread.

"Okay," David agreed, throwing his covers off, exposing his bare legs to the chilly air. "I'm on my way! I… I'll be there soon."

Before he could say more, the line went dead.

David stared at the screen, his thoughts swirling. *This had to be some kind of prank, right? But who would go through all this trouble to drag him out of bed in the middle of the night?*

The clock on his phone blinked back at him—3:33 a.m.

The "witching hour." According to lore, this was a time when the sky was the darkest and the stars nowhere to be seen, leaving the world shrouded in a thick, malicious atmosphere. He paused to consider the significance of a strange phone call at such a time, but only for a moment. Shaking his head, he dismissed the thoughts. It was just a coincidence, it had to be!

He tossed the phone onto the bed and lay back down, hoping the buzz of confusion would fade if he gave it a minute. But it didn't. With a groan of frustration, he sat up.

"This is so stupid," he muttered. But his curiosity was already winning. If he didn't check it out, he'd just lie awake all night wondering what the hell was going on.

He stumbled out of bed and shuffled to the small dresser in the corner of the room, his feet getting caught by the previous day's outfit he'd thrown haphazardly on the floor. He muttered nonsensically to himself as he reached for a pair of pants to put on. A hiss escaped his mouth as the zipper scraped against his thigh and he pushed a sock smelling of sweat out of his pant leg.

"I'm on my way. Why would I say that? I'm on my way," he mumbled to himself in a tone meant to mock his earlier reply to the caller. "Three in the morning and I tell someone that I'm on my fucking way to the hospital!"

David huffed and puffed a couple of times as he searched his drawers for a clean shirt, or one without any noticeable stains or strong odor. After some time, he found it and was glad that it didn't make his nose turn up as he threw it over his head, coupled with a hoodie. His reflection in the cracked mirror caught his eye—a mop of messy brown hair, dark circles under tired eyes, and a general aura of disarray. He looked exactly like someone woken up in the middle of the night for something absurd.

"Perfect," he muttered sarcastically.

After fixing his hair a bit, he was ready to leave. He fumbled with the locks for a moment before finally getting the door open, and he rushed down the hall, only to turn around a few seconds later and head the other way instead.

He'd only been in that dorm room for a couple weeks. His name had finally come up on the waiting list for a single dorm and he had taken it. Though he preferred his last room and building, he didn't want to pass up living alone; besides, his last roommate spent more time partying than studying. On this brisk, dark morning, he was more concerned about the absurdity of calling someone to the hospital at such a time with no explanation.

His mind ran wild with thoughts, questions, and possibilities as he stuck the keys into the ignition and pulled the car out of the parking lot. All traces of sleep had since left him.

•••

The streets were eerily quiet as David drove through the city. The streetlights cast long, stretching shadows across the pavement, and the occasional flicker of a bulb added to the unsettling atmosphere.

He kept glancing at the clock on the dashboard—3:55 a.m. Why did it feel like time was crawling? The radio was off, leaving nothing but the hum of the car engine and the faint whistle of wind slipping through a small gap in the windshield.

His thoughts spiraled as he tried to make sense of the call. *Who could possibly know his name? And why would they want him at a hospital, of all places?* Far from home he didn't have any sick relatives in the area. Lastly, they knew his name. *How did they know it?*

Despite the confusion fogging his thoughts, he continued driving, pressing his foot on the accelerator gently. The lights stayed green, all the way through, as if some cosmic force was urging him to seek out answers.

"Maybe it's a mix-up," he said out loud, trying to comfort himself. "Wrong David Bishop. Happens all the time."

But deep down, he wasn't convinced. The woman on the phone had sounded too sure, too deliberate. This wasn't a mistake. He tapped his fingers on the steering wheel, the rhythm speeding up with his growing anxiety. The fluorescent green exit sign for Mass General Hospital loomed ahead, and he turned into the near-empty parking lot.

•••

The hospital lobby was sterile and unnervingly quiet, lit by a harsh overhead glow that made David wince. His sneakers squeaked on the polished floor as he moved through the hospital's halls as though he'd been there before. According to him, all hospitals were the same, and if you'd been in one, then you'd been in them all. He approached the front desk, where an attendant sat, typing something on her computer.

"Excuse me," David began, clearing his throat.

A young woman, no older than himself, barely glanced

up over the wide brim of her square glasses. Their gazes met for a second before her strained eyes proceeded to look him over, prompting her nose to wiggle and lips to purse. Her name tag read Cindy, and by the look of things, she was too busy to exchange greetings.

"It's not yet visiting hours," she said flatly, returning to her screen.

"I know," David replied, trying to keep his frustration in check. "I received a call from here, about 30 minutes ago, requesting I come to the hospital immediately."

The lady continued to stare at him, as if waiting for more information.

"They didn't tell me why," David added with a shrug of his shoulder.

Cindy sighed, clearly unimpressed and turned slightly to face the computer in front of her. "Name?"

"David Bishop."

"Oh right, David Bishop. The ICU told me you might show up. Wait here for a moment. I'll fetch Faith for you."

"Thanks…" David said as he watched the woman get up and stroll off, the hunched-over seated position she was in barely changing. "…I guess."

David stuffed his hands in his hoodie pocket, rocking slightly on his heels as he waited. The distant sound of machines and the faint smell of antiseptic made his stomach churn. Hospitals had always unsettled him, and tonight was no exception.

He had been waiting for a few minutes before a soft pitter-patter of flat shoes in haste warned him that someone was coming. He scanned down the hall where he'd watched the front desk woman disappear. The nurse that returned in her place was shorter in stature, slimmer in figure, and stood with a straight spine and upright chin.

She didn't stroll toward David so much as floated. This, coupled with her pale appearance and hasty walk, made her resemble a ghostly messenger.

"David Bishop?" she asked, her voice softer than a whisper.

David gave a single nod, opening his mouth to respond, but he found that his vocals weren't cooperating.

"I'm Faith," she smiled, lighting up her deathly complexion. "If you'll follow me, please."

She turned and began walking without waiting for acknowledgment or agreement from David. Seeing this, he dashed forward, trying to catch up with her. Amazingly, it seemed that Faith's short legs could carry her long distances in a short time. Perhaps this was one of the traits of working as an ICU nurse—the ability to move fast while staying calm.

Once they were side by side, David took a moment to examine his surroundings. The halls were sparse and clean. Not a soul in sight and barely a chair to sit on. He tried to ignore the discomfort creeping up his spine as he glanced at the closed doors and dim lights. If he didn't know any better, he'd liken the place to a long since abandoned building. The few signs he could see indicated where they were going.

He sought confirmation. "Are we going to the ICU tower?"

"Oh yes!" Faith hummed and nodded like a bobble-head doll.

Her name gnawed at his thoughts. It seemed a perfect blend of cruel irony and strange destiny that a woman named Faith would guide him through a hospital in the dead of night for some unknown purpose.

"I'm sorry…" David chuckled, trying to sound light and knowing the next words to come out of his mouth would probably sound ridiculous to the lady. "Why am I here exactly?"

"What do you mean?" Faith kept her attention on the path ahead, never slowing down or looking back at him.

"I don't know what I'm doing here. I don't even know anyone who would be in this hospital."

"One of my patients asked for you by name," she admitted. "An older gentleman. Been here for a while now. He requested that I call you."

"Older gentleman? Are you sure he asked for me? Could he have meant another David Bishop?"

"That's unlikely," she snickered. "I wouldn't have made that mistake. Perhaps he's a relative of yours. Someone you didn't know about. Could that be possible?"

"Seems unlikely," David mumbled.

"'Get me David Bishop from MIT.' That's what he said, and here you are. David Bishop from MIT."

David paused, a flash of shock hitting him square in the face, but he couldn't let it slow him down for more than a second or else he'd lose Faith completely. It didn't seem possible, but she was right. He was David Bishop, and he was currently studying at MIT. She'd known to call him. Perhaps this older gentleman did know him.

"Maybe he is a relative… but I doubt it," he said, trying to sound convincing but failing.

"I take it you're not from a big family," Faith deduced.

He shrugged.

"I was adopted. They told me my parents died when I was still an infant."

"It could be your adoptive father!" There was a hint of joy in her voice.

"He's currently living in California with my adoptive mother, so I think it's safe to say it's not him. What's this man's name? Maybe that will ring some bells."

"Not unless you know many John Does." Faith giggled, her obvious glee in the situation beginning to bother David. "He came in from the street without any form of identification. He wasn't even in the system."

David frowned. "That doesn't make sense. I don't know anyone in the hospital, let alone someone with no ID. Are you sure—"

"I'm sure," she interrupted, her tone firm but not unkind. "He asked for you specifically."

"That's… helpful…" he said dejectedly.

What felt like the longest walk David had ever had finally came to an end as Faith turned sharply in front of him, throwing one of the many doors along the hallway open. He followed her through as they left the dimly lit, silent hallway behind to find a small, private room.

A John Doe in a private room?

•••

At first, the lights were blinding, but David needed

only a moment for his eyesight to adjust. The bareness of the room caught him off-guard. There was nothing adorning the tables: no flowers, no balloons, no get-well-soon cards, or tokens of any kind. There was only the old man in the bed, positioned against a wall of monitors, IVs, and cords.

He lay still, hooked up and wired into those machines like some kind of robot. Tubes snaked from his nose and arms to the monitors surrounding the bed, their rhythmic beeping the only sign that he was still alive.

The air in the room was unnaturally still, and if it weren't for the soft sounds coming from the machines, David would have thought they'd arrived a little bit late. The old man neither stirred nor twitched. His eyes stayed close and stuck, indicating a quiet sleep with no dreams to pass the time. His chest barel moved, as if he weren't breathing. David squinted, focusing on his lips for a quiver, and his neck for some sort of movement like swallowing. Whoever this guy was, he looked like he was hanging on by a thread.

"What's wrong with him?" David mumbled, a mixture of curiosity and concern in his voice.

Faith looked at David, her eyes filled with a sadness that tugged at his heart.

"I'm afraid he's dying."

"Dying?" David whispered to himself, glancing back to the old man. "Is there nothing you can do for him?"

"We're doing all we can." Faith shrugged. "He checked himself in not too long ago complaining of severe abdominal pain. We did all the tests, CT scan and all, and the doctors diagnosed him with pancreatic cancer."

"Oh God," he said, the words floating out his mouth like a breath.

Faith nodded, and there was something almost... pitying in her expression.

"He underwent emergency surgery, but it wasn't successful. The cancer was far more invasive than we originally thought and, worse, it's spread. Even worse than that, he developed an infection after the surgery... sepsis... and we just can't get control of it."

Silence filled the room for a few seconds as she let all that information sink in.

"Seems like luck is not on his side," David eventually responded.

"Or time," Faith agreed. "We're maintaining his vitals, but his body's giving out. There's nothing more we can do for him... aside from keep him comfortable, but he's running out of time."

"Why would a John Doe on his death bed ask for me?" David only heard the harshness of the words after they'd left his lips.

"You don't recognize him then?" He shook his head, and she shrugged. "When I started my shift at 11 p.m., he was out cold, and I wasn't expecting him to regain consciousness at all, but he did. He woke up and kept saying the same thing, over and over again: 'Get me David Bishop from MIT.' That was it. That was all he would say for over an hour before passing out again."

"This makes no sense." David's neck ached from how often he was shaking his head.

"He wanted me to find you, and I did."

"How does he know me? I've never seen this man before in my life!"

"He must know you somehow. He called for you by name."

"He called for a David Bishop; maybe you've got the wrong one."

Faith shook her head intensely.

"Not possible. When I called the Massachusetts Institute of Technology directory and asked for you, they said they only had one David Bishop on file, and that's you."

David opened his mouth to respond but instead ended up spitting out a series of unintelligible gasps, grunts, and groans. He knew the words he wanted to say, but his mouth had different ideas.

He swallowed hard, hoping his tongue would go down his throat, and ran his fingers through his hair, his eyes widening. He could already feel stress wrinkles forming above his brow.

"This makes no sense. I was adopted. My parents died."

"Maybe he is an uncle or distant relative of your birth parents," Faith offered. "I've seen it before. If you were young when your parents passed, it's possible that you were offered up for adoption and your distant relatives wouldn't have known."

"Maybe..." His voice trailed off. "I just... I don't know. This whole thing is very strange!"

"There's only one way to find out." Faith stepped

forward, putting herself between the old man and David. She leaned in close, placing her hand gently on his shoulder. "Sir… Can you hear me, sir?"

David peered over her shoulder.

The old man's eyes snapped open, his wide gaze instantly landing on David. His head lifted off the pillow, and his arms flailed around while subtle strained moans escaped his throat. David lost his footing, shocked by the sight, and stumbled backward into the wall. The old man's eyes followed him, unblinking.

Faith stepped aside as the old man's arm lifted gently. His skin hung off the bone, and David feared it might break if he moved too quickly. The old man pointed a single steady finger in David's direction. His eyes widened more as that finger retracted, his hand taking the shape of a fist scribbling words in the air.

"He is trying to tell you something!" Faith stated, quickly retreating from the room, leaving David to stare at the man as he continued to write gibberish in the air.

She returned shortly afterward with a notepad and pen, handing them to David instead of the old man.

"W-w-what?" David's eyes filled with fear, his knuckles going white from clutching the pen so tightly.

Faith placed a gentle hand on his back, nudging him toward the old man. He began to wheeze, eventually motioning for David to come closer. After examining him for a moment, David realized the old man's wheezing was a result of him trying to talk. His lips moved slowly, the wheezing mixed with strained whispers.

David, although confused, once again let his curiosity

take control of him as he leaned in close to the old man. He continued to motion for David to move closer and closer, until his ear was right beside the old man's gaping mouth. Pen ready, David listened intently.

Eight sets of words spilled from the old man's lips in a whisper so low David wasn't even sure he'd heard any of them correctly at first. The words seemed so random. Unconnected in any way. He must have gotten them wrong, or the old man's mind was dancing a little too close to the edge of insanity.

He glanced down at the list he'd just written. A list of eight items. David only had a moment to study the page before the old man's chest deflated with an exhale and chaos ensued.

His eyes finally left David and slowly closed. At that exact moment, a monitor began flashing red and alarms began to blare from the machines. David took a step back, his mouth falling open. Faith pushed him out of the way in her haste to rush to the old man's side. His hands went numb, almost dropping the list to the floor.

"Code blue!" Faith cried out, her voice and all the other sounds in the room muffled to David's ears.

More nurses rushed into the room, filling it in no time and pushing David closer and closer to the door.

"He's crashing," Faith explained while the others got to work.

A heavy hand landed on David's arm, ushering him out the room.

"I'm sorry, sir, but you can't be in here," an unfamiliar voice informed him. "You'll have to go back to the waiting area."

David was thrown out into the hall, the door shutting behind him as the last nurse flew into the room. He backed away slowly.

"Stop!" The last nurse to walk in cried out with a hint of superiority in her voice. The room fell silent, a pause in the chaos. "He's listed as a 'Do Not Resuscitate (DNR)' in his file. There's nothing more we can do."

David never took his eyes off the door, until he turned and began walking back down the hall toward the waiting area. He glanced back over his shoulder, keeping his sights trained on the old man's room. Eventually, he picked up his pace and the door vanished from his sight. He turned, now looking down at the list in his hands.

"What does it mean?" he muttered to himself in the silence.

He made his way back to the waiting area and sat there for a bit. He held the list tentatively, using only the tips of his fingers pressed gently against the page's corners. Over and over again he read the list to himself, each item more confusing and stranger than the last. They made no sense. They weren't connected at all, and yet he couldn't take his attention away from it… from any of it. The man with no name, the mysterious call in the middle of the night, and the list of eight items in his hands. *What did it all mean?*

Only a few minutes had passed since he had left the old man's room, but it felt like an eternity. There was no reason for him to stay. He didn't know the John Doe, and there was nothing the hospital staff could tell him that he didn't already know. He folded the list gently and tucked it into his pocket.

As he turned to leave, his eyes caught a glimpse of Faith down one of the halls. She gave him a nod, her face mimicking what he was feeling. David forced a smile, though his mind was far from this place, trapped in a whirlpool. Though he didn't know what the old man wanted from him, he could tell there was a sense of urgency to it all.

The night sky greeted him as David left the hospital. The stars shone in the sky, cold and indifferent, but they could not outshine the city lights. There was not a car in sight as the cold air blew through the parking lot. David made his way to his car and climbed in. He thought about how he would probably share his story with his parents, and that perhaps they would be able to shed some light on the strange mystery.

He sat in his car for a while, wondering what his next steps would be. The weight of this mystery tugged heavily on his conscience, but he had classes and a life to lead. He glanced upward, the hue of a dawn sky bringing him back to reality. There was nothing for him to do but return to his dorm room, to his routine, and get ready for the first class of the day in only three hours.

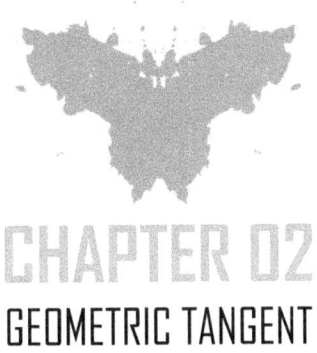

CHAPTER 02
GEOMETRIC TANGENT

One year later...

The rain was unrelenting, slamming against David's windshield in thick, endless sheets from the dark, cloud-covered sky. His wipers worked tirelessly, but the water kept coming, streaking across the glass faster than they could clear it. He gripped the steering wheel tightly, shifting in his seat as his damp hoodie clung to his back. The air inside the car was clammy, carrying a faint smell of wet fabric and old air freshener. Confined inside the car, watching the windshield wipers swipe back and forth furiously, David regretted his decision to leave his dorm room that day.

Ahead of him, the glow of red taillights stretched into the distance. The cars were packed so tightly they seemed frozen in place, their exhaust fumes curling up in thin clouds that quickly disappeared into the rain. The sound of horns could be heard faintly in the background, though most drivers had resigned themselves to the slow crawl of Boston traffic—a norm to those who lived in the area.

Pedestrians hurried along the slick sidewalk, their umbrellas straining against the wind. Rain lashed down, turning the street into a river. Whether stuck in traffic or scurrying along the roadside, no one was immune to the misery of the downpour.

David exhaled through his nose, glancing at the dashboard clock. It was barely past five in the afternoon, but the storm had turned the day into something closer to midnight. The rain had begun in the early hours, and the weather had gone downhill.

His eyes flicked to the road ahead. The rain blurred the world outside, smearing colors and shapes together until everything looked like a moving watercolor painting. He leaned forward slightly, trying to see better, but it didn't help much. The storm was suffocating, and the traffic wasn't helping his nerves.

David's mind began to drift, the rhythm of the wipers lulling him into his thoughts. One year had passed since the night he had found himself standing beside an old man's hospital bed in the middle of the night. His mind often wandered to that moment; however, he couldn't dwell on the past and life had to go on. Besides, he had many other things to focus on.

His classes had grown more difficult, but he'd worked very hard to make his way to the top of the class, working even harder to stay there. Moreover, his final project—an architectural capstone—was due in just a few weeks, and the weight of it sat heavily on his shoulders. It wasn't just a project; it was the culmination of years of hard work. Everything—his grades, his reputation, his chance at graduating with honors—rested on this one design.

Will it impress the judges? he wondered. He had poured every ounce of energy he had into the project, staying up late, skipping meals, and isolating himself from his friends to make sure it was perfect. But was it enough?

His jaw tightened as the thought settled into his mind. He hated doubting himself, but it was hard not to when so much was on the line. He took a deep breath, trying to push the anxiety aside, but his chest felt tight, like it wasn't letting the air in properly.

He suddenly gasped, realizing he'd been holding his breath the whole time. In front of him, a gap opened up. Through subconscious movement, he shifted gears and moved forward, filling the tiny opening with the front of his car. He knew, behind him, other cars would do the same until they were all tightly packed together once again like a trail of ants moving in a single file.

His mind went back to his project. He knew they'd love his design. He had to believe they would. He'd reached his breaking point, burning the candle at both ends to maintain his number one spot at the top and constantly impress with every single project, so there was no way he could allow himself to believe in anything other than his success.

In truth, he dreamed about the day it would all come to an end. He would attend his last class and he would ace his exams. He would then graduate with honors and never have to worry about turning in a college assignment on time ever again. He would then move on with his life, sleep in late on the weekends, and perhaps catch a Red Sox game with his friends or just do something for himself for a change.

The sound of a loud horn jolted him in his seat, ripping him from his thoughts and bringing him back to reality. The car in front of him lurched forward, and without thinking, David eased his foot off the brake, letting his car roll forward a few feet. The gap was barely a car's length, but still, he rolled forward to fill it. His eyes were fixed on the glowing red taillights ahead, their blurred edges shifting as the rain streaked his windshield.

The next instant, a figure appeared in his headlights.

David's chest tightened as the dark shape materialized out of the rain, standing motionless in the middle of the road. He froze, his mind struggling to process what he was seeing. The figure was drenched, the water cascading off what looked like a long coat that clung to their frame. They didn't move, frozen like a deer caught in the headlights.

David's car crept forward, inching closer, and for a brief moment, his body refused to respond.

Move! his mind screamed, but he sat frozen, his foot still hovering over the gas.

The figure suddenly slapped their hand on the hood of David's car, making a loud thump and trying to get him to stop the car before it could hit him.

"Oh shit!"

The words broke free as his body snapped into action. His foot slammed on the brake, jolting the car to a sudden stop, inches away from hitting the figure. The tires squealed, their sound syncing with the chorus of angry horns from the cars behind him.

He glanced in his rearview mirror for only a second to ensure he hadn't caused any accidents; however, when he turned his attention back to the road, the figure was gone.

He scanned the road, and even hoisted himself up using the steering wheel to peer over the edge of the hood, but there was no sign of anyone—or anything—in front of his car. The thought that he had hit the figure and now whoever it was, was lying under his car came for brief moment, but it left as soon as it crossed his mind. He doubted that there was anyone down there.

As he wandered where the figure had gone, a larger gap opened up in front of him, and before he could fill it a car pulled out from a parking space on the side of the road in front of him. One gap closes, and another opens, he thought.

David waited for the cars to inch forward once again before pulling into the now open parking space beside him. As he put the car in park and pulled the key out of the ignition, a soft breath escaped his quivering lips. He slumped back into his seat, his hands still gripping the wheel tightly. His chest rose and fell quickly as he tried to steady his breathing.

"That was too close," he muttered, his voice barely audible over the rain.

His eyes flicked to the side mirror, catching his own reflection. His damp hair stuck to his forehead, and his face looked pale under the harsh glow of the lights ahead. The reflection distorted slightly as rain splattered the mirror, but one thing was clear—he looked like someone who needed a break.

As he stared at his reflection, something else caught his attention. In the mirror's corner, barely visible through the rain, the dark figure he had almost struck had just finished crossing the street.

David turned in his seat, craning his neck to get a better look. The figure had reached the sidewalk and stood under the bright blue awning of a shop. They were still, their silhouette highlighted by the studio lights behind them. The red glow of the traffic lights reflected off their soaked coat, making them appear unearthly in the storm.

For a moment, David felt like they were staring directly at him. The feeling was unsettling, like the stranger could see straight through the car, straight through him. He swallowed hard, his mouth suddenly dry. He stared back at the stranger, wondering if they were actually staring back at him, and then, with a twist of their body, they began walking down the street, disappearing into the dark, rainy night.

His eyes shifted to the storefront the figure had been standing in front of. The blue awning belonged to an art store named Newbury Studios, its large windows glowing warmly against the cold, gray day. However, the windows and lights were not what caught David's eye; it was what hung on the walls of the studio that he could not pull his attention away from. Inside, bright lights lit up walls lined with artwork—posters, prints, and paintings hung in neat rows, their colors standing out brightly against the white walls.

David's gaze was drawn to one piece in particular.

It was a large, square print framed in a metal trim and hung high on the wall. Its surface seemed to be alive with swirling patterns and colors that exploded like a supernova, with shapes he'd never known existed blending into each other like waves crashing together. It was a unique piece of art, and he just had to have it.

Without giving himself time to second-guess, he reached for the door handle and pushed it open. The storm hit him immediately, cold rain soaking his hair and seeping through his hoodie within seconds; however, he wasn't bothered by the rain or the cold. He jogged across the street, ignoring the loud sound of brakes and the sharp honking of a car's horn as it sped past, splashing water onto his jeans.

When he finally reached the studio's entrance, he was drenched. The awning provided little relief, but the sight of the artwork pulled him forward. Without hesitation, David pushed the door open. A small bell jingled above him, its sound almost drowned out by the rain outside.

Inside, the air was warm and smelled faintly of wood and paint. The soft hum of a heater running in the background was the only sound besides his own wet shoes squeaking against the polished floor.

David looked around, shaking the water from his hands. The space was bright but simple. The walls were painted a clean white, and every inch of them was covered in framed artwork. The pieces were arranged neatly, each one displayed with care, but his attention was locked on the painting he'd seen from outside.

It was even more incredible up close. The colors seemed to pop off the surface, creating shapes and patterns that didn't quite make sense but worked together in a way that was impossible to ignore. He stepped closer, tilting his head slightly, as if a different angle might help him understand how it all fit together.

"Hey there, can I help you?"

The voice startled him, and he turned quickly to see a woman standing nearby. She was small—barely reaching his shoulder—with curly auburn hair tied into a loose bun. Her green apron bore the studio's name, Newbury Studios, embroidered neatly on the front. She had an easy smile, one that made David feel like he was already welcome here.

"Uh, yeah," he said, his voice coming out a little hoarse. He cleared his throat and pointed toward the art piece, unsure what to call it. "This... this piece, I saw it from outside. It's… incredible."

She followed his gaze and grinned, walking toward the piece as if she had a personal connection to it. "You've got a good eye," she said, folding her arms and tilting her head to admire the work. "This one's my favorite."

They stared up at the artwork together, the woman's unusually small size making it look that much larger. David quickly swallowed the lump in his throat and tightened his lips in an effort to hide his smile.

"I don't even know how to describe it. The way it plays with shapes, the movement—it feels alive somehow," he voiced.

The woman laughed softly, the sound warm and

genuine.

"Most people just say, 'Wow, cool colors.'"

David chuckled, though he felt his cheeks flush slightly. "Well, I am studying architecture. Guess I'm used to looking at shapes and lines a little too much."

She turned to him, her eyes lighting up. "Architecture? That explains it. You see the structure in it. I bet you even noticed the geometric formulas hidden in the background."

David blinked. He hadn't, but now that she mentioned it, he leaned in and squinted, spotting faint mathematical notations fused into the design. "I, uh... was about to notice them."

She laughed again, and David found himself smiling back, more relaxed now.

"I'm Page," she said, holding out a hand.

"David." He shook her hand, noticing how small it felt in his. "Nice to meet you."

"Likewise." She let go and gestured toward the painting. "This is Geometric Tangent, by Malik Farnsworth. Local artist, pretty well-known in the area. And this"—she pointed to a tiny, scrawled signature in the corner—"is proof that it's one of his."

David leaned closer to see the signature, nodding as if it meant something to him. "Never heard of him," he admitted, then quickly added, "but his work is... something else."

"It is," Page agreed. "Between you and me, I'd take this one home if I could."

Her playful tone caught him off guard, and he glanced

at her, half-smiling. "Why don't you?"

"Oh, I don't think it would fit in my car." She grinned.

David turned his head, looking back outside and across at his car. "Good point!"

His head drifted back to the print. It felt like it was meant for him, like it was waiting for him to find it. He cleared his throat and deepened his voice. "How much it is selling for?"

Page walked over to the small tag on the frame and checked it. "Well... you're in luck. It was $350, but we've just marked it down to $200. It's a hard sell due to its unusually large size, but this is a print of the original, which makes it far more affordable."

David's heart sank a little, even as his excitement rose. Two hundred dollars wasn't much in the grand scheme of things, but for a student living on a tight budget, it was a lot. His brain started doing mental math: How much was left in his checking account? How much would ramen noodles cost for the next few weeks if he had to stretch his grocery money?

"I know it's not cheap," Page said, sensing his hesitation. "But honestly, for a piece like this? It's a steal. The frame alone is worth almost that much, and it's mounted and glazed already."

David ran a hand over his face, feeling the dampness of his rain-soaked skin. "It's more than I was planning, but I really love it!" he said, half to himself.

Page smiled. "Love is a powerful thing!"

"That is very true... I'll take it," he said suddenly, the words surprising even himself.

"Great!" She clapped her hands and leaped into action. "Let me ring it up for you. I hope you have a big enough car so you can get it home safely."

David's smile faded as his eyes returned to the window and road. The rain poured, more relentless than ever. His little Honda Civic hatchback sat parked across the street from the studio. The car was small, and the painting was huge.

"Uh… it'll be tight, but I'll make it work." I guess where there's a will, there's a way, he thought to himself.

Page grinned. "Now that's the spirit."

CHAPTER 03

HANNAH

The X-ACTO blade felt heavier than usual in David's shaking hands. It was a tool meant for precision—sharp enough to slice through wood and delicate enough to shape the smallest architectural details. But in that moment, precision and delicacy felt just out of reach. His fingers twitched slightly, his grip tightening around the slim handle as he forced himself to steady his breathing.

The room was quiet, save for the soft creak of his chair as he leaned closer to his work. His chest rose and fell in measured breaths as he carefully positioned the blade over the row of wood coffee stirrers he had glued to a foam core base earlier. He needed to slice off their uneven tips, ensuring they lined up perfectly. Even the smallest misalignment would ruin the effect of the wooden slats, which were meant to mimic real-life redwood siding.

With slow precision, he pressed down. The blade easily cut through the coffee stirrers, separating the excess wood cleanly. He breathed a small sigh of relief upon seeing this, which was confirmation that the glue was dry. He had little to no patience when it came to things drying, whether it be glue or paint. As an architecture student, it was always a gamble when working with glue—too soon, and the wood would tear; too late, and the blade would struggle to cut through hardened lumps.

David leaned back for a moment, stretching his shoulders. He had been at this for hours, hunched over his worktable, meticulously assembling the miniature lake house model for his capstone project. His eyes flicked to the surrounding mess—bottles of wood stain, tubes of glue, various knives, and rulers scattered across the desk. A small desk lamp created a warm glow over his workspace, illuminating every tiny detail of his creation.

It wasn't finished yet. The roof needed more detail, the second-floor balcony needed its railing, and the interior—though mostly unseen—was still incomplete. But it was coming together. Slowly.

His fingers absentmindedly drummed against the desk as he examined the model. A small part of him wanted to keep working, to push through the exhaustion and get more done before the day was over. But his eyes were dry, his muscles sore, and there was still so much left to do.

Then—

A knock at the door.

David's eyes instinctively rolled before he even registered who it was. He didn't need to guess. There was only one person who knocked like that.

"Mr. D.B.! Calling Mr. Douche Bag!"

The voice outside the door was deliberately high-pitched, exaggerated to mimic that of a young, overly enthusiastic child.

"Yoho! David Bishop!"

He sighed, although a smirk tugged at the corner of his lips.

Setting the blade down, he pushed back from his desk and crossed the room, shaking his head as he opened the door.

A tall figure leaned against the doorframe, arms spread dramatically. Tufts of bleach-blonde hair hung in front of his face, slightly messy like he had just rolled out of bed—or like he had been running around causing trouble.

"Duuuuude…" Jason exhaled, dragging out the word, then he dropped his voice back into its usual deep, smooth tone. "What's up?"

Before David could answer, Jason breezed past him into the room, moving like a man who had just claimed new territory. The door shut with a soft click behind him as he kicked off his sneakers without a care for where they landed.

David barely had time to react before Jason made a beeline for the small bar fridge beside the bed, yanking it open and grabbing a can of soda. He cracked it open with one hand and took a deep gulp before collapsing onto the makeshift couch in the corner.

The entire sequence happened so naturally, so fluidly, that one would think this was Jason's dorm room rather than David's.

David simply shook his head, used to the intrusion.

"Just working on my capstone model," he answered, closing the door and walking back to his desk.

Jason slurped his soda as he made his way over to where David was hunched over the model. He stood up on his tiptoes, peering over David's shoulder.

"Looking good!" He nodded approvingly. Then, after a short pause, he gulped loudly. "What is it again?"

David's shoulders vibrated softly as he chuckled and shook his head.

Jason and David couldn't have been more different. David was meticulous, quiet, and methodical—focused on his work to the point of obsession. Jason was the opposite: loud, unpredictable, and always seeking the next big thrill. But somehow, they worked. Their differences never clashed; they balanced each other out. Besides, David couldn't have asked for a better friend to have through his college years.

"It's not finished yet, but it's going to be a lake house." He turned slightly, picking up a few of the model's wooden pieces and holding them together for Jason to see. "I've stained the coffee stirrers to look like redwood siding."

Jason let out a low whistle, clearly impressed.

"Shit, dude, I'm up to my ass in reading material for my final on global supply chain strategies, and here you are just... drawing, and model building, and whatever shit it is architects do." He shook his head and gave David a light punch on the shoulder. "I should have majored in architecture."

David shrugged and nodded, unable to hide his agreement. "Yeah, except I don't think you have the patience for it."

Jason snorted. "Probably not."

For a few moments, the room was quiet again as Jason returned to his laid-back position on the couch, stretching his legs, while David picked up his blade and got back to work, resuming his careful cutting.

Then—

"Shit!" Jason suddenly shot up, spilling a drop or two of his soda on the carpet. "Aren't you gonna ask me why I'm here? Guess what I got?"

David barely had time to react before Jason's hand disappeared into his jacket pocket, fishing around before yanking something out. He whipped his hand forward, waving two red-and-white slips of paper in front of David's face.

"Tickets, baby!" Jason announced, his entire body vibrating with excitement. "Red Sox. *Tonight.*"

"No friggin way!" David cried, trying to grab the tickets, only to have Jason hold them just out of reach. "How did you even get these? It's the Red Sox versus the Yankees. There's no way they weren't sold out weeks ago."

"Ain't no big deal." Jason puffed out his chest and did a quick slide across the room, dramatically adjusting his jacket and acting as if he was walking on stage to accept an award. "You know that girl I've been fucking around with? The one that goes to Emerson?"

David nodded, thankful for the distinction.

"Well," Jason continued, wiggling his eyebrows, "she

gave them to me. I guess her dad's company had season tickets or something like that, and he gave them to her. She wasn't interested, so she gave them to me."

"When did this happen?" David questioned. "I saw you yesterday, and you never mentioned the tickets."

Jason was one for telling lavish stories, but there was always some truth behind them. The fun was picking his stories apart to decide what was true and what was embellished.

"That's because I got them this morning, dude!" Jason chuckled, rubbing the back of his head. "Okay, so this is what happened. She called me last night, drunk as hell, but you know that doesn't bother me so we, uh... hooked up." He waggled his eyebrows again. "Then this morning, when I was getting dressed and ready to leave, I saw them sitting on her dresser, and when I asked her about them, she said she doesn't even like baseball so I can just have them. Shit! I took the tickets and ran out of there with my pants still around my ankles."

David gave him a pat on the arm, smacking his tongue against the inside of his teeth and shaking his head. "You must be one of the luckiest guys I know. Every time I see you, you have another wild story to tell."

"Living the dream, my friend! Just, living the dream." Jason grinned, draping an arm around David's shoulder as they stared back at one another for a moment. "So... are we going or what?"

David hesitated. He glanced at his unfinished lake house model, sitting on the table with its tiny wooden pieces still waiting to be assembled. The responsible thing to do would be to stay in and finish what he started. But then he thought about how stale his room felt and how long it had been since he had done anything outside of work.

"Hell yeah, I'm in!" he finally said with a shrug. "I still have another week to finish my model, so why the hell not?"

"That's what I'm talking about!" Jason whooped, slapping David's hand before pulling him into a fist bump. "Alright! The game's not until 7 p.m., so finish up here and get ready. I reckon we can hit Lansdowne Street before the game and get some drinks and meet a few girls. Pretty sure the place's gonna be packed!"

David grinned. "Let's do it!"

David picked up his blade and got back to work. Meanwhile, Jason flopped back onto the couch and whistled a tune to himself while grabbing a tube of hair gel from his jacket and running a dollop of it through his hair.

Tonight was going to be a much needed break, he thought.

•••

Jason grinned, his energy high as he and David stepped onto the Red Line, moving through the crowd to grab a spot near the door. The train was crowded, but Jason didn't seem to mind. He was already talking a mile a minute, barely pausing for breath.

"I'm telling you, tonight's gonna be huge, I can feel it," Jason said, bouncing slightly on his feet. "Maybe I'll catch a home-run ball!"

David smirked, leaning against the train pole. "Yeah, you say that every time."

"I mean it this time," Jason said as the train swayed along the tracks.

David raised an eyebrow. He was more reserved—preferring calm nights, not the chaotic energy Jason thrived in. As the train rattled on, Jason kept going, telling David all the things he was going to do, all the bets he was going to win.

When they switched to the Green Line, the train was even more packed. The closer they got to Kenmore Square, the louder and rowdier the passengers became. Someone was already leading a "Let's go, Red Sox!" chant, their voice carrying over the hum of conversations.

They eventually hopped off at Kenmore Square and walked toward Fenway Park, the harsh, bright glow from the CITGO sign shining down on their shoulders.

The crowd was thick, and everyone was aware of the upcoming game. Fans were wearing Red Sox shirts, hats, and sporting foam fingers. Some had their shirts off, showing their bodies painted with their team colors, while others had settled for simply painting their faces. The whole street felt alive and buzzing with energy.

"This place is hopping!" Jason practically shouted, his eyes wide and mouth hanging open. "This is as good as it gets, dude. Red Sox versus Yankees night game!"

"No, my friend. The Red Sox beating the Yankees at home is as good as it gets," David chuckled, glancing around.

David's statement only seemed to add fuel to Jason's excitement. He spun in the air, making ballerina twirls look manly, before grabbing David by the collar and urging him forward.

With Jason pulling him along, they stepped out onto the busy streets, heading toward Lansdowne Street. The area was packed, full of people heading to bars and cheering on the game, and loud music and voices mixed together as they made their way through the crowd.

The line outside the pub on Lansdowne Street was long, but Jason was already pushing ahead, eager to get in. They squeezed through the door, brushing past other people. The place was packed—fans everywhere, some standing at tables, others leaning against the walls. The air was loud and full of excitement.

They made their way to the bar, with David keeping pace, though not nearly as animated as Jason. Jason quickly ordered a couple of beers, then they moved to a small spot near the bar, finding a high top to settle on with just enough space to put their drinks on the countertop and do what they liked to do most—people watch.

Overhead, the TVs all displayed pre-game coverage as energy surged throughout the bar. Jason, always the social one, started scanning the crowd, looking for people to talk to and college girls to hit on, though it was harder for both of them to call out any girls due to the noise in the bar.

Meanwhile, David, ever calm and silent, sipped his cold beer while his eyes slowly moved around the room. He wasn't looking for anything in particular, just observing. He liked watching people, taking in the little details: the way someone smiled, how people moved through the crowd.

That was when he caught sight of her, and for a

moment, everything else seemed to fade away. Her eyes were an amazing shade of deep, ocean blue, and when their gazes met, something inside David shifted. It was strange, almost like he had known her before, but he couldn't explain it.

Their eyes locked for only a second, and she smiled at him.

David couldn't help but hold her gaze as she walked past them, eventually joining the crowd.

"Oh my god!" he blurted out, his tongue almost hanging out of his mouth.

Jason glanced up from his beer, his eyes moving with David's as he followed the girl through the crowd. She moved with elegance and graceful movement, and finally, she managed to reach her friend on the other side of the bar without needing to shove or push her way through.

David pulled his eyes away from her and turned to Jason.

"Did you see that girl?" He slapped Jason's arm repeatedly as if he didn't already have his attention. "Oh my God, she is amazing!"

Jason simply shook his head as he tried to take another sip of his beer. He eventually gave the girl with the blue eyes and her friend another look and turned back to David.

"She's cute, I guess. But dude, her friend? Total butter face." He grinned at his joke, waiting for David's reaction. "Get it? Everything but her face!"

Jason poised himself for a full belly laugh, but David gave him a light punch to the shoulder and rolled his eyes.

"Give me a break, man." David scanned the crowd for

her once more, this time catching her eyes again. He quickly looked away. "Do you think she noticed me? I think she might have."

Jason scoffed. "Why does it matter?"

"Come on, man, you know me. You know I'm not like this, but when I saw her... when we made eye contact... I don't know. I felt something." David paused for a moment, hoping to find the right words. "It felt like butterflies or déjà vu or something. I don't know. I just know I felt something that I haven't felt before."

Jason pursed his lips in the most uninterested way while he peered over David's shoulder. "I'd say she's noticed you."

David snapped around just to see those blue eyes again, staring right back at him. She smiled softly, with her head tilting slightly to the side, allowing her long, silky brown hair to flow freely down her shoulder.

"I should go say something," David said to Jason without taking his eyes off of her. "I have to! I can't just let this moment pass."

"Oh yeah, sure," Jason rolled his eyes, his expression purely skeptical. "You said the same thing about that abstract monstrosity you bought and hung in your dorm room. The one that looks like a kindergarten crime scene."

David rolled his eyes. "It's not the same."

"Dude. You said you couldn't imagine yourself going home without it. That it was destiny," Jason reminded him.

"Your sarcasm is noted." David grinned brightly. "Doesn't change my point. When I saw that print, I could see it hanging in my living room, over my sofa. Almost like it belonged in my life to admire every day."

"Yeah. Uh-huh. Not sure the best way to flirt with a girl is to compare meeting her to buying that monstrosity of a painting," Jason said, nodding profusely.

"No, it's not like that, man. How can I explain this? It... it's like lightning striking the same place twice or something. It's like seeing her made me feel the same way, you know?"

Jason pointed his finger in David's face. It took David a moment to realize that Jason wasn't pointing at him but rather at something behind him.

"Turn around, dude," he whispered, his lips curled into a sneaky sneer.

David felt a lump instantly form in his throat, with a slight throbbing sensation confirming that it was in fact not a lump in his throat but his heart beating. He was far too aware of how wide his eyes were; he could swear that they were almost popping out of their sockets.

Slowly, he turned to face what was behind him. She was walking toward them now. Her eyes were still on David, and she smiled, bright and warm.

"Hey," she said upon reaching them, her blue eyes staring directly into his soul, accompanied by a radiating smile fit to outshine the sun. "Can my friend and I join you two?"

She seemed to address both of them, but her eyes remained fixed on David.

He swallowed hard, his mouth suddenly dry. He wasn't sure what to do with his hands or his feet, but somehow, his body managed to stay rooted to the spot. He glanced at

Jason, who was grinning like he'd just won a prize.

David opened his mouth to say something, but his mind went blank. All he could do was nod, too focused on the girl in front of him. She was even more beautiful up close. The way her eyes held his, like there was something there she wanted to share. He felt like she was waiting for him to say something, anything.

"Uh... sure," David finally managed to croak, his voice barely louder than a whisper. He cleared his throat. "You guys can sit here."

Her smile widened, and she motioned to her friend, who had been standing behind her, waiting patiently. Her friend was shorter, with a more reserved look, but she smiled too, a little shyly. They both slid into the seats beside David and Jason.

"I'm Hannah," she said smiling.

David swallowed hard, his mouth dry, trying to keep it together. "Uh, I'm David. This is, uh, Jason." He motioned awkwardly to his friend, who was already halfway into a conversation with Hannah's friend, a look of amusement plastered on his face.

Hannah's smile didn't fade. "So, are you guys here for the game?" she asked, the tone casual, but with an edge of interest that made David's heart beat a little faster.

Jason, ever the charmer, immediately leaned back, his legs stretched out as if he owned the place. He raised his drink. "Yup, how about you two? What brings you to the game tonight?"

The girls exchanged a quick glance, then Hannah spoke first. "We're just here for the experience," she said, shrugging lightly.

Jason laughed. "Oh, you've got that alright," he said, winking. "Red Sox-Yankees? This is as real as it gets. The atmosphere here is electric."

David didn't say much. He couldn't seem to tear his gaze away from Hannah, her eyes still locked on him. There was something about her—something that felt different. He was no expert at this, but he could tell she wasn't just making small talk. Her smile was warm, her body language open. She was genuinely interested in the conversation, but David's thoughts kept drifting.

He'd never felt so out of place before, even though he had been in plenty of social situations like this. The words felt like they were stuck in his throat. It wasn't that he didn't know how to talk to girls. It was that this felt... different. Like there was something more at play.

"So," Jason began again, sensing a shift in the mood, "You two in school around here or just visiting?"

"We're students," Hannah replied, her tone light.

"Cool," Jason said, leaning forward and grinning. "I'm from around here, too. But David here is a transplant." He shot David a knowing look, which made David's cheeks flush slightly. He couldn't help it; he was used to being the quiet one, but now he felt like he was in the spotlight.

David cleared his throat and shifted in his seat. "Yeah, I guess," he said, trying to steer the focus back on Jason. "I'm just finishing up school. Architecture."

Hannah nodded, her smile still there. "That's really cool. I've always thought architecture was interesting."

Her words felt like they cut right through the noise

around them. The chatter of the crowd, the hum of the TVs on the walls, it all faded for a second. He could only hear her voice, soft but clear. It felt like the beginning of something, but he wasn't sure what yet. All he knew was that there was a pull connecting them somehow.

"You should show me your work sometime," she added, her voice just a little quieter. "I'd love to see what you've done."

David blinked, surprised by her interest. He hadn't expected her to say something like that. He'd been too caught up in trying to figure out why he felt so drawn to her, but now he was also wondering if he could keep his cool enough to show her what he was working on.

Jason, thankfully, broke the tension by slamming his empty glass on the table with a laugh. "Well, now that we've got the introductions out of the way, what do you say we hit the game?"

David could tell Jason was trying to shift the conversation, but his mind was still stuck on Hannah's words. He needed to stop overthinking it. He didn't even know if she was serious about wanting to see his work, or if she was just being polite. But for once, he didn't mind the uncertainty. He was... intrigued. "Well, I guess the game's about to start. Do you have tickets?" he said, breaking his own silence. He gave a half-smile, hoping she would say yes.

Hannah smiled back at him, her blue eyes sparkling with slight disappointment. "No, we're just bar hopping, but if you need to get going, I understand."

David felt a jolt of disappointment. He couldn't help

but feel like she was trying to say something more without saying it at all. It made his heart skip a beat. He had never felt this way before, and now the thought of walking away, never knowing what could come of this, made him reconsider. "Hey, Jason, I decided that Hannah and I are going to watch the game right here."

Jason looked at David, surprised, but then not so surprised. He turned to Hannah's friend and asked, "Wanna join me? Looks like these two would rather watch on the big screen." The friend cried out in excitement, and they both waved goodbye as they headed for the door.

David and Hannah returned to their gaze. "You didn't have to give up your tickets for me," she whispered in a kind tone.

"I wanted to. I hope you don't mind. I just wanted to get to know you more," he smiled.

She smiled right back.

He couldn't shake the feeling that something had shifted inside him. This wasn't just another casual night out. This felt like the start of something—something he wasn't quite ready to understand, but something he knew he wanted to explore.

CHAPTER 04

THE LIST

The late afternoon sunlight spilled through the half-empty apartment, sending out long streaks of gold across the hardwood floor. The living room, once cozy and familiar, was now in a disorderly state, full of cardboard boxes, packing tape, and scattered belongings. The couch, the one they had cuddled on during movie nights, was stripped of its pillows. The bookshelves, once lined with Hannah's novels and David's architecture magazines, stood bare, exposing faint outlines where dust had settled over the years.

David stood near the kitchen, hands on his hips, surveying the cluttered space. It was strange how a place could feel so different when it was being packed away. For years, the small third-floor apartment, off Fayette Street near Inman Square, had been home—their first real place together after getting married. Now, with each box sealed and labeled, it was slipping further into memory, making way for something new.

They were excited to be moving to their first house nestled in the suburbs of Arlington, Massachusetts. The new house was in an ideal location for the young professionals. It would be a short drive from Alewife's T terminal, where David would be able to take the train to Boston's Back Bay, where he worked as an architect. It was also a few blocks from Hannah's job at a local specialty school for the deaf and blind.

He couldn't help but reminisce about how good the previous years had been to the both of them. David had graduated near the top of his class with a Bachelor of Architecture degree. He then spent some years taking his licensure exams and working his way up at one of Boston's well-known architecture firms, the Beacon Design Group. Hannah, on the other hand, had earned her bachelor's in education, as well as her certification for teaching the deaf. It had been her lifelong dream to become a sign language teacher, since she had grown up needing to use it to communicate with her deaf grandmother.

David and Hannah's love had grown stronger each day, and he was sure that she was his soulmate. He would tell all who would listen how in that moment they first met— at that pub on Lansdowne Street during a Sox game—he was certain that she was the one. Although they had both felt it was love at first sight, they had agreed to simply date until they were both out of college and had good jobs. Hannah knew her father would never hesitate to pay for her wedding; however, it was important to her that she and David be able to pay for their own wedding.

"Babe, I need more boxes!" Hannah's voice rang out from the back bedroom.

David shook his head with a small smile. They had bought more boxes than they thought they'd need, but somehow, it was never enough. He stepped around a pile of folded clothes, moving through the maze of packed and unpacked items, and made his way down the short hallway toward the bedroom.

When he reached the doorway, he leaned against the frame, watching Hannah for a moment before responding. She was on her knees in front of an open closet, her brown hair tied back in a messy ponytail, a streak of dust smudged across her cheek. She was sorting through a pile of old sweaters and mismatched shoes, tossing some into a donation bag and others into a half-packed suitcase.

David cleared his throat, smirking. "Here you go, sweetheart," he said, handing her the last empty box they had. "But that's it. We're officially out. The rest will have to be put into bags."

Hannah groaned dramatically, flopping onto her back against the pile of clothes. "How do we have so much stuff? We've only lived here for a few years!"

David chuckled, stepping into the room. "That's what happens when you combine two lives into one small apartment. We accumulate things."

Hannah lifted her head, eyeing him playfully. "Are you saying I have too much stuff?"

He grinned. "I'm saying we both do."

She sighed, sitting up again. "I just want everything to be organized for the new house. I don't want to bring junk with us."

David crouched down beside her, placing a hand on her knee. "It's going to be great, Han. The new house, the space, everything. We're doing this together."

Her face softened, and she nodded. "I know. It just feels... big, you know? Like we're closing a chapter."

David understood what she meant. Moving wasn't just about shifting locations—it was a symbol of change, of growing into a new phase of their lives. They had spent their college years and early marriage here, making memories in this small space. Now, they were stepping into something bigger—into a future that held things they had dreamed about for years.

Hannah suddenly sat up straighter, her expression shifting from nostalgic to mischievous. She wrapped her arms around David's neck and pulled him close then pressed her lips against his. "You are the best thing that has ever happened to me. I am here, freaking out about moving and everything, and you're handling all this so well, bringing me bags and boxes without a single complaint!"

David just smiled at her. "Thank you, my love. For better or worse, right?"

Hannah loved it when he smiled. Her playful expression turned sensual. "Honestly, babe, I love you so much! Thank you for making me so happy and making all our dreams come true! I am so excited about our new house and starting a family someday."

"Me too, babe. Me too," David replied, the mood

shifting into something carnal.

Hannah then leaned in for a quick kiss, but David was having none of that. He sat down on a rolled rug and grabbed her by the hips, settling her right over his waist. Feeling the bulge through the clothing between them, she gyrated her hips on him, sending a shot of pleasure straight into her depths.

David grabbed her chin and pulled her in for a long kiss, slanting his mouth over hers in a way that had her core clenching and wetness seeping between her thighs. She returned his kiss with the same intensity, while still rubbing her panty-clad crevice over his sweats until they both had to come up for air.

Hannah giggled, her laugh turning more devious. She then slid her hand between them, taking hold of David's hard bulge and giving it a squeeze. His eyes widened, before momentarily closing as a moan escaped his lips.

"You know what I want to do tonight?" she whispered against his lips.

David raised an eyebrow. "What's that?"

She grinned, sliding a hand down his chest. "I want to decommission this place, to remember all the memories and moments we've shared here."

David's smile widened. "Oh, do you now?"

Hannah giggled, nodding. "Mm-hmm. Last night in our old apartment? I say we make it memorable."

David's hands slid to her waist, pulling her closer, before moving to her butt cheeks and giving them a squeeze. "I like the way you think."

For a moment, the stress of packing and moving faded

into the background. They shared a deep kiss, wrapped up in the warmth of each other, until the sound of something falling in the closet broke the moment.

Hannah sighed, reluctantly pulling away. "Okay, okay. Back to work."

David laughed, rubbing his thumb against her cheek before standing up. "Let's finish this."

They returned to work, wrapping up their packing.

Then—

Hannah pointed to the top shelf. "Babe, can you please help me grab that shoebox back there? I think it's just old papers and junk, but I want to go through it before we toss anything."

David reached up, fingers grazing the dusty cardboard before pulling it down. He set it on a nearby box and lifted the lid. Inside, a jumbled collection of old photographs, receipts, and faded greeting cards sat in no particular order. Some of the pictures were still in their processing envelopes, complete with film negatives.

Curious, David flipped through them, smiling faintly at the memories—college events, old vacations, random snapshots of nights out with friends. As he reached deeper, a folded piece of paper slipped from the pile and fluttered to the floor.

He bent down to pick it up.

The moment his fingers brushed against the paper, something shifted in his mind. A strange, almost dizzying sense of recognition washed over him, like stepping into a forgotten dream. He unfolded it slowly, his eyes scanning the handwritten words.

And then he stopped breathing.

"Oh my God," he muttered.

There, in faded ink, was a list. Eight items, written in neat but slightly rushed handwriting.

His eyes locked onto the first word.

Hannah.

A cold wave passed through him, sending goosebumps across his arms.

His grip tightened on the paper. This wasn't possible.

"Babe?" Hannah's voice pulled him back. "What is it?"

David didn't answer. He just stood there, staring at the list as if it held some secret he had long buried and forgotten. His heart pounded against his ribs, his mouth suddenly dry.

Hannah frowned, sensing something was wrong. She reached for the paper, but David hesitated before letting her take it.

Her eyes moved across the words, reading them out loud. "Hannah…?"

She looked up at him, confused. "Why is my name on this?"

David swallowed hard. "I never told you about this."

"About what?" Hannah's voice grew uneasy.

He exhaled slowly. "This list… it's six years old."

Hannah blinked. "Six years?"

He nodded. "I got this from a man… a man who died right in front of me."

A heavy silence filled the room. Hannah held the paper between her fingers, her grip tightening as she stared at it.

David continued, his voice low and uneasy. "But… I

met you five years ago."

Hannah's face paled.

Neither of them spoke. The air between them grew thick with an unspoken dread.

David licked his lips, forcing himself to say the only thing that made sense—except that it didn't.

"So how the hell did your name end up on this list a year before we even met?"

She swallowed hard. "I think you need to tell me everything."

David exhaled through his nose, running a hand through his hair. He shared the details of that incident from six years ago—the strange phone call in the middle of the night, the visit to the hospital, the elderly man without a name who recited the list before flatlining.

A long silence followed.

Hannah finally spoke, her voice softer now. "And you never figured out who he was?"

David exhaled sharply, shaking his head. "Never. They called him a John Doe. No ID, no family, nothing. Just a man who came in alone and died alone. I tried asking and digging deeper about him, but no one knew where he came from. No one even knew how he got to the hospital. He just… appeared."

Hannah's gaze dropped back to the paper in her hands. She traced her finger over the words again, her expression unreadable.

David took a step closer. "Hannah… I put that list in a box and forgot about it. I didn't even think about it again until now." He gestured toward the paper. "And yet somehow, your name is the first thing on it."

Hannah exhaled through her nose, staring at the list as if it might change under her gaze.

David's voice was quiet. "That's why I don't know what to think."

Hannah swallowed, her throat bobbing. "It doesn't make sense."

David nodded. "I know."

Another silence fell between them, heavier this time.

Finally, Hannah spoke, her voice more resolved. "We need to figure out what the rest of this means."

David studied her for a moment before nodding. "Yeah. We do."

They both looked down at the list, taking note of each of the items.

Hannah
Hermit Lake
Ladybug tattoo
18 Vassar Street
Leonard Friston
Emmitt Poole
Cathedral Rock
Kill him

Hannah traced her finger over the items, her touch hesitant, like she was afraid the ink might smear under her skin. "This is beyond strange. I mean, some guy you never met, who is dying of all things, gives you a list. And the first thing on the list is my name?"

"I know, it's really weird," he added, at a loss for words.

"Weird?!" Hannah cried out, "No, this is like *Twilight Zone* bullshit!"

Her words were enough to ease the tension in the room. David laughed because it was unusual for Hannah to swear.

Hearing him, Hannah laughed too, and for a moment, the atmosphere felt lighter.

David then cleared his throat. "I think we need to try and figure this thing out. We met five years ago, which was a year after I was given the list. Obviously, I tossed the list in the shoebox and honestly forgot about it. Now years later, I find the list and your name is number one on it. What if it's some sort of prediction?"

"Prediction? Do you think these items are predictions of the future?" Hannah asked skeptically.

"Maybe, or it's just a crazy coincidence."

"If that is true, then what is Hermit Lake, or ladybug tattoo? And oh my God! Did you see number eight? 'Kill him?' I mean, this is outright creepy. And I don't recognize any of these, except for my own name," Hannah added, her tone turning somber again.

David looked at the list again, jaw tight. "You're right, this is all creepy. And I also don't recognize any of the items." His eyes moved up the page again from the last entry, stopping at a particular one on the top part of the paper. "Except... maybe this one." He tapped the fourth line.

18 Vassar Street

Hannah looked up at him, brow furrowing. "That means something to you?"

David hesitated before answering. "There is a Vassar Street that cuts through the MIT campus. I think 18 Vassar would be near the Stata Center."

Hannah bit her lip, her mind racing. David could see the concern on her face, and he added, "Okay, let's not read too much into this. I mean, it could mean nothing. Maybe we can just start by checking out an item or two on the list and see if it's legit."

Hannah nodded and pulled out her cellphone, her hands still slightly shaky as she tapped on the search bar. "Hermit Lake," she said, typing the words in.

David leaned over, watching as the results popped up.

"It's a real place," she confirmed, her voice tight. "It's in New Hampshire, north of Manchester. It's a small, isolated lake near the White Mountains." She scrolled through images, her pulse quickening. "There's a campground. Some old cabins. A hiking trail."

David sat back, rubbing his hands over his face. "So, what? The guy who gave me the list wanted me to go there?"

Hannah exhaled. "Maybe it's a clue. A starting point."

David scoffed, though there was no humor in it. "A clue to what, Hannah? This isn't a scavenger hunt. This is a piece of paper from a dying man. A man I didn't even know. And now, after six years, it just happens to show up again? This isn't normal."

Hannah nodded. "I know it's not. But that's why we need to find out what's going on with this list."

She turned the phone toward him, and he stared at the image on the screen for a few seconds. He wanted to dismiss the whole idea, to say no and throw the list away, forgetting this ever happened. But the pit in his stomach wouldn't let him.

Hannah, noticing how conflicted he was, continued. "I think we should do this in order, beginning with checking out Hermit Lake first, just to see if anything feels off. If it's nothing, we will forget about it."

David reluctantly agreed. "Fine, we'll do that."

•••

The rest of the evening passed in slow motion. They went back to packing, but the mood had shifted completely. The apartment, once filled with warmth and nostalgia, now felt different.

David taped up a box, his mind only half focused. Hannah sat across from him, folding clothes into a suitcase, but she wasn't really paying attention either.

Every so often, their eyes would drift back to the list placed on one of the boxes. Neither of them spoke about it.

By the time they crawled into bed, exhaustion weighed heavily on their bodies, but sleep didn't come easy.

Hannah lay curled against David's side, her fingers tracing absent patterns on his arm. The steady rhythm of his heartbeat should have been comforting. But her mind was still spinning.

She swallowed, her voice barely above a whisper. "David?"

"Yeah?"

She hesitated, then finally asked the question that had been clawing at the back of her mind.

"What if the last thing on that list… 'Kill him'… is something you're meant to do?"

David didn't respond.

He just stared at the ceiling, his mind replaying the moment he first held that paper in his hands all those years ago.

Back then, he had assumed it was meaningless. A dying man's last act of delirium.

But now, as the weight of the mystery settled onto his chest, he wasn't so sure.

Because if the list had been right about the name Hannah…

Then what if it was right about everything else…?

CHAPTER 05
HERMIT LAKE

As the days trickled by, there was a rhythm to their new life. The usual but expected slowness that accompanied the workweek seemed more noticeable than ever, as David and Hannah settled into their new house.

The house, nestled on a tree-lined suburban residential street just down the road from Crosby Park in Arlington, felt like a dream come true. The move had been exhausting, but the unpacking was progressing smoothly. The rooms, once filled with cardboard boxes, were slowly returning to normalcy. There were still plenty of odds and ends scattered about, but the furniture was in place, the kitchen functional, and the living room inviting.

David couldn't help but smile at the little touches. Hannah's books were now stacked neatly on the shelves, and the couch was just the right distance from the window to let in the perfect afternoon sunlight.

David sat at the dining room table, his laptop open in front of him as he worked through a few emails from his workplace. His eyes wandered over to Hannah, who was sorting through a stack of paperwork at the counter. She had a cup of coffee beside her, but it looked like it had long gone cold.

"Honey, are you sure you really want to drive up to Hermit Lake on Saturday?" David asked, his voice breaking through the silence in the house.

Hannah paused, glancing up at him with a small smile tugging at her lips. By the expression on her face, David could tell she had been thinking about the question for days. It was the second weekend they had since moving in, and the idea of driving hours to a remote lake wasn't exactly the relaxing weekend getaway he had in mind. Though he knew they'd talked about visiting Hermit Lake ever since they had found the list.

"Yes, I'm sure," Hannah said with a shrug. "If you think about it, if my name being on that list is a coincidence, then nothing will come of it. But if the items on that list are not coincidences, if they actually turn out to be predictions of the future, then... well, we may have stumbled onto something incredible."

David sat back in his chair, folding his arms across his chest. He turned his head, looking at her with a mix of curiosity and concern. "Then again, if we go to Hermit Lake because of the list, aren't we just engaging in a self-fulfilling prophecy?" His tone was playful, but there was an edge of doubt in it too, a hesitation about the whole situation.

Hannah gave a small laugh, walking over to where he sat, her fingers brushing against the back of his chair. She placed a hand on his shoulder and bent down, her face just inches from his. "Yes, I think that is true. We could be making the predictions happen just by believing in them," she said, her voice quiet for a moment, as if considering her words carefully. Then her expression shifted, playful once again. "But let me ask you this: if five years ago, you knew the name Hannah was number one on that list the day we met, would you have run the other way, or would you have taken a chance?"

David smiled, leaning back in his chair and looking up at her. He could feel the warmth of her presence as she hovered just above him. His heart gave a small jolt, and for a moment, he felt like he was back at that pub on Lansdowne Street, the night they had met. There was something about her smile, the way she held his gaze, that made it impossible for him to imagine ever running from her.

"That's not a fair question," he said softly, his lips curving into a grin. "Because you always had me at hello."

Hannah smiled back, her eyes sparkling. She leaned down and kissed him quickly, a brief but sweet press of lips. When they pulled apart, she kept her forehead pressed against his for a moment, both of them remained still for a bit longer.

"You know, this whole list thing... it still feels crazy," she murmured. "But the thought of knowing it's there, and maybe doing something about it, it feels... like we've been given a key to a door we didn't know existed."

David sighed, his hands reaching out to rest on her waist as he stood up, pulling her gently into his arms. He held her close, as though in that moment, the world outside didn't matter. It was just the two of them, their new home, and whatever lay ahead.

"We'll figure it out," he said quietly, his voice firm but filled with uncertainty. "We'll go to Hermit Lake on Saturday, just to see what's there. And if nothing happens, we move on, maybe to the next item on the list."

Hannah nodded against his chest. "Yeah, I fully agree with you."

For a moment, there was silence between them. They knew they were about to embark on something strange, something that would either make their lives a little more complicated or change everything they thought they knew.

David pulled back slightly, looking down at her with a soft smile. "But no matter what, you and me, we've got this. Right?"

Hannah looked up at him, her hand coming up to touch his face, and nodded. "Right. We've got this."

They stayed like that for some time, holding each other in the quiet of the room, before turning back to do what each of them was busy with.

•••

The air was crisp and cool that Saturday, the kind of early autumn morning that made it impossible to step outside without taking a deep breath. The sky was a soft, pale blue, and a thin layer of mist hovered over the quiet streets as David and Hannah walked toward their car, coffees in hand.

Their usual café had been the first stop, as it always was on mornings like this. The small corner shop, tucked between a bookstore and an old brick apartment building, smelled like roasted beans and cinnamon. The owner, an older man named Pete, greeted them as he always did, with a knowing nod and a simple, "Heading out on an adventure today?"

Hannah had laughed as she stirred a splash of cream into her coffee. "Something like that."

Now, standing in the parking lot, David double-checked the GPS on his phone, his brow furrowing as he adjusted the route settings. "Looks like it'll take us about an hour and a half. Weather looks good, but it might get chilly later." He tapped the screen a few more times before glancing at Hannah.

She took a slow sip of her coffee and smirked. "You know, for someone who claims to love spontaneity, you sure do love to over-prepare."

David rolled his eyes, slipping his phone into his jacket pocket. "It's the architect in me. Making plans is what I do." With that, he slightly smirked.

"Uh-huh," Hannah teased as she walked around to the passenger side. "Tell that to the guy who got us lost on our first road trip together."

David chuckled as he slid into the driver's seat. "That wasn't my fault. The road signs were confusing."

"The road signs were in English, David."

"Yeah, well, if we hadn't gotten lost, we never would've found that little diner."

Hannah smiled at the memory. They had decided to take a weekend trip up the coast. Somewhere along the way, a wrong turn had sent them thirty miles off course, down a quiet coastal road that led them to an old diner with faded red booths and the best fried clams they'd ever had. They'd sat in that booth for hours, talking about everything and nothing, not caring that they were off schedule.

"That place had amazing seafood," Hannah said as David pulled onto the main road.

"Yeah, and you just wanted to use their restroom."

Hannah grinned. "See? Great memories."

David shook his head, but he was smiling.

•••

Driving north on I-93, through Manchester and Concord, the change in scenery was immediate. The farther they moved away from the city, the quieter the roads became. The highway cut through rolling hills and dense forests, the trees bursting with the fiery reds, deep oranges, and golden yellows of early autumn. Sunlight filtered through the branches, creating shifting patterns of light and shadow on the pavement.

David kept one hand on the wheel, his other resting on his lap, occasionally reaching for his coffee in the cupholder. Hannah sat beside him, her legs crossed beneath her, gazing out the window at the passing landscape.

The sight of the trees, their colors vivid against the clear blue sky, made her smile. "God, babe, I love the foliage this time of year," she said, breaking the long silence.

David glanced over at her, a small smile forming on his lips. "Yeah, it's something else."

Hannah turned toward him slightly. "How much longer?"

David tapped the GPS screen on the dashboard. "We'll be getting off after Northfield soon. Then it's about ten more miles on Route 132, and we should be there."

Hannah nodded and returned her gaze to the trees, watching as they blurred together. The road stretched ahead of them, winding through the countryside. Occasionally, they passed old barns and quiet farms, the kind of places that looked like they hadn't changed in decades.

The car settled into a comfortable quiet again; the sound of the tires against the road was the only noise to be heard. There was something peaceful about the drive, despite the reason for their trip. It was almost easy to forget that they weren't just on a casual getaway.

Almost.

Just after they passed a narrow bridge over Gulf Brook, a small wooden sign came into view on the right side of the road. The paint was faded and the edges of the wood were splintered with age.

DEVIL'S DEN – NEXT RIGHT

Both David and Hannah noticed it at the same time. Without saying a word, they turned their heads toward each other, their expressions mirroring the same thought. It was an unspoken moment of recognition—something about the sign, about its presence on this otherwise ordinary road, felt… creepy.

Hannah was the first to break the silence. She smirked and shook her head. "Glad that wasn't on the list."

David chuckled, his fingers tightening slightly on the steering wheel. "Yeah, no kidding."

Hannah leaned back in her seat, exhaling. "You know, I would like to say this whole thing has been fun. Like a scavenger hunt. But…" She trailed off, her voice quieter now. "I know we don't know what will come of this yet, but all the items seem harmless. All except for number eight."

David didn't need her to say it. He knew exactly what she was talking about.

Kill him.

The words from the list had stuck with them both.

David glanced at Hannah, making a point to meet her eyes, even as he kept one hand steady on the wheel. His voice was firm when he spoke. "I agree. If these items turn out to mean something, if they really do predict the future somehow, we are not going anywhere near number eight."

Hannah held his gaze for a moment before reaching over and taking his free hand in hers. Her grip was warm, steady. "You promise?"

David gave her hand a small squeeze. "Yes. I promise."

She held onto him for a few more seconds before letting go, leaning back against the seat. The road stretched ahead, the sign fading from view in the rearview mirror. The unsettling feeling it left behind, however, remained.

•••

As David and Hannah finally arrived at Hermit Lake, the road narrowed. The trees, with their leaves turning shades of gold and red, framed the lake ahead. The water was calm, smooth like glass, reflecting the overcast sky.

David pulled the car into a small clearing at the end of the road. There were only a few houses here, spread far apart, each with open yards leading to the shore. He turned off the engine, and for a moment, there was nothing but silence.

Hannah stepped out first, stretching her legs. The air was crisp, carrying the scent of pine and damp earth. Leaves crunched under her boots as she took a few steps forward. David joined her, glancing around at the houses. He had always admired different styles of architecture, and these lake homes were no exception.

His eyes landed on one house in particular. It was modern but still had a cozy feel—wood siding, large windows, and a perfect spot overlooking the lake.

"Look at these homes," he said, nodding toward it. "I've always wanted a lake house, ever since my capstone project at MIT."

Hannah smiled, slipping her hand into his. "You spent an entire school year on your capstone design. Do you think you still have those drawings somewhere?"

David chuckled. "Probably."

They followed a narrow dirt path leading toward the water. Along the way, they passed a small, old barn. The wood was faded, and the roof sagged slightly, like it hadn't been used in years. Beyond it, the lake stretched out in front of them, lined with houses, each with its own dock.

Some docks looked newer, while others were worn down by time.

David and Hannah stood by the shore, taking it all in. The lake was still, with only the occasional ripple. The quiet was different from the city—it made everything feel slower, more peaceful.

David broke the silence. "Well, here we are at Hermit Lake, and the sky hasn't fallen."

Hannah smirked. "Yet."

She looked around, then back at him. "You do realize if nothing happens here, we're going to have to look for item number three. Ladybug tattoo."

David chuckled. "Great. A permanent reminder of a very weird weekend."

They both laughed softly. The place was beautiful, calm. But something about it felt just a little... off. Neither of them said it out loud, but they both felt it.

As they stood side by side, a comfortable silence settled between them, leaving only the sound of water gently lapping against the shore. A breeze stirred the trees, rustling the golden leaves overhead. In this moment, it was just the two of them, standing before Hermit Lake. But then, out of nowhere, a voice broke through the quiet.

"Well, aren't you two a lovely young couple?"

David and Hannah turned toward the sound. Emerging from the trees was an older woman, her movements steady and full of purpose. She looked to be in her late seventies, maybe older, but there was something youthful about her, perhaps in the way she carried herself. She had a small smile on her face, giving her an inviting demeanor. She wore a simple white, long-sleeved shirt and loose blue pants, the kind of outfit chosen for comfort rather than fashion. Her gray hair, streaked with highlights, was neatly styled, framing a face lined with years but still full of warmth.

Hannah smiled at the unexpected compliment. "Oh, thank you."

David, always more aware of their surroundings, felt the need to explain why they were there. After all, they could be standing on her property. "I hope we are not intruding. We saw the path and just wanted to get a closer look at the lake."

The woman waved off the concern with a gentle laugh. "Oh no, not at all. You are both just fine."

Hannah relaxed even more at the woman's kindness. There was something instantly familiar about her, as if she were the kind of person who made everyone feel at home.

The three of them fell into easy conversation, exchanging introductions with handshakes and friendly smiles. The woman was Mae Miller, and as it turned out, she lived in the house right next to the path. It was a beautiful home—one David had already admired without realizing who it belonged to.

Mae shared a little about herself, talking about how she and her husband, Paul, had always wanted to have a beautiful house by the water and how they had ended up doing just that—building a house by the lake. She spoke with fondness but also with a quiet sorrow that didn't need to be explained. Paul was gone now, and Mae lived alone, though her family visited from time to time.

David and Hannah, in turn, shared that they had just wanted a day away from the city, leaving out the real reason they had come to Hermit Lake.

As they spoke, the sharp bark of a dog echoed in the distance. The sound was high-pitched but determined, coming in short bursts with little pauses in between.

Mae glanced toward the trees. "Oh dear, that's just Lucy, my Shih Tzu. She doesn't usually bark much. I think she is feeling left out because she loves meeting new people."

"Oh, how cute!" Hannah's face lit up. "We love dogs! We have been living in apartments since college, so we never had the space for one." She grabbed David's arm playfully. "But now that we've just bought our own house, maybe it's time to start thinking about getting one."

David simply smiled, knowing this conversation was far from over.

Mae laughed. "Well, congratulations to you both. How exciting! A new house, newly married... and maybe a dog in your future. Who knows? A new baby could be next!"

David and Hannah both chuckled, their smiles widening, though neither commented on that last part.

As they began walking back up the trail together, David glanced at Mae's home once more. It was even more impressive up close, the details of the craftsmanship standing out. Unable to help himself, he said, "I really love what you and Paul did with your home. It looks like you completely renovated both the interior and exterior."

Mae's eyes brightened. "Oh, Paul was obsessed with the idea of a lake house. He and I would take long drives down the back roads of New Hampshire looking for the perfect location. I will never forget the moment we saw Hermit Lake; we just knew. But when he first showed me this house—my goodness, it was a dump. I thought he was crazy! But that didn't stop him."

David paused on the trail path to take in the full view.

"I must say, this location is incredible. And I love the way the design captures the aesthetics of a contemporary New England barn."

Mae stopped mid-step and turned to look at him, surprised. "My goodness, you sound just like Paul! He was an architect, and that is exactly what he was going for—a New England barn-style home."

Hannah's eyes widened in shock. "Paul was an architect? David is an architect too! What a coincidence!" She shot David a look, as if urging him to acknowledge how bizarre it was.

Mae smiled. "Well, isn't that something? Pure serendipity." She hesitated for a moment, as if debating something, then seemed to make up her mind. "If you two have moment, I would love to show you something."

Curious, David and Hannah followed as Mae led them toward the old barn at the edge of her property, not far from the path. The structure was small, the wood weathered with age, but the bones of it were strong. It had character—something that could be brought back to life.

Mae placed a hand on the worn-out siding. "Paul always wanted to renovate this old barn to match the house. He had plans to convert it into a guest cottage, but he never got the chance." She turned back to face them, her expression thoughtful. "But you both seem like a wonderful couple, and for some reason that only God knows, you ended up here today. Now, you can say no, but I'm going to ask anyway."

She paused before continuing.

"Would you be interested in remodeling this old barn into a guest cottage that matches the main house? And before you answer, hear me out. I am willing to sign a contract stating that I will pay for all the construction, and in exchange for your time and expertise, you and Hannah could use it whenever you'd like."

David and Hannah froze, stunned. The idea of having their own lake cottage—something they had always dreamed about—was suddenly being handed to them.

Hannah gasped. "Oh my God, yes! Deal!" She laughed, realizing how quickly she had responded. "Sorry, David, this is your thing. What do you think?"

David was equally shocked at the offer, but deep down, he already knew the answer.

"If that is what you really want," he said, looking at Mae, "then yes, I'd love to."

Mae held out her hand with a satisfied smile. David and Hannah each shook it, sealing the deal.

"Very well then," Mae said, her voice full of certainty. "We have a deal."

•••

On the drive home, David and Hannah were still riding the high of Mae's offer. The road stretched ahead of them, the trees on either side now just dark shapes against the night sky. Streetlights became more frequent as they neared the outskirts of the city, but neither of them paid much attention. Their minds were still at Hermit Lake.

Hannah leaned back in her seat, her hands fidgeting in excitement. "I can't believe our luck. A chance to have our own cottage on a lake," she said, shaking her head.

David, gripping the wheel, hadn't stopped smiling since they left the place. "I know. It feels so surreal. I mean, what are the chances?"

"The list led us there," Hannah pointed out. "And now this? It's like fate or destiny!" She glanced over at him. "It's crazy—I was just thinking about that time you told me how you fell in love with lake houses. About your adoptive mom's home magazines and how you saw one in a magazine and knew that's what you wanted someday."

David let out a small chuckle. "I was just thinking about that too," he admitted. "She used to have stacks of those magazines, always flipping through them for ideas. She redid our kitchen once: restored the cabinets, painted them bonnet blue, added white bead board and subway tiles. I used to sit at the table and watch her plan it all out."

Hannah smiled, resting her chin in her hand as she listened. She loved hearing stories about his childhood. They had spent hours, back when they were dating, just talking and getting to know every little thing about each other. It was one of the things that made them fall so hard, so fast.

David continued. "I used to flip through those magazines too, but what fascinated me most were the before and after pictures. The way a space could be completely transformed. And then there were the floor plans; I loved those. I think that's part of the reason why I pursued being an architect."

Hannah nodded, squeezing his arm. "I remember you telling me that."

David hesitated for a moment, then said, "But I never told you the rest."

Hannah turned to him, curious. "What do you mean?"

David took a deep breath. "One night, when I was a kid, I was lying in bed, flipping through one of those magazines. I saw the most incredible lake house, and I just... I fell in love with the idea of it." His fingers tapped lightly on the steering wheel. "That night, I had the most realistic dream. I was standing in the doorway of a beautiful lake house, looking out at the view. There was a patio, a stretch of grass, and this crystal-clear lake. And in the yard... I saw a woman, a little girl, and a dog. They were playing and laughing."

Hannah's expression softened. "David…"

He glanced at her quickly, then back at the road. "I woke up, and for some reason, that dream stuck with me. I always wondered if it meant something. If maybe, one day, that could be my family."

Hannah reached for his free hand, lacing her fingers through his. "It can be," she said softly. "That can be us someday."

David turned to her, his expression full of something deep and unspoken. "I would love that," he said. "I think... being adopted makes me want it even more than most."

Hannah's grip on his hand tightened. "Someday, my love," she promised.

•••

The following weeks had been filled with productive trips to Hermit Lake, where David and Hannah meticulously measured the old barn, captured its essence in photographs, and excitedly brainstormed designs for their future lake cottage. Their recent return to Arlington, however, took a disquieting turn. Each visit had been a delightful adventure, fostering a growing friendship with Mae and allowing them to discover the charming back roads and local establishments of Tilton Northfield. However, the tranquility of these excursions shattered as they stepped inside their Arlington home. Evidence of an intruder was immediately apparent. Though not completely ransacked, the signs of forced entry were undeniable: drawers stood ajar, their contents spilling onto the floor, and clothes draped precariously from their openings. Closet doors hung wide, and furniture had been inexplicably shifted.

Hannah stood frozen by the front door, a knot of dread tightening in her stomach. David disappeared into the coat closet, the muffled clink of something solid echoing in the sudden silence. He emerged clutching an old wooden baseball bat, its familiar weight now a stark symbol of the unknown threat. His pulse hammered against his ribs, a frantic drumbeat against the suffocating quiet. Sweat slicked his palm as his fingers tightened around the worn wood.

Each footfall was a deliberate act as he moved through the house, the bat held ready. Shadows stretched and danced in the dim light, turning familiar shapes into menacing figures. He cleared each room with agonizing slowness, peering into yawning closets and the inky blackness of corners where danger could be lurking. A grim resolve etched his face as he continued his methodical sweep, the silence amplifying the frantic thrumming in his ears. Finally, in the back of the house, he found it – a partially opened window, a dark gash in the wall, whispering of intrusion.

Catching his breath, David voiced the question hanging in the air, "All clear...I don't see anything missing, do you?"

Hannah sighed, a mixture of relief and unease in her voice, "No, nothing... nothing noticeable at least."

Puzzled, David continued, "I don't understand. Why would someone ransack our house and take nothing?"

"Perhaps they did take something," Hannah offered, her brow furrowed in thought, "We just don't know what it is yet."

"Good point," David conceded, a new sense of vigilance hardening his gaze. "Looks like we need to make sure we check all the windows from now on... make sure they are completely locked."

Hannah nodded in agreement, the weight of the intrusion settling upon them.

A tense silence hung in the air as David and Hannah moved through their violated home, each misplaced object a fresh stab of unease. They worked in tandem, putting things back, but the order they restored felt fragile, a thin veneer over a deeper chaos.

"We need to change the locks," Hannah said, her voice

tight, the words a shared mantra against the lingering fear. The police would need to know, a formal report against the phantom who had breached their sanctuary.

As David righted a fallen picture frame, a disquieting question gnawed at him. Nothing was missing. The realization sent a chill deeper than the initial shock. *Why break in and take nothing?* The thought pulsed in his mind, a persistent, unwelcome guest. *Were they looking for something else? Something unseen?* A prickle of unease crawled up his spine. *Could this be connected to something else, something just beyond his grasp, a half-formed shadow lurking at the edges of his memory?* The silence of their restored home felt heavy with unspoken possibilities, each more unsettling than the last.

Together, David and Hannah painstakingly returned their home to order. They resolved to change the locks immediately and notify the police of the suspicious activity, the unknown intentions of their mysterious intruder leaving them deeply unsettled.

In the following weeks, their weekend trips to Hermit Lake were put on hold. A sense of unease lingered, keeping them closer to home. David channeled his energy into his computer, focusing intently on drafting the construction plans. His goal was to have them ready to present to a contractor by spring, a tangible project to anchor him amidst the lingering uncertainty.

CHAPTER 06
FIRST NIGHT

O ver the past year, David and Hannah had settled into their new routine. Life had become predictable in the best way possible. The days passed quietly, with no more surprises or strange incidents, and the ladybug tattoo had become nothing but a distant thought. They had built a life for themselves that felt balanced and calm, something they had both longed for.

David had finished the architectural plans for their lake cottage over the winter, and by the time summer arrived, construction was complete. The cottage was everything they had imagined: a cozy escape on the edge of Hermit Lake, tucked away from the noise of the city. It was the perfect retreat for both of them. They spent their weekends there, enjoying the lake, the peace, and the sense of having something just for themselves.

They had also gotten closer to Mae. She had invited them over for dinner several times, and in return, they'd spent weekends at her place, sharing stories of their past while taking walks by the water. Mae was easy to talk to, and over time, they found themselves more comfortable with her. Mae's dog, Lucy, became a regular part of their weekends too. David and Hannah enjoyed having a dog around, even though they didn't have to care for her full time, which was a nice experience for them. And since Lucy was a sweet companion, always ready to cuddle up on the porch or run around the yard, being around her without the added responsibility of taking care of her was just what they needed at the moment.

Life for them had returned to "normal." Hannah had been promoted at work, taking on more important duties at the school, and those often kept her busy during the week. She had moments of stress, but the quiet weekends at the lake made it easier to recharge. David, too, had his share of work to do. As an architect, his schedule was packed with deadlines, but there was always time to get away for a few days. His most recent project had been a condo development in Cambridge, but he still made it a point to spend time at the lake whenever possible. The cottage had become a place where both of them could escape from the rush of daily life.

Still, every so often, a small thought would creep into Hannah's mind. It wasn't something she wanted to focus on, but she couldn't quite shake it.

The list.

The piece of paper that had started it all—hang under

a magnet on the refrigerator, the strange man at Mass General, the mention of her name, and Hermit Lake. The more she thought about it, the less it seemed like coincidence. But she pushed the thoughts away. Life was good. Their time at the lake, their quiet evenings, and their growing connection with Mae and Lucy were all enough for now.

The sun was just beginning to rise, casting soft light across the water. Hannah sat in an Adirondack chair, wrapped in a blanket while watching the mist rise from the lake. Everything was still, calm, and perfect. This was what they had wanted, what they had worked so hard for.

But then, as she sat there, the thought of the list entered her mind again. She frowned slightly, trying to push it aside. The peacefulness of the morning was exactly what she needed, and yet, a small unease settled over her. *Had it all really been just a coincidence? Her name, the lake, everything that had happened?*

For a moment, she let herself think about it. But then she shook her head and closed her eyes, choosing to focus on the sound of the birds in the trees, the gentle ripple of the water, and the warmth of the morning sun on her face. The list wasn't worth dwelling on. She stayed on the porch a little longer, letting the warmth of the sun soak into her skin. Eventually, she stood, stretched, and went inside, leaving the morning behind.

That had been months ago. Now, a bitter cold Boston winter had settled in, and the year was coming to an end.

•••

Hannah's heels clicked against the wooden floor as she

hurried from the bedroom to the bathroom, trying to finish getting ready. Tonight, she and David were going out to celebrate Boston's First Night, the city's annual New Year's Eve festival. They had dinner reservations at their favorite seafood restaurant down by Rowes Wharf, and Jason and his new date, Amber, would be joining them.

David stood near the bedroom door, already dressed, waiting for Hannah to finish. He had learned by now that standing too close or rushing her would only slow things down. Instead, he paced lightly, keeping his hands in his pockets.

"You look amazing, dear," he said when she passed by him again.

Hannah flashed him a quick smile. "Thank you, babe."

She stepped into the bathroom, leaning toward the mirror as she added the final touches to her hair and makeup. The soft light above the sink reflected in her eyes as she carefully smoothed her mascara. She glanced at her reflection, tilting her head slightly as if examining more than just her face.

"I can't tell you how wonderful this past year has been," she said, reaching for her lipstick. "All our trips to Hermit Lake, getting to know sweet Mae... having our own little lake cottage. It still feels surreal."

David leaned against the doorframe, watching her with a smile. "It really does. Mae has been great. And the cottage... I don't think we ever expected things to turn out like that. It indeed was a very unexpected outcome considering what inspired us to make the trip."

Hannah met his eyes in the mirror. "You always told

me you felt like someone was watching over you."

He nodded, crossing his arms. "Yeah. I've always believed that."

Hannah pressed her lips together, blending the color before setting the tube down on the counter. "You know, I was thinking about the list again."

David raised an eyebrow. "Oh?"

She turned slightly, still facing the mirror but watching him through the reflection. "Yup. I was thinking that thus far, it seems that the first two items on the list turned out to be good things," she continued. "You met a Hannah, and we got your dream of a lake cottage out of our trip to Hermit Lake."

David studied her for a moment before speaking. "You're worried about number three, aren't you?"

She nodded, finally turning to face him. "Yes. And I was thinking... maybe we should stop looking. Just live life, be happy, and let things happen on their own."

David exhaled, rubbing his jaw. "I don't know. It's hard to refrain from looking out for some of the items. I am just too curious, I guess." He hesitated before adding, "I mean... I was actually thinking about the list last week... about 18 Vassar Street."

Hannah's brows furrowed. "What do you mean?"

"I was near MIT for a meeting, and I thought about stopping by. Just to see what's there."

Hannah's expression hardened. "David..."

"I didn't do it," he quickly added. "I just thought about it."

She crossed her arms, watching him carefully. "Babe,

promise me you're not going to do that. We agreed that we would at least follow the list in numerical order."

David let out a small sigh but nodded. "I know, my love, and I promise."

Hannah studied his face for a second longer, making sure he meant it. Then she stepped forward, wrapping her arms around his shoulders. "Thank you."

David hugged her back, resting his chin lightly against the top of her head.

As she pulled away, she glanced at him with a small smile. "Maybe we should keep the list to ourselves tonight. I know Jason is a close friend, but we've never met his date, Amber."

David nodded in agreement. "That's probably a good idea."

Hannah gave one last glance in the mirror, straightening the strap of her dress. *Tonight was about celebrating, about enjoying the moment*, she thought.

Adjusting her heavy winter coat, she took David's hand, moving through their apartment toward the front door, and together, they stepped out into the cold night.

•••

The Seaside Restaurant was alive with energy, with the dimly lit dining room offering some respite from the chilling cold outside. The dark water outside reflected the lights through the large windows, with some small traces of snow hanging onto the boats docked in the harbor. Inside the restaurant, the smell of grilled seafood mixed with butter filled the air while the waiters swiftly moved between tables with steaming trays of food.

David and Hannah arrived first and took their seats in the corner of a booth that had a view of the waterfront. The restaurant had always made their list of favorites; it was elegant but relaxed, with an atmosphere somewhat familiar to their own little world.

A few minutes later, Jason arrived, leading Amber by the hand. As soon as he spotted them, he smiled.

"There they are, my two favorite lovebirds!" he called out, clapping David on the shoulder before leaning in to give Hannah a quick hug and making the introductions. "Babe, meet my friends, David and his beautiful wife Hannah. Guys, this lovely lady right here is Amber."

Hannah smiled warmly. "It's great to finally meet you, Amber. Jasons talked about you a lot."

Amber, a petite blonde with sharp eyes and an easy smile, took the seat next to Jason. "All good things, I hope," she said playfully, tucking a strand of hair behind her ear.

"Mostly," Hannah teased.

Jason laughed, waving down a server as they all settled in. "Alright, let's get some drinks going. It's New Year's Eve, after all."

They started with a round of drinks—a Boston Lager for Jason and David, wine for Hannah, and a Moscow mule for Amber. As the server placed the drinks down, Jason raised his glass high.

"To the new year, to new friends, and to nights we probably won't remember but will pretend we do."

They all clinked glasses, their laughter mingling with the sound of conversation around them.

The evening unfolded with light conversation, getting to know Amber better, sharing stories about work, travel, and the past year. She was friendly, quick-witted, and had a way of slipping into their dynamic with ease. Hannah instantly liked her.

Then, as expected, Jason took center stage.

With a mischievous grin, he leaned forward, resting his elbows on the table. "Alright, listen up, because this is *gold*," he said. "Summer break of 2017, Cape Cod. Absolute *scorcher* of a day. I'm talking 90 degrees, windows down, shirts off because, you know—AC is for pussies."

David chuckled, already knowing where this was going.

"So, we roll up to Nauset Beach in Chatham," Jason continued, using his hands as he spoke, his Boston accent thickening as his excitement grew. "We meet up with the rest of the guys, get a prime spot on the beach, and park my dad's Cadillac Escalade, and then we start partying. I mean *really* partying—beers, music, beach volleyball, the whole deal. Around sunset, we all decide to hit the bar up the dunes. Live band playing and hot girls everywhere. *Absolute* perfection."

Amber raised an eyebrow, but Jason was too deep into his story to notice.

"So, there I am, three Jolly Rancher shots deep, destroying some poor guy at beer pong, when David taps me on the shoulder and goes—'Dude, your dad's *Escalade* is in the friggin ocean.'"

The entire table laughed out loud, and people at the neighboring tables couldn't help but crack a smile at the energy of their conversation. Jason threw his head back, barely able to finish his sentence. "I shit you not! I was so drunk I forgot about the whole low tide, high tide thing. Left it parked too close, and the next thing you know, whoosh—the ocean owns it."

Hannah wiped tears from her eyes, laughing so hard she could barely speak. "I can't believe that actually happened! I've never seen David drunk before."

Jason pointed at David. "That's 'cause he wasn't drunk. Mr. Responsible over here? Maybe two beers at the most. He was the one keeping us all in line." He clapped David on the back. "Matter of fact, it was your fucking fault, dude. You were supposed to be the designated driver, and you didn't notice either!"

They all broke out in another fit of laughter.

David shook his head, grinning. "Yeah, that one's on me. But I also remember you trying to bribe a lifeguard to 'help get it out.'"

"Hey, desperate times, man." Jason took a sip of his drink, still laughing. "$50 and a six-pack didn't cut it, though."

Amber, who had been mostly quiet, let out a small, amused sigh, though she seemed to be enjoying the evening with her new friends. "You guys were a mess," she said, but there was something slightly tight in her voice—maybe irritation?

Trying to shift the conversation, Amber turned to David. "What about you? Any funny stories?"

David leaned back, shaking his head. "Not really, Jason has always been the storyteller."

Jason, not one to let a moment pass, snapped his

fingers. "Oh, I got one for ya! David, tell Amber about that giant framed poster you bought—the one with the math formulas... the cool abstract piece?" Then he turned to Amber. "This is a cool story... you gotta hear how he got that thing home."

Hannah immediately smiled. "Oh yeah, I love this one."

David chuckled. "It's not as dramatic as an Escalade in the ocean, but here goes. So, I'm sitting in traffic on Mass. Ave one evening, completely miserable. It's raining and everything's moving at a crawl. I look out the window, and across four lanes of traffic, I see this brightly lit art studio. It was one of those upscale Newbury Studio stores. You know, all white walls and big glass windows. Inside, the walls were full of framed posters, prints, and lithographs. So I notice this huge, framed, 4' x 4' print on the wall."

He paused, giving Hannah a quick glance. "It was like love at first sight."

Amber smirked. "With the print?"

"With the print," David confirmed. "I mean, I just loved that thing, the primary colors, the lines, the use of abstract mathematical formulas and geometric shapes; it drew me in. I just had to have it. Kinda like when I met Hannah," he said, winking at her.

Everyone at the table smiled as David continued. "I had no idea who the artist was, or how much it was, or whether it would fit in my car; I just had to have it. So I found a parking spot, parked my car, ran into the store, and bought the poster."

Amber tilted her head. "Who was the artist?"

"Malik Farnsworth. The piece is called *Geometric Tangent*. He painted a series of three of them, but I only have that one."

Jason leaned forward, grinning. "Dude, tell her how you got it home."

David sighed dramatically. "Oh, yeah, so I walk in and I see a lady; she tells me it's the last one and it was just put on sale for like $200, marked down from $350. So, I was super excited to buy it. Now, at the time, I was driving this old Honda Civic hatchback. Very tiny car. Mind you, this thing is framed and matted—way too big to fit in the backseat. So, I had to unscrew the frame and take it apart. I then had to take the foam board with the print on it and slide it like a glove into the hatchback. It barely fit across the top of the headliner. Not to mention this all happened in the middle of a rainstorm. But I was so determined to get it in the car and get it home... that I drove home with it resting on my head the entire way."

The table burst into laughter again.

"Forty-five minutes in traffic," David continued. "I had to tilt my head sideways just to see the road. But it was all worth it."

Amber shook her head, smiling. "That's dedication. Do you still have it?"

"Oh, he's obsessed with that thing," Hannah said playfully. "He's dragged it to every apartment he's ever lived in."

David nodded. "That's true. And now that we finally have our own home, it has a proper place, hanging front and center in our living room."

Jason clapped his hands together. "Alright, Hannah, your turn."

She hesitated, sitting back in her chair and feeling all eyes on her. "I don't really have any good stories."

"Come on, Hannah, there's gotta be something," Jason pressed.

David glanced at her, a small, knowing smile playing on his lips. Then, he gave her a slow wink. Hannah suddenly realized what he was suggesting.

The list.

They had agreed not to bring it up tonight, but… something about this moment, this conversation, made her feel strangely at ease. Hannah sighed, setting her glass down carefully on the table. She could feel the way Jason and Amber were looking at her with anticipation. A small part of her wanted to brush it off, make a joke, and change the subject. But another part of her felt ready to let someone else in on it, even just a little.

"Alright," she said, offering a small smirk. "You win, Jason. I actually do have a story I can share. It's a very strange one, so be open-minded. And it's about something that David and I are both currently involved in."

Jason grinned triumphantly, throwing an arm around Amber's shoulders. "I knew it! It's always the quiet ones." He leaned in, his tone teasing. "So? What is it? You two join a cult? Become spies? Wait—" He gasped dramatically. "Don't tell me… swingers?"

Amber groaned, swatting at his arm while the rest of the table broke into laughter. Hannah shook her head, rolling her eyes. "Don't you wish," she shot back playfully.

David chuckled, but he was watching her carefully now, sensing her hesitation beneath the humor.

"But seriously," Hannah continued, her voice softening, "it's... actually pretty strange."

The laughter faded. Jason and Amber straightened in their seats, their attention sharpening. The shift in Hannah's tone told them this wasn't just another funny story. This was something different, maybe juicier.

She took a breath. "It started years ago. Seven, actually."

Jason raised an eyebrow.

"At Mass General," she continued. "David received a phone call in the middle of the night, and the caller requested his presence at the hospital. He met an old patient there, a John Doe, to be specific. And this strange man gave David a list."

Jason frowned. "A what?"

"A list," David answered.

Amber tilted her head. "Like a grocery list?"

Jason smirked. "If it says 'bread, eggs, and milk,' I'm walking out."

Hannah let out a small laugh but shook her head. "No. It wasn't anything like that." She hesitated for a second, then pressed on. "It had names. Places. Just a short list of things that, at the time, meant nothing to him."

Jason's playful grin faded slightly. He wasn't laughing anymore. "Shit, you never told me this story," he said while glancing at David.

Hannah glanced at David, then back to them. "He kept it. Didn't think much of it. It got stuffed away in an old shoebox and forgotten about. Until recently."

Amber's brow furrowed. "You found it?"

David nodded. "A year or so ago. Just by chance."

Hannah tapped her fingers lightly against the table. "And here's where it gets weird," she said. "The first item on that list? Was my name."

Amber's lips parted slightly, her expression shifting from mild interest to something closer to intrigue.

Jason let out a low whistle. "Okay. That's *weird*. But maybe it was a coincidence?"

Hannah shook her head. "We thought so too. At first. But then we saw the second item on the list."

David leaned forward slightly. "Hermit Lake."

Jason blinked. "Okay..."

Hannah continued. "We decided to investigate and took a trip to Hermit Lake, where we met a lovely elderly lady named Mae, who asked us to help her renovate her cottage, and in turn, we get to use it anytime we want."

Jason leaned back. "The lake cottage you told me about... I get it now..."

Amber let out a short, breathy laugh. "Okay... that's a little creepy. You guys can totally write a book!"

Jason rubbed his chin. "Damn. That's actually kind of crazy."

Hannah shifted uncomfortably, suddenly feeling exposed. She hadn't meant to share this much, but now it was out there.

Jason narrowed his eyes playfully. "Alright. Now I have to know. What's item three?"

Hannah hesitated.

David was the first to answer. "We don't know yet."

Jason raised an eyebrow. "You mean, you haven't looked for it?"

Hannah forced a small smile. "We're just… taking things as they come."

Jason scoffed. "Come *on*. If this list is actually leading you somewhere, you're just gonna sit back and wait?" He smirked. "Does it have any six-digit numbers? Something I can play in the lottery?"

David chuckled. "No. Nothing like that. Just clues. Vague ones."

Jason leaned in. "Like what?"

David hesitated for half a second before answering. "Ladybug tattoo; stuff like that."

The moment the words left his mouth, Hannah shot him a sharp look. David felt it immediately, the shift in her posture and the way her eyes narrowed ever so slightly. He had said too much, and he could tell that his wife didn't approve that he had revealed the third item.

Hannah's stomach twisted. They weren't supposed to say anything else. They had already gone further than planned, and now Jason and Amber were looking at them with a new kind of interest: *curiosity*.

Jason's eyes widened, his entire expression shifting from curiosity to something closer to shock. He sat up straighter, his hands resting flat on the table as if steadying himself.

"No way." He shook his head slightly, like he was trying to process what he'd just heard. "Did it really say 'Ladybug Tattoo'?"

The table fell silent.

David felt his pulse quicken. "Yeah. Why?"

Jason didn't answer immediately. He glanced around the table, his jaw tightening as if debating whether or not to say what was on his mind.

"Dude." His voice was lower now, more serious. "You need to tell me. Because if that's true... I think I've seen it. I *know* someone with a ladybug tattoo."

David leaned in slightly. "Who?"

Hannah was already gripping the edge of the table, her knuckles white. "Jason, *who?*"

Even Amber looked interested now, though there was something else in her expression—something guarded. She tilted her head slightly, watching Jason carefully.

"Yeah," she said, her tone just a little sharper than before. "I would like to know as well. Who exactly are you talking about?"

Jason exhaled and lifted his hands slightly, palms out, as if to reassure her. "Relax, babe, it's not like that. It's not someone I *know* personally." He paused, looking back at David and Hannah. "It's this journalist. A blogger. She writes for *The Boston Rag*—you know, that indie news site that covers local bands, arts, and underground stuff. If you look up her blog, you'll find it."

David narrowed his eyes. "What's her name?"

Jason thought for a second, then snapped his fingers. "I think she goes by *Nella on the Net*, or something like that. She's got this profile pic—kinda iconic, actually. A black girl, around our age, hand under her chin. And if I remember right... she's got a ladybug tattoo on the back of her hand."

For a moment, nobody spoke. Hannah's breath felt caught in her chest. David stared at Jason, then slowly turned his head to look at Hannah.

Their eyes met.

Neither of them had to say anything. The feeling was instant, the moment pressing down on them the same way it had before—when they found the lake cottage, when they first realized Hannah's name was on the list.

Hannah could already see it in David's face. The shift. The spark of excitement. The gears turning in his mind. She knew what this meant to him. She also knew what it could lead to.

Her stomach twisted.

This was happening again.

First her name. Then the lake. And now—this.

Another item. Another coincidence.

What could it all mean?

•••

David and Hannah stepped into their home, the warmth of the night's events still lingering between them. The house was quiet, a stark contrast to the laughter and noise of the restaurant. Neither of them spoke as they took off their coats and shoes, but the tension in the air was unmistakable.

Hannah's mind was restless, still replaying everything Jason had said about the ladybug tattoo. It had shaken her more than she wanted to admit. She felt like they had crossed an invisible line tonight, moving deeper into something unknown. The excitement in David's eyes earlier made it clear—he believed in the list more than ever. And that scared her.

David turned to her, watching her closely. "You okay?"

Hannah hesitated before nodding. She didn't want to talk about it. Not right now.

David stepped closer, reaching for her hand. His touch was steady, grounding. "We don't have to figure it all out tonight," he said softly.

She exhaled, nodding again. But she didn't let go of his hand. She held onto him, needing the comfort, needing to feel something real—something that wasn't tied to the list, or fate, or whatever strange force seemed to be pulling them forward.

David's fingers traced small circles along the back of her hand. His touch was gentle, but there was an unspoken intensity beneath it. He could sense her unease, and in his own way, he was trying to pull her back to him, to this moment.

Hannah took a step forward, closing the space between them. She placed her hands on his chest, feeling the warmth of his skin beneath his shirt. She looked up at him, searching his face.

She didn't need to say anything. He understood.

David leaned in, pressing his lips to hers. The kiss started slow, but there was something deeper behind it— something urgent. Hannah let herself sink into it, into him. She needed this. She needed to drown out the uncertainty, even if only for a little while.

David's hands moved to her waist, pulling her closer. Her body melted against his, the warmth of his touch spreading through her. They moved together instinctively, their kisses deepening and their breaths growing heavier.

Hannah slid her hands up his chest, fumbling with the buttons of his shirt. David helped her, slipping it off his shoulders before reaching for the hem of her dress. He pulled it up and over her head, letting it drop to the floor.

They didn't speak as they moved through the house, their bodies finding each other in the dark. By the time they reached the bedroom, there was nothing between them.

David guided her onto the bed, his body pressing against hers. The air between them was thick with heat, but there was more to it than just desire. This wasn't just about passion—it was about needing each other, holding onto each other.

In one swift move, David slid on top of her, his weight pinning her to the mattress. He began feathering her with soft kisses, his lips brushing ever so lightly over her skin. "I love your skin," he murmured, pressing his mouth against her. She shivered in pleasure.

"He kissed her neck, working his way down to her breasts. Cupping her breasts in his hands, he suckled the ruby tips, nipping at them gently.

"Oh," she gasped. "That feels... oh."

"Yes, it does, doesn't it?" He trailed kisses down her stomach.

He slid down so his face was between her thighs and spread her legs gently. He loved how she would surrender so easily to his tongue, feeling a throbbing between his legs as his excitement escalated.

"I love pleasing you," he said into her, and claimed her

with a long, slow stroke of his tongue. Hannah sucked in a gasp of pleasure as his mouth moved against her, her thighs quivering under the strong grip of his hands.

Hot pleasure swirled through her body, and she felt light as air. Was that her voice urging him on shamelessly? It must have been. Hannah tangled her fingers in his hair as he pleasured her, and the sensation built inside her until she was ready to peak. David's tongue slowed as he felt a gush of wetness on his lips...he could hardly wait to be inside her.

"Oh, David!" she cried out.

He smiled, then moved up, straddling her and trapping her between his thighs. He adjusted his hips, sliding his tip against her entrance. Hannah cried out as he slid inside her.

He moved his hips hard and fast, his breath harsh and guttural in her ear. Several times he paused, and she grabbed his ass and urged him on. He chuckled quietly.

"Don't stop," she cried out.

The dam broke, and waves of pleasure washed over them in a tsunami of sensation. Hannah came hard, her muscles spasming and gripping him. David's answering cry of pleasure sent a jolt of triumph through her. They were so tightly wrapped in each other as they found their release, it was impossible to tell where one ended and the other began.

Time blurred. There was no past, no future. Just this. Just them.

When it was over, they lay together, their bodies still tangled, their skin damp with warmth. Hannah rested her head on David's chest, listening to the steady rhythm of his heartbeat. His arms were wrapped around her, holding her close. And for the first time that night, she felt calm.

As the night wore on, they made love again, a new exploration of their shared desire, a reaffirmation of their bond. They laughed, they cried, they whispered words of love and adoration, their bodies and souls entwined in a dance of passion that lasted until the first light of dawn crept through the window.

When they finally drifted off to sleep, it was with a sense of peace and contentment. The new year had brought them more than just a new beginning; it had brought them a reminder of the passion that still burned brightly between them.

As they lay there, their bodies intertwined, David traced soft patterns along her back, his fingertips barely grazing her skin. The sensation was soothing, almost hypnotic."

Then she felt it. A small circle. Then another.

Hannah's breath caught in her throat.

She stiffened slightly, but David didn't seem to notice.

"What are you drawing?" she asked, her voice barely above a whisper.

David's fingers paused for a moment before he answered, his voice heavy with sleep.

"A ladybug."

She swallowed, her mind racing, but she didn't say anything.

CHAPTER 07

LADYBUG TATTOO

The office was quiet. Most of David's coworkers had already left for the day, and only a few people remained, typing on their keyboards or making quick phone calls. The soft hum of computers filled the space, mixed with the occasional shuffle of footsteps in the hallway.

David leaned back in his chair and let out a deep breath. It had been a long day, but at least he was heading home earlier than usual. As he reached for his coat, his eyes landed on the framed wedding photo on his desk. In the picture, Hannah was laughing, her eyes full of happiness. He stood beside her, smiling, his arm around her waist. It was one of his favorite photos—one that reminded him how lucky he was.

Life was good.

They had a strong marriage, a comfortable home, and

steady jobs. Everything felt settled. Perhaps even safe. But lately, something inside him had started to shift. It wasn't dissatisfaction, exactly; more like restlessness.

The list was always on his mind, like a thread hanging loose, just waiting to be pulled. He kept finding himself reaching for it, but he feared what unraveling it might reveal. And ever since they had found the list, nothing had felt the same again. He couldn't help but remember how at first, it had seemed like just an old note from his past and the items on the list just a strange coincidence. However, as he and Hannah had worked through the items, each step had felt too connected, too intentional.

And now, there was the latest clue.

Nella on the Net with the ladybug tattoo.

His mind kept replaying Jason mentioning it at New Year's dinner last weekend. David hadn't even seen it himself, but the moment Jason described it, something had stirred inside him.

Why did that detail feel important?

He didn't know. But ever since that night, the thought had followed him everywhere. David ran a hand through his hair, pushing the idea away. He had promised Hannah they would go through the list in order. No jumping ahead and no skipping steps. Still, the feeling wouldn't leave him.

With a sigh, he grabbed his coat and turned off his computer. He needed to go home, relax, and stop overthinking everything. But as he walked out the door, left the office building, and slowly walked down Boylston Street toward the T terminal, he already knew the truth.

He wasn't going to let this go.

•••

David stepped onto the subway car just as the doors slid shut behind him with a soft hiss. The space was packed with commuters, their faces blank with exhaustion after a long workday. Some scrolled through their phones, their fingers moving absentmindedly across screens, while others sat motionless, eyes closed, perhaps lulled by the sway of the train.

David found a spot near the door, and he gripped the metal pole as the train lurched forward, rattling and squeaking down the tracks. His body swayed slightly with the train's movement. The air inside the car was heavy with the smell of stale breath and damp winter coats. However, David barely noticed.

His eyes were fixed on the window beside him, watching the darkness outside rush past. Every few moments, dim yellow lights flickered along the tunnel walls, breaking up the blackness in quick flashes. The repetition was almost hypnotic, a pattern of movement that matched the low hum of the train.

But David's mind was elsewhere, tangled in the thoughts of the list.

Suddenly, the tunnel gave way to an open sky, and the sudden shift from darkness to light made him blink. The train had emerged onto the Longfellow Bridge, revealing a stretch of open water below. The Charles River shimmered beneath the setting sun, the orange glow reflecting off its calm surface. The view was fleeting—beautiful, but temporary. Within seconds, the train would slip back into the tunnel, and the moment would be gone.

David felt a tightening in his chest as he became anxious. The next stop was Kendall/MIT.

His body reacted automatically. His fingers tensed on the pole. His legs were prepared to move. Years of commuting had conditioned him to step off the train at this stop, to take the familiar route through his old campus. Even now, years later, his body still remembered the routine. He had a small inkling deep in his mind, telling him to explore item four on the list.

18 Vassar Street

He knew the area. He had probably passed by it dozens of times on his way to class during his college years. But if he was being honest with himself, he had yet to find out the meaning of the street when it came to the list and why it was important—if it really was.

The brakes screeched as the train slowed down and the conductor's voice rang through the overhead speaker.

"Next stop, Kendall/MIT."

David's pulse quickened. He could get off. Just step out onto the platform, take a short walk, and see it for himself. Perhaps just to look, just to get ahead. He knew it would be so easy.

The doors slid open with a soft chime, and he stared at the platform outside. The opportunity was right there, he just had to move.

But then, Hannah's voice came back to him. The promise they had made to do one thing at a time, in numerical order. David exhaled through his nose, tightening grip on the pole.

The doors stayed open for a few seconds longer, the cold air from outside rushing in. Then, with another chime, they slid shut.

The train pulled forward and David stayed in place. A small part of him felt relieved now that he had made up his mind. He had done the right thing. But another part of him felt something else.

Frustration.

However, with the decision settled, he pulled his phone out of his pocket. His fingers moved quickly as he opened the search app and typed in "Boston Rag." The first link that came up was what he was looking for.

He clicked on it, and the website loaded right away. The page was filled with bold headlines, some articles, and photos of different spots around Boston. It looked rough, like the kind of website that didn't try to impress but just got to the point. He could almost feel the city's energy through the screen—raw and alive.

His eyes moved quickly over the page until he found the link he wanted under the news tab on the drop-down menu: *Nella on the Net.* He paused for a moment then tapped it, and the page shifted to reveal the photo Jason had talked about. It was Nella, just as his friend had described. She was a young woman, black, confident, with sharp, dark brown eyes that seemed to see straight through the camera.

She was standing with her hand lifted just below her chin, the back of it facing the camera. On it, clear as day, was a small ladybug tattoo. It was delicate but stood out on her skin. The ladybug seemed to rest there as if it had some sort of quiet importance. David stared at it, his mind connecting the image to the list he had been following for so long.

He kept scrolling, his thumb moving quickly as he passed through a few more links, looking for more information. At the bottom of the page, he found what he was searching for—an address for the *Boston Rag*. The office was just blocks away from his own office. David leaned back in his chair, staring at the address for a moment. It was closer than he thought, and the thought of walking over there made his heart beat faster.

This was it, he realized. This was the next step. Tomorrow, he would go to the address and try to find her. He placed his phone back in his pocket and sat quietly for a moment, letting the weight of the decision sink in.

Tomorrow... tomorrow, he would try to meet her.

•••

The next day, David's workday ended just like all the others, quiet and routine. He shut down his computer, gathered his things, and stood up from his desk. The office was still buzzing with activity, but David felt like he had already checked out mentally. His phone buzzed in his pocket. He pulled it out and saw a text from Hannah.

Hannah 5:04 PM
Thinking about you my love!

David 5:05 PM
Thinking about you more!

A small smile crossed David's face as he quickly typed back. Then he hit send. His phone screen went dark, but the smile didn't leave his face. He knew he shouldn't be keeping secrets, but he couldn't help it. Today, he just didn't want to bring up the list. He didn't want to worry Hannah. She had been feeling tired lately, and he didn't want to add anything else to her plate. It was easier this way, for now.

David grabbed his coat, slipping his arms into the sleeves as he made his way out of the office. He paused at the door for a moment, looking out at the city. Boylston Street was busy as usual, people walking quickly, wrapped in coats against the cold. David adjusted his collar and stepped outside, letting the chill of the air hit his face. He had a plan for the evening—he wasn't going home right away.

He had thought about it all day, and now he was going to act on it. He would stop by the *Boston Rag*, just to see if Nella was in the building. He wasn't sure what he expected, but he had to do something. The curiosity was eating at him. Every time he thought about Nella, about the ladybug tattoo, it felt like a piece of the puzzle was finally in reach.

David walked down Boylston Street, the familiar surroundings offering little comfort. The street was full of people: office workers finishing their day, tourists looking for a good dinner spot, the usual crowd. But David's mind was elsewhere. The more he thought about the list, the more it seemed to pull him toward something... something important. He couldn't explain it, but he knew it was real.

The Boston Rag was just a few blocks away. Now that he

was aware of it, he remembered that he had walked by it a hundred times before without giving it a second thought. Now, it felt different. Each step brought him closer to something he couldn't quite put into words. The thought weighed heavily on him, but he pressed on.

As he reached the building, he paused in front of the entrance. The door was glass, framed by dark metal, and the lobby beyond was lit with the soft glow of overhead lights. He couldn't help but feel like he was stepping into a world he wasn't quite a part of, but he was determined to find out more.

He pushed the door open and walked inside, the sound of the door chime barely registering in his mind. The air in the lobby had a musty, old feel, a blend of nostalgia and creativity that lingered in every corner. The floors creaked beneath his feet as he made his way to the front desk, his eyes taking in the walls that were lined with framed photographs.

Local rock bands from the '80s and '90s grinned from the glossy black-and-white prints, their faces caught in moments of raw energy on stage. It was the kind of place that made you feel like you had stepped into a different time—a time when Boston's music scene was thriving, when graffiti art was an expression of rebellion, not just decoration.

The walls also held legendary sports moments, such as shots of iconic players like Larry Bird and David Ortiz in mid-action. There were faded concert posters, the kind you would find stuck to telephone poles in the neighborhood. Photos of film producers and newsworthy moments also lined the walls leading to other corridors, with some of the more recognizable editorial writers.

David stood for a moment, taking it all in. It was a strange contrast to the clean, modern office he had just left behind. Here, it felt like the past was alive with stories untold. He was out of place, a little like an intruder. This wasn't his world, but he couldn't help but be fascinated by it.

There was a receptionist behind the front desk, a woman who looked up from her computer as he approached. "Can I help you?" she asked, her voice calm but direct.

David hesitated for a second, realizing how unlikely it was that his request would be taken seriously. He had no plan beyond simply seeing if Nella was there, but the words came out anyway.

"Yes," he replied, confidence waning. "I was wondering if Nella is in the building today. Nella on the Net, I mean."

The receptionist raised an eyebrow. "She works remotely most of the time," she said, but then quickly added, "But I can check with her editor to see if we are expecting her. Do you have an appointment?"

David shook his head. "No, I don't. But I don't mind making one. Actually, I was just in the area and thought I'd stop by and see if she's available."

The receptionist gave him a look that seemed to say she wasn't sure what to make of his request. She picked up the phone, dialed, and spoke into the receiver, her voice soft but firm. "Is Nella in today? Do we have her scheduled?"

David stood awkwardly by the desk, watching as the receptionist spoke. It felt strange to be there, uncertain of what would happen next. The conversation was quick, the kind of exchange that suggested this wasn't anything unusual for her, with a few moments of back-and-forth banter between her and the editor on the line. Before long, the receptionist looked up at him again, this time with a different expression.

"Wait, what was your name again?" she asked suddenly, turning her attention fully toward David.

"David... David Bishop," he answered, unsure why it felt important to say his full name.

There was a pause on the other end of the line as the receptionist listened to the editor on the other side. David's nerves tightened. The minutes felt like hours as the phone call stretched on, and he wondered if he had made a mistake coming here and if Nella was truly as elusive as her reputation suggested.

Finally, the receptionist placed the phone back on its base. She looked up at David, her face unreadable.

"Nella is actually here today. She'll be down in a minute," she said. "If you want to wait in the lobby."

David's heart skipped a beat. He wasn't sure what he was expecting, but it certainly wasn't this. He nodded, offering a simple, "Thank you," and moved to the side to find a place to sit.

He wandered around the lobby for a few moments, feeling nostalgic, before taking a seat in one of the chairs near the wall, his hands folded in his lap, his mind racing.

The minutes seemed to drag on as he waited, his eyes moving from one picture to the next, but his mind was elsewhere.

Each time the elevator door opened, his head snapped up. He couldn't help it. He was waiting for her, for Nella. The woman whose ladybug tattoo may be a match to the third item on the list.

Finally, after what felt like an eternity, the elevator doors opened, and Nella stepped out. She was younger than he'd imagined, but just as striking. Her dark brown eyes met his, and she smiled, her hand lifting in a wave.

David stood up, suddenly unsure of what to say. He opened his mouth to introduce himself, but before he could, he saw the tattoo. The small ladybug, on the back of her hand, just as Jason had described. It was her. His phone vibrated in his pocket, but he ignored it, too keen on conversing with Nella now that she was right before him.

"Hi, you must be Nella?" David asked, his voice steady despite the rush of thoughts in his head.

Nella smiled again, her handshake firm and confident. "The one and only," she said, her voice light and easy. She seemed at ease, as if she was used to being recognized, to people knowing who she was. David's heart once again raced, but he forced himself to stay calm and smile.

They stepped into a quiet corner near the entrance of the lobby, and Nella explained that she wasn't usually at the *Rag* but happened to have stopped by this afternoon for a meeting. Then she asked David how she could help him.

David, standing across from Nella, felt slightly

unprepared. He hadn't really thought through what he was going to say, and now that he was standing here, face-to-face with her, he found himself rambling.

Nella listened without interrupting. She nodded occasionally, her dark eyes fixed on him, showing genuine interest. She wasn't just being polite, she was actually paying attention, absorbing every word. David could tell.

He kept the story simple, only sharing a watered-down version. He left out items four through eight on the list. He didn't mention how much this whole thing had been weighing on him, how it had started to feel bigger than just a coincidence. He just gave her the basics, hoping she might have some insight.

His phone buzzed again in his pocket. He ignored it, rubbing his hands together instead. *Not now... very bad timing,* he thought. He wanted to finish his conversation, to hear what Nella had to say.

"Do you need to get that?" she asked, raising an eyebrow.

David shook his head. "No, it's fine."

Nella took the distraction as a chance to jump in with some of her own questions. "Well, what a story…" she said, stepping back slightly. "I mean, as you know, I am a blog journalist, so I have a natural interest in strange stories. I write about this kind of thing all the time, and I must say, some of the things you brought up are very interesting. But I have to be honest—I am not sure how they are related, but some of what you're telling me sounds like a bunch of strange coincidences." She tilted her head. "Except for one thing."

David watched as she tapped her fingers against her chin, thinking. Then she looked back at him.

"Your wife's name," she said. "Hannah. You said it was on the list a year before you actually met her?"

David nodded.

Nella hesitated, as if deciding how much to say. "I have to confess," she continued, "there's something interesting about the name Hannah you might not know…"

Before she could finish, David's phone vibrated again, cutting her off. He hesitated, glancing at Nella, then sighed. It was unusual to get so many calls back-to-back. Maybe it was work. Maybe it was nothing. But something in his gut told him he needed to answer.

"I am sorry, I think I better take this," he said, already reaching for his phone.

Nella gave a small nod, watching him curiously.

David swiped to accept the call, not recognizing the phone number. "Hello?"

The voice on the other end was frantic, rushed. A woman. He didn't recognize her. The words spilled out too fast, overlapping each other, and rising in pitch.

"Wait—slow down," David said, trying to calm her and gripping the phone tighter. "I can't understand you."

But as she spoke again, he began making out some of what she was saying. His body tensed and his breath caught. His face grew hot, then suddenly cold. The room around him felt like it was shifting, tilting.

"It's Hannah," the woman said, her voice steadier now but still urgent and her words now recognizable. "Something happened to Hannah as she was leaving. An ambulance took her to Brigham and Women's Hospital."

David's heart slammed against his ribs. For a moment, he didn't speak; he couldn't. Everything around him blurred. The noise of the phone ringing at the reception desk, the chatter of people coming and going from the elevators, Nella's face before him—it all faded into the background. Seeing this, Nella's brow furrowed.

"David?" she asked, voice cautious.

David's fingers curled around the phone. His grip was so tight it hurt, and he hung up the phone.

He didn't respond, couldn't respond. His body moved before his mind caught up. He stepped back, closer to the lobby doors. His eyes met Nella's, and whatever was on his face made her expression shift from confusion to concern.

In that moment, he didn't say a word. He simply turned and ran out the doors.

CHAPTER 08

ONLY 28

David pushed through the sliding glass doors of Brigham and Women's Hospital, barely feeling the rush of warm air that hit his frozen skin. His lungs burned from running, each breath sharp and uneven, and he had a runny nose. His chest rose and fell too fast, his body struggling to keep up with the panic surging through him. His clothes were a mess—his jacket unzipped, his shirt sticking to his back with sweat, and his shoes damp from the slushy sidewalks outside. His hands trembled slightly as his fingers curled into fists at his sides.

He didn't stop moving. His feet hit the tile floor hard, each step making a sharp, hollow sound that bounced off the high ceiling. His legs ached from pushing himself, but he barely noticed. His thoughts were racing too fast for his body to feel anything else.

Where is she? What happened?

His eyes darted around the crowded emergency room, scanning the space with frantic urgency. People sat slumped in chairs, some holding their heads in their hands, others staring blankly at the walls. Nurses moved quickly, their expressions focused and their hands full of clipboards and IV bags. The smell of disinfectant was thick in the air, mixing with something else... something metallic and bitter.

David stumbled to the front desk, his heart slamming against his ribs. A nurse sat behind the counter, tapping at a keyboard, her expression neutral, almost bored. She didn't look up. David slammed his hands onto the counter. "Hannah Bishop!" he gasped. His voice was rough, barely more than a breath. "I was told she was here!"

The nurse's eyes flicked up at him, but her expression didn't change. She was older, with lines around her mouth and eyes, her gray hair pulled into a tight bun. She had probably seen this before: people panicking and demanding answers.

But David didn't care how many times she had seen it.

She glanced at her screen, typing something, then looked back at him. "Family waiting area." Her voice was calm and flat, sounding like she was just giving directions to a grocery store.

David's fingers curled against the counter. "What does that mean?" His chest felt tight. His breathing too fast, too shallow. "Is she okay? What happened to her?"

The nurse didn't answer right away. She only motioned toward a hallway to the left. "A doctor will speak with you soon as soon as they get a chance."

David's stomach twisted. His mouth opened, but no words came out. *They weren't telling him anything.*

His hands strongly gripped the edge of the counter, turning his knuckles white. The room felt too bright, too loud, and too still at once. A woman in a chair nearby was quietly crying. Somewhere behind him, a child was coughing. The steady beeping of a monitor came from one of the triage rooms. It all blurred together, background noise against the pounding in his head.

God damn it, what the hell is going on! Why won't they just tell me what happened to her?

His breath hitched, and his fingers twitched from the nerves assaulting him. *He should have answered his phone.* He should have been there and not ignored the persistent calls trying to reach him.

But he had, and the guilt ate at him.

His pulse roared in his ears, drowning out everything else. His feet felt frozen to the ground, his body stuck between fighting for more answers and the sinking dread that was dragging him under, suffocating him.

Finally, he forced himself to move. He turned toward the hallway the nurse had pointed to. His legs felt like lead and his body was stiff and heavy.

Each step took more effort than it should, and each step brought him closer to the truth.

A truth that he wasn't sure he was ready to hear.

As he approached the family waiting area, he found it packed, filled with people he didn't recognize. He could feel their stares even though they were mostly lost in their own thoughts. The room was too small and too cramped, as if it were meant for a handful of people, not the dozens scattered across the seats with barely enough space to move. Each family seemed to be caught in their own moment, and in their own world of quiet tension, with some people sitting still, others fidgeting and shifting nervously.

David took in the scene quickly, his eyes jumping from face to face, and none of them seemed familiar. But the air was thick with the same feeling of unease. The silence was heavy, broken only by the occasional cough or the soft shuffle of shoes against the floor. It felt as if there was an unspoken understanding in the room—everyone here was waiting for bad news. Like their lives were waiting to be changed in one moment.

David's chest tightened as he scanned the room.

Where were Ed and Cathy?

And then he saw them. Cathy—his mother-in-law, hunched over in a chair, her face pale, her hands wringing together tightly in her lap. Ed—Cathy's husband and his father-in-law—was sitting next to her, his face stoic but his eyes wide, filled with something like fear. They were a picture of controlled chaos, holding it together but not for much longer.

David didn't even think about it; his body moved before his mind could catch up. He walked to them quickly, his heart pounding in his chest. His feet felt heavy, but they carried him forward, toward the two people who meant everything to Hannah and him.

As soon as Cathy saw him, she was on him. She stood

quickly, and in one motion, threw herself into his arms. Her body shook with a force that caught him off guard. She wasn't just crying; she was sobbing uncontrollably, her whole body wracked with grief. The sound was raw, painful, and it shook David to his core. He could feel the wetness of her tears soaking through his shirt as her face rested on his shoulder and her arms tightened around him, as if she was trying to hold on to something she was about to lose. This act intensified his fear and concern about what was going on with Hannah.

After some time, Ed and Cathy gathered themselves and returned to their seats, with David walking behind them and standing in front of their chairs once they had settled down.

Cathy began sobbing again, and her voice came out in broken gasps, each word trembling with pain. "Where were you, David? They called you first!"

David froze. For a moment, he couldn't move. The words hit him harder than he expected as an image of Nella flashed through his head, and a rush of guilt flooded through him. He had missed the call. He had been running an errand and had been distracted. But that excuse didn't feel right. It felt like a lie, like a weak attempt to cover up his failure.

His mouth went dry, and he stood still, unsure of how to answer. His eyes moved to Ed, who had stood up, his face drawn and his expression tense. Ed's hand landed on David's shoulder, a grip so tight it almost hurt, but David didn't pull away. Ed needed him.

Ed's voice was low and barely audible over the noise

that had suddenly erupted across the room. "The school called us after they tried reaching your phone to no avail. Well... that's what they told us. The school administrator then told us that Hannah was struck by a car as she crossed the street in front of the school, she was heading home." His voice cracked slightly, but he fought to keep it steady. "Apparently, it was a hit and run."

"Oh my God," David replied.

"It was bad, son. They rushed her into emergency surgery on life support," Ed continued, seeing that David had not understood the seriousness of the situation.

David felt the ground shift beneath him. *Life support?* He had hoped it wasn't so serious. But Ed's words crushed that hope like a heavy rock pressing down on him. Cathy's face was pale, her body trembling. She voiced the words in disbelief, as if hearing them might make them different, or make them hurt less. "She is only twenty-eight."
David's heart twisted. He couldn't help but think how everything had been fine just last night and this morning. They had been laughing and happy before he had left for work. She had even sent him a thoughtful and loving text while they both were at work. *How could this have happened? How could something so serious happen so quickly?*

David's mind raced and his thoughts felt scattered. He wasn't sure what to think or feel. He opened his mouth to speak, but the words got caught in his throat.

Instead, it was Ed who spoke again, his voice thick with emotion. "Her head hit the windshield, David. She has a massive hemorrhage."

David's stomach dropped. The air left his lungs in a

rush, and suddenly, he was dizzy.

His knees felt weak, and he had to sit down quickly, his body dropping into a nearby chair. His hands were shaking, and he gripped the armrest tightly, trying to keep himself steady. He didn't want to look at Ed and Cathy, didn't want to see the fear in their eyes, and the grief that was becoming a part of him too.

All he could think about was Hannah. Hannah, the woman he loved, the woman who was supposed to be strong, healthy, and full of life. And now, she was fighting for her life in a hospital bed, her body connected to machines, and her future uncertain.

Cathy's sobs were quieter now, but they still shook her whole body. She buried her face in her hands, her shoulders trembling with each cry. Ed stood beside her, his hand on her back, trying to comfort her, but it was clear he was struggling too. David didn't know what to say. There were no words to make this better, no words to take away the fear that was eating at him from the inside. He had missed the call.

What if he had answered it? What if he had been there when it happened? Could he have been in time to see her? To hold her hand?

David closed his eyes, but the image of Hannah, lying unconscious in a hospital bed, her body hooked to machines, kept playing in his mind. And with that image came a deep, hollow fear—the fear that he would never see her smile again, never hear her laugh again, never hold her hand again.

And then it hit him—the full weight of the words Ed

had just spoken.

A massive hemorrhage.

David's breath caught in his throat, and before he could even process what was happening, his legs gave out. It wasn't a slow fall, a gradual collapse. It was as if the world had pressed down on him all at once. He sank to his knees on the cold tile floor, his hands reaching out to steady himself but finding nothing to grip. The hard surface of the floor felt like it was pressing into him, forcing him lower, forcing him to feel the full impact of the moment.

This wasn't real.

His mind repeated the words like a mantra, trying to convince himself that this was just some horrible nightmare. People survived things like this, didn't they? There was still time, wasn't there? She could still make it.

He closed his eyes, trying to shut out the room around him, trying to hold onto that little shred of hope that things might still be okay. But then he opened them again, his gaze drifting to the sterile surroundings. The cold, hard floor tiles stretched out in front of him. The sharp lines of the walls, too white and too bright. The hum of the vending machines in the corner, the faint sound of a distant phone ringing, the hushed whispers from other families.

His body trembled on the floor, and he felt a sting in his eyes—tears. The pressure behind them was unbearable, and for a moment, he fought to keep them back. He couldn't break down. Not here. Not in front of them.

But the tears came anyway, running down his cheeks as the emotions he had been holding in for so long finally overflowed. There was no more holding it in. The pain, the fear, the guilt—it was too much. His body gave in completely, and he fell apart.

David's face pressed into his hands, his whole body shaking as the sobs that he had been holding in finally broke free. He didn't care anymore who saw him, who heard him.

His world was breaking. And as much as he wanted to believe things could turn around, he knew deep down that nothing would ever be the same again.

•••

The hours dragged on, one after another, with each minute feeling like an eternity. David, back in his chair, couldn't stop fidgeting. He tapped his foot nervously against the floor, his fingers twisting a crumpled tissue in his lap. Every time the double doors at the far end of the room opened, he flinched, his body tensing involuntarily. He was not sure if it was the sound of the door or the anticipation of what he would hear that caused it, but each time, he couldn't help himself. His heart raced, and his chest tightened with the need for news.

Doctors and nurses passed through the doors, their faces hidden behind the cool masks of professionalism. Every now and then, a name would be called. Some families stood up, relief flooding their faces, as they were led into a small room for updates. The others, the families left behind in the waiting room, looked at each other for a moment, exchanging nervous glances. Some shook their heads or whispered to each other. A few families crumbled, their faces contorting with sorrow. David's stomach twisted in response to the pain around him. The cries, the anguish, it all blended into quiet background noise as David tried to focus on his thoughts.

In the corner of the room, an older couple hugged each other tightly, tears streaming down their faces, but those were tears of relief. They smiled through their grief, holding on to each other as if they had just been given a second chance at life. David watched them for a long moment, his eyes fixed on the way they held on, the way they clung to each other like they were the only ones who understood.

The sight of them, so joyful and full of relief, was a huge contrast to the emptiness David felt. The sharp difference made his stomach turn. The pain and confusion in his chest only grew as he watched them. It was not that he was angry at them, but something about the happiness in their eyes dug into him, twisting the knife already lodged deep in his heart.

Why wasn't I with her? Why didn't I answer my phone? The thought hit him like a slap, and he quickly shook his head, trying to push it away. But it kept coming back, again and again. Why hadn't he been there when she needed him?

How fast things changed; now, neither meeting Nella nor the list seemed that important anymore. The guilt ate at him, burrowing deep into his chest. It was like a weight he couldn't lift, a heavy stone lodged in his heart. Why had he been so distracted? Why had he chosen to deal with everything else, the stupid list, the conversation with Nella, instead of picking up his phone? Why hadn't he realized how important this moment was, how much he should have been there for her?

Suddenly, the double doors opened and a woman in blue scrubs stepped into the waiting area, her face calm and her movements controlled. She looked around, her eyes scanning the crowd, before she spoke.

"Bishop."

The name was loud and clear, and the room had suddenly gone quiet. David's heart skipped a beat. His body froze and his mind couldn't grasp the words immediately. He looked at Ed and Cathy, who stood up quickly, their faces drained of color, and they shuffled toward the woman.

David didn't move. His legs felt too heavy. His body felt like it was made of lead. Every step toward that private room felt like wading through water, thick and slow. His thoughts were muddled and jumbled together in a haze of confusion. Why did it feel so slow? Why did his feet feel like they were stuck?

The woman's footsteps echoed in his mind. He followed them with his eyes, barely able to move. He watched Ed and Cathy go ahead, their faces full of expectation. But David didn't expect anything good. Deep down, he was already preparing himself for the worst.

The walk to the small room was long, even though it was just a few feet away. Every step felt like it took forever, his pulse pounding in his ears, drowning out the soft sounds of the hospital. The tile floor underneath his feet was cold, slick, and hard, each step he took only amplifying the emptiness in his chest. He wanted to run. He wanted to scream. But his body wouldn't obey him.

The door opened, and the doctor stood there. Her face was soft but firm, her eyes kind yet distant, as if she'd done this a thousand times before. She didn't look surprised, and she clearly didn't look like she was giving bad news for the first time. She'd been here before, with other families, other broken hearts.

David's body froze again when she spoke. Her words were gentle but firm, like a punch to the gut.

"I'm sorry, she didn't make it."

For a moment, it felt like the world had stopped spinning. The room around David blurred into the background. His mind couldn't seem to process what the doctor had just said. The words didn't feel real.

David opened his mouth, but nothing came out. His tongue felt thick in his mouth. His body trembled, but he still couldn't seem to move. His eyes were fixed on the floor, the tile beneath him sharp and hard. His legs felt like they were going to give out. He didn't even know if he could stand. He felt like he was floating, disconnected, as if his body was no longer his own.

Cathy's scream ripped through the air, a raw, broken cry of pure pain. It was a sound David would never forget. A sound that shook him to his core, made his stomach lurch and his chest tighten with an almost unbearable grief.

He looked up, but the scene around him didn't register. He saw Cathy crumple into Ed's arms, her sobs shaking her body, her hands gripping at him for support. Ed, who had always been the strong one, the calm one, was now shaking. His face was crumpled with grief, his own sobs breaking through the façade of strength he had always worn so easily.

David was still frozen. He couldn't speak. He couldn't move. His mind was in disbelief. The room around him was muted and distant, like he was hearing everything from under water. The doctor's voice, Ed's and Cathy's sobs, they were all muffled, as if the world had been silenced. All he could do was stare at the table in front of him.

On the table, there was a stack of pamphlets. The words were printed clearly on the front, but all David could see was the title of one pamphlet: *Understanding Grief.*

The words didn't make sense. How could they? He didn't want to understand grief. He didn't want to be there, hearing those words and seeing his world crumble into nothing.

The pamphlet was bright and clean, its edges sharp and untouched by time. It didn't belong in that room. He wanted to push it away, but he couldn't bring himself to move. He just stared at it, his chest tight with the weight of the words he'd just heard.

Suddenly, a deep, bone-chilling loneliness took over. It was overwhelming and suffocating. It felt like the air in the room had been sucked out, leaving nothing behind but a hollow emptiness.

It was not just grief. It was something deeper, something colder. It was the feeling that, in that moment, in that room, David was completely alone. Even though he was surrounded by people, by family, the loneliness was suffocating. No one could feel the way he felt. No one could take the pain from him. It was his, and his alone.

His stomach churned and his body went cold. His

heart was a hollow space, empty and aching, with no place to put the pain that was flooding his chest. All of it—every thought, every piece of guilt, every ounce of grief—had settled in one place. And that place was alone.

No one could help him. No one could take it away. And the truth of that was the most painful part of all.

•••

David moved through the next few days in a fog. Time stopped making sense. Morning and night blurred together. Sometimes, it felt like only minutes had passed since the hospital, and since the doctor had said those six words. Other times, it felt like a lifetime ago. But no matter how much time moved forward, he felt stuck and frozen in that moment.

People came and went. Ed and Cathy handled the arrangements for the funeral, but David was there, nodding when needed and signing papers when asked. He barely registered what he was doing. He heard people talking, but their words sounded distant, like a conversation happening in another room. He answered when necessary, but the words came out hollow, as if someone else was speaking for him.

At night, he barely slept. He lay awake, staring at the ceiling, his body too tired to move but his mind refusing to shut down. Sometimes, he closed his eyes and expected to hear Hannah's voice, to feel her shift beside him in bed. But when he reached for her, there was nothing but cold sheets. The emptiness was unbearable.

He stopped sleeping in their bed. The first night he tried, he lasted less than ten minutes before he got up and went to the couch. He couldn't do it. The bed still smelled like her. Her pillow still held the faint scent of her shampoo. It was too much. Too real. So he grabbed a blanket and made the couch his home.

Every morning, he woke up stiff and sore, the position unnatural, the couch too small. But he didn't care. Anything was better than that empty bed.

The house didn't feel like home anymore. Without her, it felt foreign. Too quiet. Too still. Every corner reminded him of her. The kitchen where she used to hum while making coffee. The bathroom mirror where she used to leave little notes for him in lipstick—small things like *Have a good day!* or *Miss you already!* He found one of them still there, faded but readable. It made his chest tighten so painfully he had to leave the room.

He caught himself reaching for his phone to text her. Out of habit, his fingers moved automatically, ready to type something simple—*What do you want for dinner?* or *Heading home, need anything?*—but then reality came crashing down hard on him. He gripped the phone tightly in his hand, staring at the screen, the empty message box open, waiting. But there was no one to answer. He put the phone down without typing anything.

He barely ate. People brought food, casseroles, sandwiches, things they said would "help," but none of those mattered. He only ate when Cathy pushed him to, when Ed insisted, but the food tasted like cardboard. He chewed and swallowed because he had to, not because he wanted to.

Hannah's words sometimes echoed in his head. He

remembered how she used to tease him for getting too serious over little things. *Life's too short to stress, babe,* she'd say with a laugh, nudging him playfully. The words used to make him roll his eyes, used to make him smirk. Now they felt like a cruel joke.

Life's too short.

He started avoiding people. Jason as well as other friends called, but he let the phone ring. He knew they meant well, but he didn't have the energy to talk. Their voices would be full of pity, full of questions he didn't want to answer. *How are you holding up? Do you need anything?* He didn't have an answer for them. He didn't know how he was holding up. He didn't even know what he needed.

The days passed, but David didn't feel like he was living them. He was just moving through them, one after the other, waiting for something to change. But nothing did. And finally, came the day of the funeral.

The small catholic chapel was full, and every seat was taken, with people standing along the walls, their heads bowed and their faces somber. A low murmur of voices filled the space as people whispered to each other. Some dabbed at their eyes with tissues, and others sat in silence, staring ahead and lost in their own grief.

David sat in the front row, his hands clasped together and his fingers gripping each other tightly. He hadn't let go since the service started. His knuckles had turned white, but he hadn't loosened his grip. It was the only thing keeping him grounded.

Cathy sat beside him, shaking. She clutched an old stuffed rabbit in her lap, its fur worn and faded from years of love. It had been Hannah's favorite toy as a child. Cathy held onto it like it was the last piece of her daughter she had left. Her shoulders heaved with quiet sobs. Every so often, she let out a sharp, broken gasp, like she was trying to breathe through the pain but failing.

Ed sat on Cathy's other side, his arm wrapped around her, holding her together. He hadn't cried, not in front of everyone, but his eyes were red and his face pale. He stared straight ahead with an unreadable expression.

David barely processed the words being spoken. A priest stood at the front, talking about life, love, and loss. But the words didn't reach him. It all sounded muffled and distant.

People took turns speaking. Friends. Family. One of Hannah's coworkers even talked about how much she had loved teaching, how much her students had adored her. A young woman—one of Hannah's former students—had stepped up to the podium with a sign language interpreter, and signed how Hannah had inspired her, how she wouldn't have been where she was today without her.

David heard all of it, but none of it felt real. Then his name was called.

He blinked, his head snapping up as the priest gestured for him to come forward. His stomach clenched. For a second, he thought about staying seated, about shaking his head and refusing. But people were looking at him now, waiting.

Slowly, he stood. His legs felt weak and unsteady, like they might give out at any moment. He took a shaky breath and forced himself to walk. Each step felt heavier than the last. When he reached the podium, he gripped the edges, his fingers pressing into the wood. His hands were shaking, and his heart pounded so hard it rang in his ears.

The paper with his speech was tucked in his pocket. He had written it the night before, staring at the blank page for hours before forcing himself to put words down. But now, as he stood in front of everyone, he knew he wouldn't read it. The words on that page felt cold and distant. They didn't match the ache in his chest and the weight in his stomach. He swallowed, looking out at the sea of faces. Some were familiar to him, but some were strangers. However, all of them were mourning Hannah.

His throat tightened, and his mouth felt dry. He gripped the podium harder. And then, somehow, he found his voice.

"Though my heart aches, and tears flow freely around us," he began, "I want to share a memory of Hannah, a memory of joy amid this mountain of grief. Not long ago, Hannah and I discovered our sanctuary, a hidden gem called Hermit Lake in New Hampshire. Away from the city's hustle and bustle, we'd escape to the mountains, and to the hiking trails that filled our souls with peace."

Clearing his throat, he continued, "On our last trip there, I'll never forget the way Hannah's face lit up as the mountains came into view on our drive to the lake. She turned to me, smiling like she had just figured something out and said, 'I get it now. I get why people fall in love with the mountains.'"

He exhaled shakily, his breath unsteady.

"After she was gone, my mind kept going back to that

moment. But this time, I didn't see the mountains the way she had. I saw them cloaked in sorrow, as towering peaks of grief that none of us could have anticipated and that seemed impossible to climb. Right now, it might seem like we are at the base, and that we cannot find a way around this mountain; however, we must climb it. I believe that together, we will ascend, step by step and hand in hand with those we love, finding strength in each other's presence. Some may reach the summit faster, while others may take longer."

David took a long pause as he tried to steady emotions that threatened to spill over. He glanced toward Cathy and Ed. Cathy gripped the stuffed rabbit even tighter, her face buried against Ed's shoulder. Ed stared down at his lap, his jaw clenched, his shoulders stiff.

"One day, we will all look back and see the imposing peak behind us, as a testament to our resilience. In time, the mountain of grief may transform. With enough healing, perhaps we'll remember not just the pain, but the joy Hannah found in the mountains. The joy she brought into our lives. Perhaps we'll recall her love for those peaks with a smile, a glimmer of peace in this sorrow."

He took another moment to wipe a tear from his eye, "But right now..." He exhaled shakily. "Right now, all I see is that mountain of grief and my heart reminding me of just how much I miss her."

As David's words came to an end, the chapel fell silent. No one moved, and no one spoke. David gripped the podium, his hands shaking, and his heart pounding in his chest. He looked down at the wood, not wanting to meet anyone's eyes. The lump in his throat grew, and he swallowed hard against it, but it didn't go away.

Somewhere in the back of the chapel, the sharp click of a door opening broke the silence. The sound echoed, cutting through the stillness. David glanced up, just for a second, his eyes catching a dark figure slipping out of the side door.

Before he could process it, before he could think about it, Cathy broke down into sobs, and the sound of grief filled the room.

CHAPTER 09
PALINDROME

David lay in bed, motionless. The sheets under him were wrinkled and twisted, with the blankets barely covering him. He had been in this exact position for hours, maybe even the whole day. He wasn't sure. Time didn't make sense anymore. The only thing that existed was the crushing weight in his chest, the emptiness in his stomach, and the thick silence that filled the room.

The curtains were drawn shut, letting only a faint, dull light seep through the fabric. However, it wasn't enough to brighten the room. The air inside was stale, heavy with the smell of unwashed clothes, the faint mustiness of sweat, and the remaining traces of Hannah's perfume. That was the only thing that still smelled like her. He hadn't touched her side of the bed. He hadn't washed the pillowcase, which still held the slightest scent of her shampoo, something floral, something warm. He should have thrown it in the laundry days ago, but he couldn't. He didn't want to lose that last piece of her.

His body ached. His muscles felt stiff and sore from lying in the same position for too long. His arms felt heavy and his legs numb. It was as if his body had given up, refusing to move unless absolutely necessary. He had barely eaten. The thought of food made his stomach churn, not with hunger but with a hollow discomfort. The last meal he had was… what? A piece of toast Cathy had forced on him two days ago? Maybe three? He didn't know. His stomach had stopped growling a while ago. Now, it just felt like an empty pit. His lack of food had taken a toll on his weight.

His beard had grown out, rough and unkempt, covering his jaw and neck, showing that it had been a while since his last shave. He hadn't even looked in a mirror. Well, he didn't need to. He knew what he'd see—sunken eyes, dark circles, a face that barely resembled the person he used to be. But none of it mattered.

He wasn't himself anymore. He was something else. Something hollow. Something left behind.

Outside, a car passed by, its tires humming against the pavement. The sound came and went, distant, and barely registering in his mind. It didn't matter. Nothing mattered anymore. He stared at the ceiling. The same ceiling he had been staring at for what felt like forever. His thoughts circled the same empty track, the same questions, and the same guilt.

This is my life now.

A ghost of what it used to be.
I should have been with her.
Maybe I would have done something.

The thoughts came and went, dull and relentless, weighing heavily on him. They didn't spark any reaction anymore. They didn't even bring tears. They just existed, like everything else in this empty, lifeless space. His breath was slow and shallow. In, out. That was all he could do. Breathe in, breathe out. Even that felt like too much effort sometimes.

Then the doorbell rang.

The sharp, sudden sound cut through the silence and made him flinch. His body stiffened for a moment, but he didn't move. His eyes flickered toward the bedroom door, but that was it. He lay there, still, listening.

The bell rang again.

Louder this time.

He exhaled through his nose, slowly and shakily. His hands curled into the blanket, gripping it slightly, but he didn't sit up. He didn't answer. Maybe if he stayed still, if he didn't make a sound, whoever it was would just go away.

But the doorbell rang a third time.

Longer. Followed by a knock.

David clenched his jaw, and his fingers tightened around the fabric of his duvet. Whoever it was, they weren't leaving. He didn't have the energy for this. Didn't have the patience. But the ringing wouldn't stop, and the knocking only grew louder.

His heart beat sluggishly in his chest, not from panic, not from fear, but from frustration. From exhaustion. He didn't want to deal with this. With anyone.

But the knocking kept coming.

Finally, with a slow, stiff movement, David forced himself to sit up. His muscles protested and his joints ached. His head felt heavy, like it was full of sand. He rubbed his face, feeling the roughness of his beard against his palms. His body swayed slightly as he sat on the edge of the bed, dizziness washing over him.

The knocking continued.

With a deep breath, he pushed himself up. His legs wobbled under him, weak from days of barely moving. He steadied himself, placing one hand on the bedpost, and exhaled.

Then, slowly, he made his way to the door. Each step felt like it took longer than the last, as if his legs were too heavy to lift. This was an unexpected distraction in his current state of misery, one he wasn't sure he fully welcomed. However, a small part of him felt warmed by this gesture of sorts, that perhaps someone was concerned with his well-being. He simply wanted a chance to feel human again.

He reached for the doorknob with his right hand, fingers stiff and unsteady. A dull ache ran up his arm as he turned it, reminding him that his muscles had not had any sort of movement in a while. The door creaked softly as it swung open. He rubbed his eyes with the back of his hand, trying to chase away the constant fog in his mind. His eyelids felt like they were glued shut, and his head was aching. The noise of the world outside felt muffled, distant. It didn't matter. Nothing did.

There, standing just outside the door, was Nella.

She was dressed in a simple black jacket and dark jeans, her long hair falling loosely around her shoulders. Her face was soft, with an expression full of concern, and for a moment, the world around David seemed to pause. He could see the hesitation in her posture, the way she was shifting her weight from one foot to the other, almost like she wasn't sure if she should be there. Her hands were clasped tightly in front of her as if she was unsure of what to do next.

"Hi, David," Nella said in a voice so quiet it almost didn't reach him. Her words seemed to hang in the air, awkward and unsure. "I heard what happened... and I'm so sorry for your loss."

Her words hit him like a wave, but they didn't seem to make much of an impact. He wasn't sure if it was the numbness that had settled deep in his chest or the way his mind kept replaying the same thoughts over and over. Either way, her voice didn't sound real. It was just another sound, another thing in a world that didn't feel like it belonged to him anymore.

David didn't know what to say. The silence between them stretched on, thick and uncomfortable. His mouth felt dry. The usual words he might say—words of gratitude, of acknowledgment—weren't there. He didn't even know if he wanted to say anything. His eyes drifted to the floor for a second, then back to her, but he couldn't bring himself to meet her gaze fully.

Nella shifted slightly, still standing there, waiting. He could see the tightness in her shoulders and the way her fingers twitched, as though she was about to say something else but wasn't sure how to continue.

He didn't know if he should invite her in. The space felt too small, too empty. His body tensed, as if the thought of being close to anyone was more than he could bear. His gaze drifted past her, his mind still foggy. He didn't have the energy to deal with company, not now, not like this. But he couldn't just stand there, staring at her without saying anything either.

Finally, he took a deep breath, the sound barely audible in the heavy silence. He stepped aside to open the door wider, just enough for her to step in. His movements were stiff and reluctant, like every action required an effort far greater than it should.

"Come in," he muttered, his voice hoarse from lack of use. It wasn't an invitation, not really. It was just a way to break the silence, to make some kind of movement in the stillness. His voice sounded foreign to him, like someone else was speaking.

When she hesitated, he moved from the door and stepped back inside. After a moment, Nella followed him in and closed the door behind her, taking note of his wrinkled sweatpants and t-shirt.

She glanced around his house, seeing that the living room curtains were still drawn, which kept out what little light the outside world offered. A thin layer of dust coated the coffee table surface, which showed that it had been untouched for days. She also took note of the way David had moved, slow and heavy, and how his clothes hung looser on him, his arms thinner than she remembered.

"I did a web search a few days after you ran off," she said finally, breaking the silence. Her voice once again sounded careful, as if she wasn't sure if she should be saying anything at all. "I was curious why you never came back."

David didn't react. He stood near the couch, staring at the floor.

"Your last name came up in an obituary, and that's how I found out what had happened. I was shocked. I tried calling, I even texted you, but you never responded," Nella continued, softer this time.

David barely nodded. His fingers twitched slightly at his sides, but that was the only sign he had even heard her. His eyes stayed down, focused on nothing.

"Yeah, sorry... I've been depressed, I miss her so much," he muttered. His voice was quiet, rough from disuse. It was a simple answer, but it held so much beneath it.

Nella studied him for a moment. She could see the exhaustion in his face, the deep lines under his eyes, and the hollowness that grief had left behind. He looked like he had barely been holding himself together.

Without thinking, and without planning it, she stepped forward and wrapped her arms around him, giving him a hug. David tensed at first, his body stiff against hers. It had been so long since he had felt someone this close. But Nella didn't let go. She held him firmly, her arms steady and offering warmth in a space that had felt cold for so long.

For a few seconds, he didn't react. He didn't lift his

arms, didn't lean into the embrace. He just stood there, frozen, as if unsure how to respond.

Then, slowly, his body gave in. His shoulders sagged and his hands, weak and hesitant, lifted slightly before resting against her back. It wasn't a strong hug, not the kind full of energy or reassurance. But it was something. And for the first time in what felt like forever, something inside David cracked. It was small at first, then, all at once, the burden of everything he had been holding in crashed down on him.

A shaky breath left his lips, but it wasn't enough. His chest tightened, his throat burned, and before he could stop it, a sob broke free. His body jerked slightly against Nella's, the first tear slipping down his face. Then another. Then more.

His whole body trembled as he let go. The grief that had sat like a heavy stone inside him, silent and suffocating, finally spilled out. It wasn't quiet. It wasn't controlled. It came in ragged, uneven sobs, his breaths breaking between them, his body shaking from the force of it.

He clung to Nella without thinking, gripping the fabric of her jacket like it was the only thing keeping him from falling apart completely. His fingers curled tightly, his knuckles turning white. He pressed his face against her shoulder, trying to hold himself together even as everything unraveled.

Nella didn't say anything. She didn't shush him, didn't tell him to calm down. She just held him, her arms firm but gentle, letting him break without trying to stop it. Her hand moved slightly, rubbing slow circles against his back, grounding him.

David gasped between the sobs, his chest heaving as months of pain poured out all at once. The loneliness, the guilt, the crushing emptiness that he had buried deep, pushing it down every time it tried to surface. But now, with someone holding him, with someone there, he couldn't keep it inside any longer.

The room was silent except for the sound of his cries. The world outside didn't matter. The dust in the house didn't matter. Right now, there was only this moment, raw and painful and real.

It felt like forever before the sobs began to slow. His body was exhausted, his limbs heavy, his breathing uneven. His grip on Nella loosened slightly, his fingers uncurling from her jacket. Slowly, he pulled back, his eyes red and swollen and his face damp with tears. He wiped at them with the back of his hand, sniffling as he tried to compose himself.

"Sorry," he muttered, his voice rough and strained from crying. He didn't meet her eyes.

"Don't be," Nella said softly. "You needed that."

David swallowed hard, nodding slightly. He had nothing to say. No words felt right. But for the first time in a long time, the weight inside him felt just a little lighter. After a few minutes, they sat down on the couch. David leaned forward, his elbows resting on his knees, rubbing his face with both hands. His breathing had steadied, but his body still felt drained. He didn't know what to say. He didn't know if there was anything left to say.

Nella shifted slightly beside him, her eyes wandering

around the room. Her gaze landed on a large and prominent piece of abstract art. Along the top was the title, *Geometric Tangent*, and along the bottom was the name, Malik Farnsworth.

"That's cool," she said, pointing at it.

David followed her gaze, his eyes settling on the piece. "*Geometric Tangent*," he said, his voice flat.

Nella nodded, studying the artwork. "I like it," she said, her tone light, as if inviting him into a normal conversation.

"Thanks," David replied in the same flat voice.

For a moment, neither of them spoke. The silence wasn't awkward, but it wasn't exactly comfortable either. It was just there, like everything else in his life, something to sit with, something to endure.

Then, without looking at her, he finally asked, "How did you know where I live?"

Nella shifted slightly, tucking one leg underneath her as she turned toward him. "Well, it wasn't that hard," she said. "I found you through social media. You posted about your new house last year and your location was visible. So, I put two and two together."

David let out a slow sigh, rubbing his face. "Guess I should be more careful about what I post."

"Yeah," Nella said, shrugging. "You couldn't have said it any better. I mean, there are a lot of crazies out there." Her tone was casual, but there was something light about it, something almost teasing.

David turned his head slightly, looking at her out of the corner of his eye. "Yeah, thanks. Besides, I don't really have any enemies, so I guess I am okay."

"Well, not yet anyway," Nella replied with a smirk.

And then, without meaning to, and without even realizing it was happening, the corner of his mouth lifted. Just a little. A half-smile. Barely there, but it was the first he had smiled in weeks.

"So why are you here?" David asked.

She hesitated for a moment before speaking. "I know the last time we spoke, you told me quite an interesting story," she said, her voice measured and careful. "And I wanted to talk to you about it."

David's fingers tensed slightly. His eyes flickered to the floor, then to the painting on the wall, as if searching for an answer somewhere in the room.

"Now?" he asked, his voice quieter than before.

"Only if you're up for it," Nella said. She wasn't pushing him. She was giving him the choice. "And considering what you've just been through these past couple of weeks... I can wait for you. You know, I think it might be too soon. Maybe I should go; we can talk about it another time."

He let out a slow breath, rubbing the back of his neck. For a few seconds, he said nothing. The silence stretched between them. Then, finally, just as she was about to get up from the couch, he looked at her.

"No, please stay," he said. His voice was steady, but there was something raw underneath it. "I could use a friend right now."

Nella didn't hesitate. She nodded. "Okay then. I want to say this as delicately as possible. There was something you said the last time we spoke that caught my attention. I mean, you shared a lot... a lot of very strange coincidences. But you said one particular word that resonated with me."

David barely reacted, though he curiously asked. "What was it?"

She didn't look away from him as she answered in a calm voice, knowing that what she was about to say could possibly strike a nerve. "Hannah."

The change in him was instant. His body stiffened, and his breathing slowed, almost like he was bracing for impact. His fingers curled slightly, gripping the fabric of his sweatpants. He didn't move, didn't speak.

The name had been trapped in his mind for weeks, circling endlessly, but hearing it out loud was something else entirely. It was like a knife being dragged through his chest, sharp and unforgiving.

The silence between them stretched uncomfortably. David exhaled slowly, his hands now clasped together as he leaned forward, staring at the floor. His mind drifted back to every moment he had shared with Hannah—their first date, their late-night talks, the way she used to hum while she cooked. Every little thing about her had made his life better. And now, all of it was gone.

His throat felt tight as he swallowed. When he finally spoke, his voice was barely more than a whisper.

"I don't share my personal life with too many people," he admitted. "Now I sit here and wonder, why not? We all have only one life to live; it's a blessing, a gift from God. I should have stood on a mountaintop and called out to the world... that I loved my life, and that I loved my wife. Instead, I now sit atop a different mountain... a mountain of grief. And nobody knows what a wonderful and blessed life I had because I never shared it. I opted to keep my happiness private."

Nella didn't respond immediately. She let his words settle, giving him the space to feel them fully.

"You're sharing it now," she said softly.

David let out a shaky breath, and a single tear slipped down his cheek. He wiped it away quickly, but it didn't matter. The pain was written all over his face.

"That person... the hit and run driver... they are still out there. Free. I want to hate God for what happened to Hannah," he whispered. "I want to resent him for taking away my beautiful wife. But I can't allow myself to succumb to the darkness of the abyss. I must find the strength to forgive... to move on."

His voice cracked on the last word. He clenched his jaw, struggling to keep himself composed, but it was pointless. His grief was too much.

"You know, you can't change the past; trust me, I don't share my personal life with people either. I have shit in my past that I wish I could take away," Nella admitted, her voice quieter now.

David turned his head slightly, studying her. There was a shift in her expression, something almost guarded. "Maybe we should both start sharing then," David said with a smirk, trying to lighten the tension.

Nella smiled and then nodded in agreement.

David then continued. "Only a few people know this about me. I was adopted... I was adopted as an infant when both my parents were also killed in an accident. I have amazing adoptive parents; they live in California. You know, once they learned about Hannah's death, they got on the first flight to Boston. They have always loved and supported me, and I have always felt like I belonged with them. My life was a blessing, and that is why I must move forward."

"That's all any of us can do... move forward, I mean. Speaking of forward, that one word I was talking about that resonated with me..." Nella said, trailing off.

"Hannah?" David whispered.

"Yes, do you know the name Hannah is considered a palindrome?" Nella asked.

David looked at her, confused.

Nella, seeing this. clarified. "Well, you know I'm a journalist, which makes me a wordsmith. Basically, a palindrome is a word that reads the same way both forward and backward. For example, radar and level."

"I don't understand. Do you think this is related to the list I told you about? Was I supposed to find you so you could give me that clue?" David asked, still confused.

"Actually, I think it's much bigger than that. And if you really want to do this, you and I, then we both must be ready to go down the rabbit hole."

David's eyes widened in utter surprise at her words. "I can't believe you just said that!"

Nella was taken aback. "Said what?"

David continued, "After Hannah died, I had this strange dream. In front of me was a woman, I think it was Hannah, but she was wearing a mask. Her body, her shape, she was wearing a red dress—not a fancy dress, a sundress, like the one she used to wear on weekends. She was dancing around our bedroom, spinning and twirling. It was strange, like most dreams sometimes are. But it was the mask that was the most bizarre. She was wearing a rabbit mask. It didn't just cover her face, either; it was covering her entire head. Big ears and big dark eyes. Those eyes! I called out to her, and she kept dancing around. Then I walked over to her and tried to remove the mask, and she reached up and held it on. I called her name again, and she finally spoke. She said, 'Down the rabbit hole you must go!'"

Nella looked in awe.

David leaned forward, eyes widening, because, for the first time in weeks, his mind had found a speck of light beyond the darkness he had been enduring. "I am ready."

"Okay, here it goes. You told me that Hannah was the first item on the list, and Hannah is a palindrome. You also came looking for me because of my ladybug tattoo, which was item three on the list. Well, what makes this so intriguing is that my full name is Nella Allen. My first and last name is also a palindrome. My father was strangely obsessed with palindromes, and he used to tell me that my name was special because of it. I recall my mother telling me a story that happened after my brother was born. How my dad had hoped for a daughter next because he wanted to name her Nella. Thereby making my first and last name a palindrome," Nella said in one breath.

She then inhaled deeply and continued. "My father is Robert Allen. He was a respected healthcare administrator at a prominent Boston hospital."

The name sounded vaguely familiar, but David couldn't place it right away. He glanced at her, searching her face for clues. Then, a memory surfaced. The name. The news reports. The scandal.

"Wait..." David started slowly. "Is he that guy that was in the news, the one that was on trial and went to prison?"

Hearing David say this, Nella grew uncomfortable. "Yes, he is the one. So you can see why I don't share my personal life with too many people either. My father was an amazing dad, David. Believe me, I was a daddy's girl for sure. I even got this ladybug tattoo on my hand because of him. He used to call me ladybug. Our life was perfect until 2007 when we lost Marcus, my older brother. He was a Marine, and he was killed in Iraq. It broke our family for a while. I could tell something had changed in my father, understandably so. But then one day, about six years ago. I'm on my way to English Lit. at BU, my dad's alma mater. I got a text from my mom, telling me to call her ASAP. Well, you know the rest; it was all over the news for years," she said, voice tight.

"Something about conducting an illegal surgery, right? Where some woman ended up dying," David said.

"Yeah. Sometime after 2013, things took a turn for the worse. He became obsessed and started talking about neurosurgery. About how he always wanted to be a brain surgeon but never got the chance. I know he was in medical school when my mom got pregnant, and he cut short his plans to be a doctor, but he never spoke of it until then. I mean, it started to get really weird. Bringing up over dinner his desire to do brain surgery on patients. I mean, how crazy was that? One day, he just walked into an operating room, kicked everyone out, and locked the door. The patient was undergoing a gall bladder removal. She was a 47-year-old mother of three. By the time they were able to stop him, he had partially removed her skull and had already cut into her brain. She went into cardiac arrest and died on the table. That, David, is why I don't share my personal life."

"Oh, Nella, you are not your father," he said sympathetically, giving Nella a hug.

Nella didn't respond to that. She just continued with the story. "Ever since that day, I have had a lot of unanswered questions. I have not seen my father since the trial. Even as he sits in prison, he refuses to talk to anyone. On the day of his arrest, I drove straight home to our house in Newton. I looked through his desk in his office. I thought I would find something, perhaps prescription drugs, narcotics... anything that would explain why he did what he did."

"And? Did you find anything?" David asked.

"More questions than answers. But I did find something, something strange. On his desk calendar, written on the day of the incident, there was a notation. It read: '*Mr. Owl ate my metal worm.*' Nella then paused before adding, "It's a nineteen-letter palindrome."

David swallowed hard. "I don't get it. Do you think these palindromes are related to why we were supposed to meet? Why item three on the list led me to you? To your ladybug tattoo?"

Nella nodded, looking him in the eyes and taking his

hand. "You said that a dying man gave you that list seven years ago and that the first three items were like predictions. It can't be a coincidence that the list led you to me and all my unanswered questions happen to be linked by interconnected palindromes."

David hesitated for a moment before getting up and walking into the next room, returning with a piece of folded paper. He sat back down next to Nella and handed it to her.

"This is the list; maybe one of the items is familiar to you," David said to her.

She unfolded the paper carefully, smoothing it against her palm and reading the entire list:

Hannah
Hermit Lake
Ladybug tattoo
18 Vassar Street
Leonard Friston
Emmitt Poole
Cathedral Rock
Kill him

Her expression shifted as she read each entry out loud. At first, she looked intrigued. Then confused. Then, when she reached the last item, her entire body tensed.

Her lips parted slightly as she looked up at David. "Kill him?" she whispered.

David nodded. "That's what it says."

Nella read the words again as if trying to make sense of them. "That's… creepy."

"Yeah," David muttered.

Nella let out a sigh. "Anyway, nothing rings a bell. I guess I was hoping for more."

She looked back down at the list before adding, "Isn't Vassar Street near MIT?"

David smiled. "Yes, it is!"

Nella then smiled back, saying, "Well, guess you already know your next stop!"

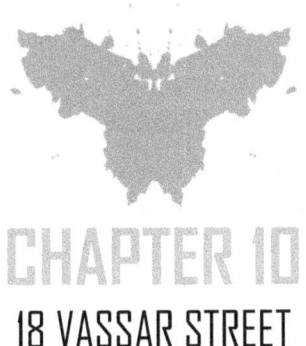

CHAPTER 10

18 VASSAR STREET

David stepped through the glass doors of his workplace—The Beacon Design Group—and immediately felt the shift in the air. The murmur of quiet conversations, the clatter of keyboards, and the soft shuffle of papers should have felt familiar.

They didn't.

Everything seemed distant, like he was walking through a place he used to know but no longer belonged to. As he moved past the reception desk, he gave a small nod to Melissa, the receptionist, who hesitated before offering a polite smile. It was the same kind of smile he had seen too often lately—the cautious, sympathetic one people gave when they didn't know what to say.

"Hey, David. Welcome back," she said softly.

"Thanks," he replied, his voice flat. He didn't stop to

chat. He just couldn't.

The open workspace stretched ahead, modern and sleek—white desks, exposed brick walls, warm pendant lights hanging low over each workstation. He had spent some good years here, poring over blueprints, sketching designs, and space-planning projects with colleagues. But today, it all felt hollow. The energy and the passion that once drove him was gone.

As he reached his desk, he saw that someone had left a small stack of folders. His name was scribbled on a sticky note on top. The note read:

Start here when you're ready.

David stared at the note for a moment before pulling out his chair. As he sat down, he felt eyes on him. He glanced up to see Mark, a fellow architect, looking in his direction.

"Good to have you back, man," Mark said, approaching. His voice was casual, but his eyes held that same concerned look everyone seemed to have.

"Yeah," David replied.

Mark hesitated, then gave a nod before walking back to his own desk. No one knew what to say. They wanted to acknowledge his loss, but they were afraid of saying the wrong thing.

David sighed and flipped open the first folder.

A commercial project. Something about a new office building in Cambridge. Normally, he would have been eager to study the site plans, analyze the structure, and visualize how it would come to life. Instead, the words blurred together. He closed the folder.

It was too soon.

•••

David checked the time. 9:42 a.m.

Had it really only been an hour since he walked in? He felt like each second was stretching longer than it should. He tried to focus, clicking open his email and finding over a hundred unread messages: project updates, deadlines, internal memos, and other junk. He scanned the subject lines, but nothing felt important.

Not anymore.

A message from his boss sat near the top.

Jim: Take it slow. If you need anything, let me know. Glad to have you back.

David exhaled and clicked out of his inbox. He wasn't sure what he needed.

By 11 a.m., he had reorganized his desk twice, sharpened pencils he didn't need, and pretended to work. His mind wasn't in the office. It was trapped between memories of Hannah, the list in his pocket, and his conversation with Nella the last time she was at his place. He reached into his coat and felt the folded piece of paper, reminding him that he was still seeking answers.

•••

By the time noon rolled around, David couldn't take it anymore. He grabbed his coat and headed out without telling anyone. The cold air hit him hard as he stepped onto the sidewalk. People moved around him, talking on their phones, rushing to grab lunch, and living their normal lives.

His normal life was gone.

David walked without a destination, letting the city

guide him. His feet carried him to a familiar spot: a small coffee shop on the corner of Tremont Street. A place he and Hannah used to visit on slow afternoons. He missed her a lot, and he knew that even his newfound friendship with Nella would not change his feelings for his wife anytime soon.

He hesitated outside coffee shop, then turned away. He wasn't ready for that.

Instead, he found a bench near a park and sat down. He pulled out the list and unfolded it carefully, his eyes scanning the items again. Each one felt like a piece of a puzzle waiting to be solved.

18 Vassar Street

That was this afternoon's destination. Maybe it would mean nothing; maybe it would lead somewhere.

All David knew was that sitting at his desk and pretending to care about office buildings, wasn't going to help. And for the first time since Hannah died, he felt something other than grief.

A need to understand. A need to find out the truth.

And that was enough to get him up from the bench and through the rest of the day.

•••

The afternoon dragged on, each minute stretching unbearably long. David sat at his desk, gripping a mechanical pencil between his fingers and tapping it against the surface of his desk. The sound blended into the background noise of the office—keyboards clicking, muffled conversations, and the occasional ring of a phone. He should have been working. He should have been reviewing plans, design ideas, or at the very least, replying to emails. Instead, he found himself staring for nearly twenty minutes at the same page of a project brief he'd opened when he'd come back from lunch, nothing making much sense.

Time kept dragging by contrary to his state of mind. Then finally, he pushed back from his desk, his eyes flicked to the clock on his computer screen.

3:42 p.m.

Almost there.

His legs bounced slightly beneath the table. Eighteen more minutes until 4:00p.m and he'd finally be free. He had made plans with Nella to meet at MIT at 4:30 p.m. Together, they were going to visit 18 Vassar Street in search of possible clues, or better yet, answers.

David no longer believed in the idea of a self-fulfilling prophecy. Perhaps he just didn't care anymore. He and Nella were now convinced that the list and the strange palindromes could not be a coincidence, but rather pieces of a larger puzzle.

A puzzle they were determined to solve.

•••

David sat in the subway car, staring at the scratched metal pole in front of him. The train swayed gently, rocking him in place, but he barely noticed. The noise in his head was louder than the world around him. Thoughts of Hannah, the list, the strange connections that didn't make sense and the feeling that something bigger was happening, something just out of reach.

"Next stop, Kendall/MIT," came a voice as the subway train slowed down.

David stood before the train even fully stopped. The doors hissed open, and he stepped onto the platform. The rush of cold air hit him immediately, stinging his skin. It was early evening, but the winter sky was already darkening. He followed the signs, climbing the stairs toward the Main Street exit.

As he came up onto the sidewalk, his eyes scanned the area. Then he saw her.

Nella stood near a streetlight, her hands stuffed into the pockets of her thick coat. A light dusting of snow clung to her dark curls, and she shifted from foot to foot, either from the cold or impatience. When she spotted him, she gave a small smile, but there was something else in her expression. Not just friendliness—concern.

David let out a breath he didn't realize he was holding. He hadn't admitted it to himself, but seeing her standing there, waiting for him, made something in his chest loosen. And for the first time that day, he felt a little more present and less like he was drifting.

She tilted her head slightly as he approached. "How was your first day back?"

David smirked, shoving his hands into his pockets. "I survived." His voice was dry, almost dismissive.

Nella gave him a knowing look. She didn't push, didn't ask for more, but he could tell that she understood.

"Well," she said, "that's something."

David let out a small huff of air, not quite a laugh, but

close. The moment passed, and Nella gestured toward the street.

"Ready?"

David nodded. He was more than ready.

They began walking side by side, heading west on Main Street, their footsteps crunching against the thin layer of snow covering the sidewalk. The cold air stung both their faces, but they barely noticed as they began chatting along the way.

"This place hasn't changed much," David muttered.

"Tell me about it," Nella said, glancing at him.

"This is where I attended Architecture School. I must have spent five years running around this campus in my day. When I saw 18 Vassar Street on the list, I had a good idea where it was, yet I don't recall anything marked 18."

Nella didn't reply to that. They reached the corner, and David slowed his pace. He scanned the area, spotting the familiar numbers on the buildings around them. On their left, they saw 32 Vassar Street, home of the Stata Center.

Then they came upon 50 Vassar Street, home of the Fairchild Building. David and Nella paused, circling in different directions, eyes focused on the address numbers of the surrounding buildings.

Nella suddenly pointed across the street and called out, "There's 15 Vassar Street! Across the street. It's the Parsons Lab building."

David frowned. His steps became hesitant. His eyes moved from one building to the next, looking for number 18.

Nothing.

He and Nella exchanged a look before both of them began circling the area, scanning every sign and checking the nearby buildings again.

"Maybe we missed it," Nella said. She turned back the way they came, retracing their steps.

David shook his head. "No. That doesn't make sense."

He crossed the street, double-checking every number. 15, 32, 50. No number 18.

He curled his hands into fists inside his coat pockets. "It's not here," he said, his voice tinged with frustration.

Nella stopped beside him, looking just as puzzled. "How can that be? I think that if it is on the list, then it has to exist."

David exhaled sharply, his breath visible in the cold air. "Maybe we're missing something."

They both stood there, staring at the buildings around them and trying to piece together a puzzle that wasn't making any sense. David rubbed the back of his neck, scanning the area one last time.

Still no 18 Vassar Street, no hidden signs.

Nothing.

"Maybe it's behind one of these buildings," he said, turning to Nella. "Let's cut through the Stata Center. If there's something we're missing, we might see it from the other side."

Nella nodded, following as he led the way toward the entrance of the Stata Center.

The glass doors slid open, and they stepped inside. Immediately, a rush of warm air met their frozen faces. The contrast was sharp; outside was cold and gray, but inside?

Inside was something else entirely.

The Stata Center was unlike any other building on campus. The walls didn't follow normal rules. They twisted and leaned, as if the entire structure was caught mid-collapse. The ceiling stretched high, slanting in unexpected directions, and large, reflective surfaces bounced light across the space, making it feel alive. Bright yellow, silver, and red walls clashed against exposed steel beams, creating a mix of chaos and brilliance.

David slowed his pace as they passed a food court and café, his eyes moving across the design.

"This place is amazing!" Nella exclaimed in awe.

David smiled. "I know, right?" he said, his voice lighter. A part of him was happy that she noticed how the inside architecture was as unique as the outside.

Nella glanced at him. "You like this place."

David nodded, his hand running over a curved metal surface. "It's one of my favorites. It is considered one of Frank Gehry's masterpieces."

"Frank Gehry?" Nella questioned.

"Oh sorry, he's a famous architect. He doesn't believe in straight lines or right angles. Everything he designs looks like it shouldn't stand, but it does. It's controlled chaos. I think you can clearly see that with this building," David said.

Nella watched him closely, noticing the way his posture had shifted. The usual tension in his shoulders had faded. And his face, so often weighed down, brightened as he spoke.

David noticed her staring and asked, "What is it?"

She smiled. "Nothing. I am just thinking how nice it is to see you smile. In fact, this is the first time I've seen you actually excited about something."

David shied away. "Architecture has always done that for me. I have always had a passion for it."

Nella nods. "I get it; journalism did the same for me."

David and Nella stepped out into the angular courtyard behind the Stata Center. The evening sky had darkened into deep blue, the last traces of daylight fading behind the sharp, uneven edges of the building. Lights from inside created long, distorted shadows, making the whole structure look even more dreamlike.

David's gaze moved over the curved walls and strange, protruding windows, their odd angles reflecting bits of light from streetlights and passing cars. It was a place that shouldn't exist—yet here it was, standing tall in defiance of traditional architecture.

Before either of them could speak, a deep voice broke the silence.

"I wouldn't want to be the guy who has to clean those windows."

Both David and Nella turned, casually laughing in response to the man's obvious attempt at humor.

A man in his late fifties or early sixties strolled toward them, dressed in blue maintenance work clothes. His gray beard and short-cropped hair were neatly kept, and a ring of keys dangled from his belt. His uniform had an embroidered patch: MIT Facilities Management.

He stopped beside them, looking up at the chaotic structure with a smirk.

Nella, always sharp, took the chance. "Excuse me, sir?"

The worker turned to her, raising an eyebrow.

"I was wondering if you could help us. We are looking for 18 Vassar Street. Would you happen to know where it is?" Nella asked.

The man let out a small chuckle, shaking his head as if amused by the question. Then, with a knowing smirk, he said something that made both David and Nella freeze.

"You're standing on it."

David blinked. "What?"

David and Nella looked at each other, as if questioning what they had just heard.

The worker shrugged. "You must be talking about Building 20, right? It's right where you're standing. This used to be Building 20. Its address was 18 Vassar Street before they tore it down back in '98."

Nella and David exchanged stunned glances.

"You're saying... it's gone?" Nella asked slowly.

"Yep. Demolished." The worker chuckled again. "Let me guess... someone told you the building's still standing, hidden under an invisibility cloaking field?"

David stiffened. "Wait—what? Did you just say an invisibility cloaking field?"

The man laughed. "Oh yeah. That was the rumor back then, started by the science majors. See, when they started knocking down Building 20, they found an elevator shaft. The weird part? It had buttons leading to secret laboratories five floors below ground. After that, the stories went crazy. People started saying the real building was still here, just cloaked by some kind of government tech."

"That's... ridiculous," Nella muttered, though her voice wasn't as confident as she wanted it to be.

The worker grinned. "Maybe. But you'd be surprised how many students back then believed it." He adjusted his key ring. "Anyway, that's all ancient history now. You guys need anything else?"

David and Nella remained silent for a moment, the conversation sinking in.

Then David shook his head. "No... thanks."

The worker tipped his head in a small nod, then strolled away, disappearing around the corner. David and Nella remained in their exact position, surprised at the wild story they'd just heard, and wondered if it could be related to the answers they were seeking.

"Okay, so Building 20 is gone," David said, breaking the silence. "But what now? What else do we do with that info?"

Nella glanced at him, her expression thoughtful. "Well, we go find more details, obviously." She raised an eyebrow. "I mean, this could be something, right? A hidden building five floors underground... sounds like the perfect place for some secret project."

David's lips twitched. He couldn't help but laugh a little at the thought. "You're buying into this conspiracy theory stuff, huh?"

Nella smiled, though there was a hint of uncertainty behind her eyes. "I don't know, David. I'm just trying to connect the dots. I mean, everything's so weird. The list, your encounters at Hermit Lake, the palindromes, 18

Vassar Street being a ghost address… We're not exactly dealing with ordinary things here."

David felt his stomach tighten. He hadn't considered it that way. Everything they had uncovered so far before and after Hannah's death—the strange list, the strange coincidences—seemed like more than just odd occurrences. Maybe there was something deeper going on. Something he didn't want to acknowledge but couldn't ignore either.

"Well, we're definitely not going to find out anything standing around here in the cold," he said, looking at his watch. "Let's hit the library or the MIT records department. They might have something on Building 20."

"I have a better idea! How about a cup of something hot from the café? I'm freezing and feel like having a caramel macchiato," Nella said, grabbing David's hand and pulling him back the way they came.

"Sounds good to me!" David replied.

•••

David and Nella sat in a cozy corner of the coffee shop, the aroma of freshly brewed coffee mingling with their quiet conversation.

David took a long sip of his coffee, the warmth spreading through him, though his mind still felt heavy. Nella was quiet for a moment, her eyes distant as she stared out the window, her fingers tracing the edge of her cup. He noticed how the soft light from the café made her look different—more vulnerable. He didn't want to push her, but he also couldn't ignore the thought that had been on his mind for a while.

He set his cup down, then spoke gently. "I've been meaning to ask you something, Nella. About your brother."

Her head snapped up, and for a moment, she looked almost surprised. Her expression was guarded, but there was no hiding the pain in her eyes. She didn't answer right away. Instead, she took a slow sip from her own cup, her fingers still gripping the warm cup sleeve, as if it were the only thing keeping her grounded. After a moment, she nodded.

"What do you want to know?" she asked, her voice quieter now, more cautious.

David hesitated, unsure of how to phrase the question. "I... I just wondered about him. You mentioned losing your brother Marcus before, in Iraq in 2007, right?"

Nella was silent for a long time. Her eyes were fixed on her coffee now, as if trying to find the right words. When she finally spoke, her voice was soft, almost as if she was trying to keep the words from slipping out.

"Yeah. He enlisted when he was eighteen," Nella began, her gaze still on the table. "He was always... looking for something. I think he wanted to make our grandfather proud. Grandpa served in Vietnam. He talked about his time in the service all the time. So, when Marcus turned eighteen, two days after graduation, he enlisted. I think it was more about honoring Grandpa than anything else. Though he knew my parents would be pissed about it."

David could see how much she was holding back, how tightly she gripped her emotions. The way she spoke made it clear that Marcus was someone she still held close, someone whose memory she carried with her every day. David leaned in, his expression encouraging her to continue. Her eyes flicked briefly to him, and then away again.

"He died two weeks into his deployment," Nella continued, her voice trembling just a little. "He was assigned to a Stryker Brigade, mostly patrolling the Mosul area. One day, they spotted something in the road and stopped. They'd been dealing with IEDs, so caution was key. Marcus got out to secure the perimeter. He was just standing there, no bomb, no gun fight, kids playing nearby... then a shot rang out. A sniper. He was killed instantly."

David felt a lump rise in his throat as he watched her. She didn't cry. But there was something raw in her voice, something that told him this memory—this story—was still sharp in her heart. He could tell it still hurt, even though it had been years.

"I was there when they told us," she said, her voice barely above a whisper now. "I was the one who had to listen to the guy in the military uniform explain it to us. It was just—" She paused, swallowing hard before continuing. "It was just the worst moment of my life."

David could see the emotions flickering in her eyes, the mix of anger, sadness, and maybe even a little bit of guilt. He wasn't sure if she was angry at Marcus for leaving or angry at herself for not being able to protect him. But either way, the pain was still there, and it was clear it wasn't something she'd ever fully get over.

Without thinking, David reached across the table and

placed his hand over hers. He didn't say anything at first, just letting the moment sit between them. His fingers were warm against her cold skin.

"I'm sorry, Nella," he said quietly. "I can imagine how much that must've hurt."

She didn't pull her hand away. Instead, she looked at him, her expression softening just a little. "It was… it was the kind of pain you can't explain. It's not something you just get over, you know? You learn to live with it. But it doesn't ever go away."

David squeezed her hand gently, his heart heavy with the understanding of what she'd lost. He didn't know how to make her feel better. There was nothing he could say that would change anything. But he knew, in that moment, that she wasn't alone. He understood the kind of grief she carried.

Nella exhaled; a weight seemingly lifted from her shoulders. "Wow. I haven't told that story to anyone before. It's just been… stuck in my head."

"Thanks for sharing that with me," David said in a steady voice.

"Yeah… anyways, time to change the subject. I wonder if we can find anything on the web about Building 20?" Nella replied, taking her phone out and beginning her web search.

David followed suit and commented, "I guess I should have tried this first."

Nella looked up at him and smiled. "It's not your fault. I'm the journalist here. I should have told you this is how I find almost everything."

They leaned over their phones, searching through page after page of results. David was the first to speak, breaking the silence. "Listen to this." His voice was low, almost hesitant. Nella glanced over at his phone, her own fingers still scrolling.

"Looks like that facilities guy was right; the cloaking rumor is true. Back in 1998, before they demolished the building, apparently students did begin spreading some rumors and even did a prank on the building. They posted a banner bearing the words:

MASS. INST. OF TECH. – DEACTIVATED – PROPERTY OFFICE

I don't know where to start; the building has a long-assorted history. The search results say the building was home to government experiments, radiation laboratories, cognitive science, cosmic microwave research, and it even had a radio-frequency anechoic chamber. Whatever that is—"

"Wait! I think I found something. Let me see the list," Nella said excitedly, cutting him off.

David pulled out the list and laid it on the table in front of them. Nella's eyes looked up at him, and she held out her phone for David to see. There on the screen was an article displaying a name: Dr. Leonard Friston, which also happened to be one of the list's items.

Leonard Friston

David's jaw dropped.

"This must be the guy from the list; the article says he

wrote a book titled, *Induction Theory and Cognitive Sciences*," Nella said, scrolling farther down. "The article also mentions that he once worked at MIT's Building 20. Oh shit, it says here that he passed away. Eleven months ago. Maybe it's the wrong guy or worse we are too late."

A wave of disappointment washed over David, and for a moment, he felt his hope slip away. Everything they had uncovered felt pointless now. *Was it all just some coincidence? Was it a wild goose chase for nothing?*

David clenched his fist, trying to push back the frustration. He couldn't give up, not now. Not after everything. There had to be more to this. There had to be another piece of the puzzle.

"There's got to be another Leonard Friston," David muttered under his breath, his voice filled with determination. "Maybe someone with the same name. Maybe there's more to his story than this. We must keep looking. After all, it took me a year to find you—the girl with the ladybug tattoo."

Nella's smile grew bigger and brighter than it had been all day.

CHAPTER 11

LEONARD FRISTON

The sound of rain hitting the window woke David. It was steady, tapping against the glass, with the wind pushing against the house. The sky outside was dark, and the dim light in his room made it feel earlier than it was.

He sat up slowly, rubbing his face. It was Saturday, and he had plans with Nella. He had hoped for better weather, but the cold air in the house told him it wasn't just rain—it was one of those chilly, damp mornings that made everything feel heavier.

He stood and walked toward the bathroom, his feet cold against the wooden floor. The house was quiet, too quiet. Not just because he now lived alone, but because the rain seemed to push everything else into silence.

He caught a look at himself in the mirror as he brushed his teeth. His hair was slightly disheveled and his eyes looked tired with dark circles, proof that he hadn't slept well. Lately, his thoughts had been too loud, running in circles between past memories and new questions.

Hannah. The list. Leonard Friston.

He rinsed his mouth, wiped his face with a towel, and returned to the bedroom.

His phone buzzed on the nightstand. A quick glance told him the time. 9:07 a.m. He was supposed to meet Nella at 9:30 a.m.

"Shit," he muttered.

David grabbed his jeans off the chair and yanked them on. He pulled a sweater over his head, then reached for a heavier coat. His usual jacket wouldn't cut it today—the cold, damp air was seeping through every crack of his old house, and he could only imagine how miserable it would be outside.

As he pulled on his boots, his mind drifted back to Nella.

She was different.

From the start, she had challenged him. She asked questions, pushed him to think, and didn't let him brush things off. She had a way of making him talk, even when he didn't want to. And she wasn't just doing it for the story—he could tell she cared.

David grabbed his phone from the nightstand and his keys near the front door, then he reached for an umbrella. It had been a while since he needed one, but the way the rain sounded, there was no way he was making it to Harvard Square without getting soaked.

As he opened the door, the wind hit him first, then the

cold. The rain was heavier than he'd thought, coming down in thick steady sheets, soaking the pavement, and turning puddles into small streams along the curb. He hesitated for just a second before stepping out, pulling his coat tighter around him.

He was already late.

•••

Nella gripped the steering wheel tighter, shifting in her seat as she tried to see through the fogged-up windshield. The defroster was on full blast, but it wasn't helping much. She wiped the glass with the sleeve of her coat, leaving streaks behind.

The rain hadn't let up since she left her apartment. It was heavy and unceasing, the kind that made everything feel slower. The old wipers on her car screeched as they moved back and forth, barely doing their job.

"Come on," she muttered under her breath, adjusting in her seat. "Shit! I can't see anything."

She wasn't sure if her frustration was because of the weather or because she was feeling restless. Maybe both. A flash of light caught her eye—her phone screen. A message bubble popped up, and she read it:

David 9:30 AM
Sorry I am running late

She exhaled, her shoulders loosening.

Good.

She had been tense without realizing it, gripping the wheel too hard and leaning forward as if that would get her there faster. Now, she could slow down. Up ahead, a car's brake lights flickered as it pulled out of a spot. Perfect. She eased into the parking space, letting out a breath she hadn't realized she was holding.

David was late, but for once, she didn't mind.

As the minutes passed by, Nella sat in her parked car, listening to the rhythm of the rain tapping against the windshield. The world outside was blurred, the passing cars distorted by the streaks of water sliding down the glass. She leaned back in her seat, her fingers drumming lightly against the steering wheel.

Up the street, past the rows of wet sidewalks and pavement, the Littauer Center of Public Administration stood in the distance. The stone building looked even colder in the rain, its large windows dark against the gray sky.

David had no idea why she picked this place. She had kept it to herself, enjoying the small power of knowing something he didn't. He would expect MIT, maybe even a library, but not this. She smirked slightly at the thought. Surprises kept things interesting.

Her phone screen lit up.

David 9:41 AM
I'm here

Nella 9:42 AM
Head up Peabody Street toward the Littauer Center, I will meet you there

She straightened, her fingers hovering over the keyboard for only a second when the message indicated... Read.

She set her phone down and exhaled. She stepped out of the car and into the rain, quickly heading toward the Center's entrance.

•••

David spotted Nella standing near the entrance of the Littauer Center, her coat spotted with dark patches where the rain had soaked through. She had her hands tucked into her pockets, shoulders slightly hunched against the cold. The hood of her coat was down, letting the rain cling to strands of her dark hair. Even in the bad weather, she looked completely at ease.

David, on the other hand, was fighting against the wind as he hurried toward her, his umbrella flipping backward with a sudden gust. "Damn it," he muttered, yanking it back into shape. By the time he reached her, the wind had already pushed his damp hair into a mess, and his coat felt heavier from the rain.

Nella raised an eyebrow, amused. "Having fun?"

David sighed, shaking his umbrella off before folding it. "Yeah, I love running through a storm first thing in the morning. Definitely how I wanted to start my Saturday." He glanced up at the building behind her. "What are we doing here?"

Nella smirked, tilting her head. "It's a surprise."

David gave her a suspicious look. "I am sure your surprises mean trouble."

Nella's grin widened, a flash of mischief passing across

her face. "Exactly! Adds a little spice, doesn't it? Now, quit your shivering and let's get inside," she said, tugging at his arm and pulling him toward the building.

David let out a dramatic sigh but followed her through the doors, shaking off the cold as they stepped into the warmth of the building. After the storm outside, the warm air inside was a relief. David saw a sign that read:

Harvard University Department of Economics

Nella then led him down a long, quiet hallway lined with wooden doors, each marked with a small nameplate. The air smelled of old books and polished floors, the kind of scent that made a place feel important.

David glanced around, not sure what to expect. His damp shoes squeaked against the floor as they walked. Near the end of the hallway, they approached one of the wooden doors, and that was when he saw it.

Dr. Roslyn Friston.

The name was printed in bold letters on a plaque beside the office door. David stopped in his tracks, reading it again just to be sure. His brows pulled together in confusion.

"Who is Roslyn Friston?" he asked quietly, looking at Nella.

Nella was already watching him, her face full of excitement. She rocked on her heels slightly, as if she had been waiting for this moment.

"She's Leonard Friston's daughter," she said. "And I found something big."

David's confusion deepened. "Wait, what?"

"We had the right Leonard Friston! I searched the MIT

records department," Nella continued, her words coming fast. "Leonard Friston wasn't just some cognitive scientist. He was part of several secret, government-sponsored brain and cognitive experiments."

David blinked at her, letting the words settle. For a moment, all he could hear was the faint crackling of heat moving through the vents above. Then, his expression shifted.

"You searched the records department?" His voice was slow, as if he was still processing.

Nella nodded.

David folded his arms. "That was my idea last week when we were at MIT. And you shot it down."

Nella hesitated, then rolled her eyes with a small smirk. "I didn't shoot it down. It was a great idea!"

David tilted his head. "You literally said, and I quote, 'I have a better idea...' then you went ahead and dragged me to a coffee shop."

She lifted her chin slightly. "Okay, fine. Maybe I dismissed it."

David scoffed. "Maybe?"

Nella sighed dramatically. "Alright, alright. I dismissed it, but in my defense, I really wanted a caramel macchiato."

David stared at her for a moment, then shook his head with a chuckle. "Unbelievable."

"Hey, caffeine is important," she said, crossing her arms. "But I got the information, didn't I?"

David let out a small laugh, rubbing a hand through his damp hair. He should've been annoyed, but he couldn't be. Not when she was standing there looking so damn pleased with herself.

He glanced back at the door. "So… now what?"

Nella's grin widened. "Now, we knock."

David shook his head at Nella's smug grin, and he was about to raise his hand to knock on the wooden office door when it suddenly creaked open. The laughter between them faded as they both turned toward the doorway.

A woman stood there, her expression unreadable. She looked to be in her late fifties, maybe early sixties, with long, dark hair streaked lightly with silver. Her sharp eyes moved between them, studying them carefully. She wore a deep blue blouse with a black blazer, giving her a professional but slightly intimidating presence.

"Excuse me," she said, her voice calm but firm. "May I help you?"

David straightened, clearing his throat. Nella, always quick on her feet, took a small step forward and reached into her coat pocket. She pulled out a slim leather badge holder and flipped it open, revealing her *Boston Rag* press badge.

"Yes, sorry. Would you happen to be Dr. Roslyn Friston?" Nella asked in a polite but confident tone. "My name is Nella Allen. I'm a journalist, and I'm working on a tribute piece about your father, Dr. Leonard Friston."

Roslyn's expression didn't change, but there was a flicker of something in her eyes—curiosity, maybe, or caution. She glanced at David for a brief second before looking back at Nella.

"My father?" she asked, her voice softer now, though still guarded.

Nella nodded. "Yes. We were hoping to ask you a few questions about his work and legacy."

There was a brief silence. Roslyn's fingers tightened slightly on the doorknob. She hesitated, as if debating whether to send them away or let them in.

David, sensing her uncertainty, spoke up. "We understand if this is unexpected," he said. "We just want to make sure your father's legacy gets the recognition it deserves."

Roslyn studied them for another moment. Then, with a quiet sigh, she stepped back and pushed the door open wider.

"Alright," she said. "Come in."

David and Nella exchanged a quick glance before stepping inside.

The office was small but packed with bookshelves that stretched from floor to ceiling. Thick academic volumes, some with faded spines, lined the shelves. Stacks of papers sat on the desk, neatly arranged, as if Roslyn was constantly in the middle of some deep research. A few framed certificates and academic awards hung on the wall, their gold lettering catching the soft glow of the desk lamp.

David and Nella stepped farther inside as Roslyn walked over to her desk and gestured for them to sit. The chairs were old and wooden, their armrests worn smooth from years of use. As David lowered himself into one, he noticed a framed photograph on a side table—a black-and-white image of a man, likely Leonard Friston, shaking hands with another scholar at what looked like a conference.

Roslyn settled into her chair, folding her hands on the desk. For a moment, she was quiet, her gaze flickering over to the framed awards on the wall. Then she exhaled slowly and spoke.

"My father was a brilliant man," she said. Her voice was steady, but there was something else beneath it—pride, mixed with something more difficult to place. "He was a dedicated scientist. One of the best in his field."

Nella leaned forward slightly, her pen poised over a notepad she had taken out once she had settled in her chair. "What made his work stand out?"

Roslyn's lips curved into a small smile, the first real one since they had arrived. "He wasn't just interested in how the brain worked—he wanted to know why we think the way we do. Why humans make decisions, how we form beliefs, what separates instinct from learned behavior. He always believed that understanding cognition at its deepest level could change the world."

David listened closely. He could hear the admiration in her voice, but there was also a distance, as if she were speaking about someone who had become more of a legend than a person.

"Now, take note of this. He was named a Fellow by the American Association for the Advancement of Science in 2002," Roslyn continued, glancing at one of the framed certificates on the wall. "It was one of the proudest moments of his career. He never cared much for awards, but that one... that one mattered to him."

She reached for a small silver pen on her desk, turning it between her fingers. Her expression softened. "I remember the day he got the news. He didn't even tell me at first. I found out because I came home and saw the letter sitting on the kitchen table, half covered by one of his research papers. I asked him why he didn't say anything, and he just shrugged and said, 'Because awards don't change the work, Roslyn. They only change how people look at it.'"

She let out a quiet breath, her fingers still moving over the pen. "That was who he was. He cared about the work, not the recognition. But I knew he was proud. Deep down, he was."

David found himself watching her closely. There was a weight in her voice, a sense that she was telling them something deeply personal, even if she kept her emotions controlled.

"He sounds like an incredible man," Nella said gently.

Roslyn nodded. "He was. That is, until his death."

For a brief moment, silence filled the office and the air felt heavier. Roslyn's fingers tapped lightly against the desk, her gaze distant, lost in thought. Then, with a slow inhale, she spoke.

"I have no evidence, mind you," she said, her voice quiet but firm, "but I never believed the police report. However, you know how it is; when a seventy-six-year-old man is found at the bottom of the basement stairs, it's easy to believe he must have fallen."

David and Nella exchanged a glance. There were no coincidences. They had both seen too much, heard too many strange connections, to brush this off as just another tragic accident.

"I am really sorry for your loss. If you don't mind me asking, is there a particular reason as to why you believe it wasn't an accident?" David asked, leaning forward slightly.

Roslyn's expression tightened. She hesitated for a second, then placed both hands flat on her desk, as if steadying herself. "A reason? Of course I have a reason. It was because of a phone call," she said. "The last time I spoke to him."

Nella frowned. "What phone call?"

Roslyn exhaled slowly, her eyes drifting toward the window. "The day before his so-called accident, my father called me. It wasn't unusual—he'd call sometimes just to check in—but this time, something was different. He sounded... off."

David watched her carefully. "Off how?"

Roslyn's hands curled slightly against the desk. "Nervous. Anxious. I could hear it in his voice. He told me that he needed to see me, that I should visit him that weekend. That whatever he had to say was important, something along the lines of a confession." She paused, as if replaying the conversation in her head. "Then he said something that still haunts me."

Nella's grip tightened on her notepad. "What did he say?"

Roslyn's gaze shifted back to them. Her voice was calm, but there was an unmistakable tension beneath it.

"He said, 'I have something extraordinary to share, but it may also be the most frightening thing you have ever heard.'"

The words hung in the air. David felt a chill crawl down

his spine. He could picture it—an aging scientist, burdened by some terrible truth, finally ready to share it. But before he could, he was gone.

Roslyn stood up and walked to the window. "I will tell you this. My father was a brilliant man, and in all my life, I had never heard him say something so profound. Deep down, I think someone didn't want him to talk about it. About whatever he planned on sharing with me. Because after that phone call, the next day, he was dead."

The room felt colder. Nella and David exchanged another glance. This was no accident. They could feel it. Someone had wanted to silence Leonard Friston.

Nella broke the silence first. "Do you think it had anything to do with his research? I also noticed on the web that he had written a book…"

"*Induction Theory and Cognitive Sciences*," Roslyn interrupted her. "I have no doubt it had to do with his research. His book was extremely controversial. Besides, the phone call wasn't the only suspicious thing. When I arrived at his house, on the day he died, I noticed a copy of his book sitting on the kitchen counter."

David and Nella waited, sensing there was more. The way Roslyn's fingers gripped her arms a little tighter, the way her jaw tensed—this memory wasn't just a detail. It meant something.

"I almost didn't think much of it," she continued. "But then I saw the post-it note stuck on the counter."

She turned back to face them, her dark eyes locking onto theirs.

"The note said, 'Thank you for giving me the answers

I seek.'"

David felt his breath hitch.

Roslyn took a slow step forward. "It was signed... Emmitt Poole. That is why I think there is more to the story. I think someone came to visit him that day, and that person brought a copy of his book with them."

A sharp silence filled the office. Nella's fingers tightened around her notepad. David's mind raced, piecing things together faster than he could fully process them.

Roslyn moved toward the large bookshelf behind her desk. She ran her fingers along the spines, pausing when she found what she was looking for. Carefully, she pulled out a thick hardcover book with a slightly worn deep blue cover.

"This," she said, setting it down on the desk in front of them, "is a signed first edition copy of my father's book, printed in 1999."

David and Nella leaned in as Roslyn opened the front cover. The pages were crisp but yellowed at the edges, showing the years that had passed since it was first printed. Then, she pointed to a handwritten message inside.

"As you can see here, my father wrote *To my friend M.F., what would you change if given the chance*, signed Dr. Leonard Friston. Now, I have been wondering, could the person my father signed this book for, M.F. be the same person that left this book on his counter the day he died? I don't know. Is M.F. the same person as Emmitt Poole? I can't tell you. But I know one thing for sure: my father did not fall down those stairs on his own."

David stared at the message again. "What would you

change if given the chance?" He repeated the words slowly, as if saying them out loud would reveal their hidden meaning. "It almost sounds... personal."

Roslyn nodded. "That's what I always thought. But I could never prove anything."

She took a deep breath, her fingers lingering on the open book for a moment before she carefully closed it. She tapped her hand against the hardcover, as if debating something internally, before finally exhaling and straightening in her chair.

"By the way, that must remain off the record. I am honored to have you write a tribute about my father. As long as it honors his legacy," Roslyn said firmly, her eyes flicking between David and Nella.

Her tone left no room for argument.

Nella felt the tension in the room shift. She had spent enough time around people unwilling to share the whole truth, but Roslyn's concern didn't feel like secrecy for the sake of hiding something. It felt like she was protecting something—or someone.

She leaned forward slightly. "Of course," she said quickly, nodding. "I have every intention of keeping it positive. Believe me, I just want to honor his legacy. That's all."

Roslyn studied her for a long moment, her sharp gaze searching Nella's face as if trying to decide whether she was being honest. Then, after what felt like forever, Roslyn's shoulders relaxed just a little. The hardness in her expression softened.

David seeing this, asked, "Is there anyone you could

refer us to? Perhaps someone who worked with him at MIT, who can help us piece together some of his achievements?"

Roslyn smiled. "Of course. I apologize for rambling on about my crazy conspiracy theories. You know what? I have a good feeling about you two."

She reached for a notepad on her desk, flipped to a blank page, and picked up a pen. She scribbled down a name and phone number before tearing off the page and handing it to Nella.

"Dr. Walter Chadwick. Give him a call and tell him I sent you," she said. "He's a retired professor. We worked together here at Harvard, and he also spent much of his early career as a doctoral student of my father's. He was a good friend to him. If anyone can help you understand his work, it's him."

David and Nella thanked Dr. Roslyn Friston for her time. Then they left her office. As they headed out of the building, they paused momentarily.

David let out a slow breath, his mind still racing from everything they had just learned. He shook his head in disbelief, then turned to Nella. "Holy shit."

Nella's eyes widened as she glanced at him. "What is it?"

"Emmitt Poole," he said in an intense voice. "He is number six on the list."

For a second, neither of them spoke.

Nella blinked. "Huh," she said, shaking her head slightly, like she was trying to process it.

David just looked at her, waiting.

Nella let out a shaky breath. "What are the odds? One in a trillion! This is weird, to be given a list from a man with no name on his death bed seven years ago. My father snapped six years ago, and Dr. Leonard Friston falls down a set of stairs and dies eleven months ago?"

David didn't hesitate. He turned fully toward her, his face serious. "Weird! No, this is some *Twilight Zone* bullshit! There is something else to consider. Had I not forgotten about the list for five years, was I meant to meet Dr. Leonard Friston before his death?"

"Do you think he may have been murdered to prevent him from talking to you?" Nella asked.

David shook his head. "Like I said, this is definitely some *Twilight Zone* bullshit!"

Nella let out a short, breathy laugh—one of disbelief rather than amusement. David couldn't help but think that something bigger was at play.

CHAPTER 12
UNFINISHED BUSINESS

David hadn't expected life to regain any sense of normalcy, not so soon. His loss still pressed heavily against his chest every morning, and Hannah's absence followed him like a shadow. The wedding band on his finger constantly reminded him of this, but he refused to remove it. However, somehow, in the past few weeks, something had changed. It wasn't a dramatic shift—just small moments, little breaks in the grief where he found himself breathing a little easier and the hours in his days becoming more tolerable.

And a big part of that was Nella.

They had fallen into a routine without really meaning to. A text from her in the afternoon would often read, "Drinks after work?" or "I need food and I need answers—meet me?" He never said no. He told himself it was because of the list, because of the mystery they were trying to solve. But deep down, he knew it was more than that. He liked talking to her.

Most evenings, they met somewhere downtown— small cafés with scratched-up wooden tables, warm lighting, and the smell of espresso hanging in the air. On other nights, they chose bars, the kind with dim lighting, worn leather booths, and a constant murmur of voices that made everything feel less lonely. Sometimes, it was just a late-night diner, where the coffee was always burning hot and the waitress knew them well enough to bring Nella a slice of pie without her even asking.

David noticed that he didn't dread these nights. They weren't something he forced himself to do; they were something he wanted to do. And that thought alone unsettled him. Because every time he caught himself laughing at something Nella said, or enjoying the way she teased him about his serious nature, the guilt would creep in.

How could he sit here, feeling okay, when Hannah was gone?

He never voiced it, but Nella seemed to notice anyway. She didn't push. She never asked him to talk about his grief unless he wanted to. She just kept showing up, making sure he wasn't sinking too deep. That was why when she texted him to meet up for drinks and a bite at their favorite seafood grill near Prudential Center, he'd accepted in a heartbeat.

•••

By the time David and Nella arrived at the restaurant, it was already packed, filled with a mix of after-work crowds, couples on dates, and groups of friends laughing over drinks. The smell of grilled fish and butter filled the air, mixing with the occasional sharp tang of lemon from fresh seafood platters being served.

David pulled off his coat as they slid into their usual booth near the window. Outside, the city was alive with people bundled up against the cold, moving hurriedly on the sidewalks, their breath visible in the cold, winter's night air. Inside, the warmth from the overhead air conditioner and the low chatter of other diners made the space feel cozy, almost familiar.

Nella was already reaching for the menu, even though David was certain she knew exactly what she was going to order. She did this every time—scanning the options, pretending to consider something different, and then always picking seafood.

"You know," David said, settling into his seat, "I think you've eaten more seafood in the past month than you've ever had in your entire life."

Nella smirked, not looking up from the menu. "That's because I like seafood."

David raised an eyebrow. "Clearly."

She finally put the menu down and leaned forward. "What's wrong, David? Scared to branch out? You gonna get the same grilled cod again?"

David shrugged. "It's a classic."

She rolled her eyes. "Classic? No, it's predictable."

David smirked. "Like you ordering shrimp scampi for the fifth time in a row?"

Nella gasped, placing a hand over her chest

dramatically. "How dare you."

David chuckled, shaking his head. Their banter had become second nature now, a comfortable back-and-forth that made these moments feel... normal.

The waitress arrived, and they placed their orders—grilled cod for David, shrimp scampi for Nella, just as he'd predicted. After the waitress left, their conversation shifted, as it always did, to the list. Dr. Leonard Friston, item number five, had been their latest breakthrough. The puzzle was starting to come together, but there were still too many missing pieces.

David was appreciative of how Nella's investigative skills had once again proven invaluable, and he was beginning to feel that perhaps he and Nella were meant to figure out this mystery together. He thought it odd that Hannah was item number one on the list and now she was gone. Yet, as if part of a divine plan, Nella had been placed in David's life at just the right moment when he was in great need of a friend.

David rested his arms on the table, leaning in slightly. "Any luck finding Emmitt Poole?"

Nella let out a sigh. "Nothing. I searched every database I could think of. If he exists, he doesn't want to be found."

David frowned. "And the initials M.F.?"

"Same story," she admitted. "I ran searches on possible connections to Friston, checked old records, even looked through university archives—nothing stood out."

David exhaled slowly, nodding. The dead ends were frustrating, but not unexpected. Their drinks arrived first—his was a Boston Lager, and hers was gin and tonic with a slice of lime.

Nella took a sip and then leaned back in her seat. "Alright," she said, tapping a finger on the table, "I have news."

David lifted his glass, taking a slow sip. "Oh?"

She grinned, stretching out the moment, clearly enjoying the suspense. "I found him."

David set his glass down. "Who?"

"Well... not him as such but his address. Dr. Walter Chadwick." She beamed.

David sat up straighter. "You're serious?"

She nodded. "Dead serious."

"That's great. Where does he live?" he asked excitedly.

"Well," she said, giving a long exhale and stretching her arms behind her head, "that's the sucky part. The guy pretty much disappeared from any academic records after he retired, but I found an old reference to him in a university alumni newsletter. Turns out that he moved to Georgetown, Maine a few years ago."

David frowned slightly, considering the distance. "That's not exactly around the corner."

"Nope," Nella said, popping the "p" sound. "But it's doable."

David leaned back in his chair, running a hand through his hair. "Georgetown, Maine... damn, Nella. It's what, two and a half hours away? We'd have to plan for a weekend."

"That's what I was thinking," Nella said, taking another sip of her drink. "Let's go on Saturday. I can call him and schedule an appointment."

David hesitated, and Nella caught the pause immediately. She studied him, her expression shifting from excitement to something more thoughtful. "What's wrong?"

David rubbed his fingers against his temple, considering how to say it. "I can't this weekend. I have… something I need to take care of."

"Something important?" Nella asked.

David nodded. "Unfinished business, I need to visit someone," he admitted. "An old friend in New Hampshire."

Understanding flickered in Nella's expression. She didn't press him, didn't ask for details. Instead, she leaned forward, resting her elbows on the table. "The woman at the lake house you told me about?"

David glanced up, surprised she remembered. "Yeah. I haven't told her, Mae, about what happened to Hannah, and they had grown close over the past year."

For a moment, there was silence between them, as the energy shifted. The list and the whole investigation had consumed so much of his time and his thoughts, that he hadn't really stopped to acknowledge the personal threads still left undone.

"I get it," Nella said softly, reaching across the table and placing her hand over his. "You need to do this. And you don't have to explain. I got caught up in all this excitement—the list, the clues—but I need to remind myself that you are still healing. I am really happy we met, David. I just wish that it had been under better circumstances."

David swallowed the lump in his throat.

"And I completely understand and support what you need to do," Nella continued. "You are more than a friend to me. If what has happened so far hasn't convinced you, it sure as hell has convinced me. The list, the clues, and the puzzle pieces are leading us somewhere, and I think we were meant to solve this together. I just hope and pray we're ready for whatever we find."

David nodded, turning his hand under hers and giving it a small squeeze. "Thank you, I agree 100%; whether it be destiny or a prediction of things to come, we are in this together till the end."

"Down the rabbit hole, Alice!" Nella added with a giggle.

David laughed too, glad that she hadn't pushed and argued that the list should come first.

"Okay then," Nella said, sobering up. "We'll go to Maine another weekend."

"Thanks," he said.

She smirked. "You can thank me by buying dessert."

David let out a small chuckle, some of the tension easing from his shoulders.

•••

The purr of the engine was the only sound inside the car as David drove along the highway, the dark pavement stretching endlessly ahead. He tightened his grip on the steering wheel. The cold winter scenery was familiar, but it carried a heaviness that he hadn't expected. He had made this drive before—last year, in a different season, with a a different life.

He could still remember the first time he and Hannah had come to Hermit Lake. It had been early autumn, the trees bursting with reds, oranges, and yellows. They had been on a quest to find out why the lake was on the list. He remembered how he had been hesitant at first, but Hannah had insisted they check it out. And they had, and that weekend had been one of the best of his life.

Now, as he drove the same road back to Hermit Lake, those memories felt distant and sharp at the same time, like he was looking through a frosted window. He swallowed hard, trying to push the emotions back. But it was impossible to ignore the heaviness in his chest.

This would be the first time he went without her.

As he neared the exit, a lump formed in his throat. He knew the lake, the cottage, Mae's house—none of it would have changed. It would all look the same, as if time had stood still. But everything *had* changed. Because Hannah wasn't here.

He turned off the highway, following the meandering road toward Hermit Lake. The farther he drove, the quieter everything became. No city noise, no rushing traffic. Just the sound of his tires on the pavement and the occasional creak of bare branches shifting in the wind.

The lake finally came into view between the trees, frozen over in a sheet of white and gray. David pulled into the gravel driveway of the lake cottage that belonged to him and Hannah. His hands lingered on the steering wheel for a moment before he finally turned off the ignition. He wasn't ready to get out. Not yet.

Across the yard, the main house stood exactly as he remembered it—Mae's house. A warm light glowed from inside, barely visible through the frost-covered windows. David got out of the car, took his suitcase from the trunk, and checked into their lake cottage.

He noticed the moment Mae took notice of his arrival through the glass of the back patio door of the main house. Even from this distance, David could see the shift in her expression. Recognition. Then something else. A small frown.

David felt a sharp sting in his chest, knowing that the frown meant Mae had noticed he was alone. Knowing that he couldn't delay the inevitable, he took a deep breath and walked across the yard, each step toward the house heavier than the last, but he forced himself to keep moving.

He reached the patio door and knocked gently.

Mae's eyes met his as she opened the door almost immediately. And before he could say a word, she pulled him into a hug.

"You look like you could use a hug, young man," she whispered.

Mae held onto David longer than usual, her arms wrapped tightly around him as if she could somehow hold him together. She didn't speak right away, just rested her chin lightly against his shoulder, giving him a moment to settle. David stood stiffly at first, his body tense, but then he let out a slow, shaky breath and allowed himself to lean into her embrace. The warmth of her presence, the familiar smells and the old wood from the house, it all felt safe. Familiar. But at the same time, painfully different.

Mae was the first to pull away, her hands still gripping his arms as she took a step back to look at him properly. Her sharp eyes, framed by deep lines of age and wisdom, searched his face. He wasn't sure what she saw, but it was enough for her to reach up and rest her palm gently against his check for a brief moment before she stepped aside and motioned toward the door.

"Come inside," she said softly.

David nodded, his jaw clenched, and followed her in.

Although it wasn't his first time in Mae's house, it seemed like it was the first time he noticed the strange piece of art that depicted a large black ink blot hanging in the dining room. He had seen it before, only in passing, but had not taken a closer look at it. The simplicity of the piece somehow felt familiar, yet it wasn't anything he would choose to hang on his wall. However, it did have an abstract form that he admired.

"I just made coffee," Mae said over her shoulder, moving to the kitchen. "Sit. I'll get you a cup."

David sat heavily on the couch, his elbows resting on his knees. Suddenly, Lucy, Mae's Shih Tzu, trotted into the room and stopped in her tracks when she saw David, her head tilting to the side. She hesitated a bit, sniffing at the air before jumping up onto the couch next to David and curling into a small ball. For David, the dog was another moment of affection he was eager to accept.

She returned with two cups, setting one in front of him on the wooden coffee table before sitting on the couch across from him. David stared at the cup, watching the steam curl upward, disappearing into nothing.

"I see it's just you this weekend. Is someone taking a sabbatical?" Mae asked with a slight smile.

As soon as the words left Mae's lips, David's eyes began to well up with tears. Mae quickly got up from where she was and sat by his side, wrapping her arm around his shoulder to pat his back. "It's okay, dear. What's going on? How can I help?" she asked.

David swallowed, then finally forced the words out, his voice low and strained, though the tears continued to roll down his cheeks. "She's gone."

The words felt foreign leaving his mouth, like they belonged to someone else. But somehow, saying them here, in this house, to Mae—someone who had known Hannah, who had cared about her—it made everything feel real all over again.

Mae didn't react immediately. She just looked at him, her brows drawing together slightly. The words had landed, but they hadn't fully sunk in yet.

David clenched his jaw, his vision blurring as he stared down at the floor. He hated this feeling. The helplessness. The ache in his chest never fully went away. He went on to tell Mae the full details of what had happened to Hannah.

"Oh, David," she murmured, her voice full of emotion.

Mae didn't say, "I'm sorry." She didn't say, "I can't believe it." She just sat there, holding him as he broke down, grounding him in the moment.

For a moment, neither of them said anything. Mae's hand still rested on his shoulder. She gave it another small squeeze before slowly pulling back.

Then she let out a quiet breath, her gaze dropping to

the floor. "You know," she murmured, her voice softer now, more distant, "I lost someone, too."

David lifted his eyes to her. He hadn't expected that.

Mae leaned back against the couch, her shoulders relaxing slightly, but there was a shift in her expression. A sadness that had been buried for years, now rising to the surface. She didn't speak right away. Instead, she reached for her own cup of coffee, fingers wrapping around it carefully, as if gathering her thoughts.

David stayed quiet, waiting. Finally, she inhaled deeply and began narrating her story.

"Twenty-six years ago, Paul and I had a beautiful baby girl. We named her Mable, and she was the apple of our eye. Over the years, life was moving according to plan. We had just bought a house in Wakefield. At the time, I was a stay-at-home mom and Paul was working in the city. Mable turned six on October 7th; I still remember the date because the day after was Columbus Day, and schools were closed. It was an unusually warm day, not a cloud in the sky. Mable had a friend from school named Heidi who lived just a few houses away.

"Heidi's mother Tammy had invited us over to her house for a play date. We went, and when we got there, she invited me inside to have a cup of coffee while the girls played on the swing set in the back yard. The kitchen door was open, and I could hear the girls through the screen. They were laughing and having fun. Mable loved visiting Heidi; she especially loved her swing set, because it had monkey bars, a rope ladder, and a swing.

"I could have sworn it only felt like a few minutes had

passed, but I know it was longer. Tammy had topped off my coffee at least once when Heidi entered the kitchen from the back door. I vividly remember glancing over at Heidi shuffling through the kitchen drawers. Tammy and I were engaged in laughter as we discussed something unimportant."

Mae took a moment to compose herself then she continued.

"I should have picked up on my surroundings, my instincts, but I didn't. Not until Tammy stopped chatting with me and asked Heidi what she was looking for in the kitchen drawers. I will never forget her words as she looked up at us and said in a soft voice, "Mommy, I need the scissors to cut the rope around Mable's neck."

David felt his chest tighten painfully and he gasped. "Oh my god!"

However, Mae wasn't deterred. She was determined to finish the story so she just continued.

"It was a freak accident. The rope ladder was tangled, and it looked like she might have fallen from the monkey bars. She had gotten caught up in the rope on her way down, causing it to wrap around her neck. The impact broke her neck, and there was nothing I could do. It was such a horrible sight. Seeing my baby hanging there, lifeless."

Mae sighed softly beside him. After a moment, she let out a small, humorless laugh. "You know," she murmured, shaking her head slightly, "after Mable died, everyone kept telling me it wasn't my fault."

"Yes, Mae, it wasn't your fault," David said.

"I would lie awake at night," Mae continued, her voice quieter now, more distant, "thinking about that moment. Wondering if I had just kept a closer eye on her..." She trailed off, pressing her lips together. Then she let out a slow exhale. "I thought about it every single day for years."

David swallowed, his throat dry. He looked down at his own hands, at the tiny tremble in his fingers. He hadn't known Mae carried this kind of pain.

Mae then placed her hand on his knee and looked him in the eyes. "It took me a long time to accept that. Don't let your guilt eat away at you, David. What happened to Hannah was out of your hands."

David let out a slow, shaky breath, followed by a small nod. He then looked around and took the opportunity to admire the array of family pictures placed around the room and on the walls. "You have a lot of beautiful pictures; did you and Paul decide to have more children?"

Mae smiled. "You can't change your yesterdays, but you can change your tomorrows! One of Paul's coworkers told us how they had adopted a young South Korean boy. I remember it was a couple days later we were eating breakfast alone and we both looked up at each other and said the same thing. 'I think we should consider adopting a little girl.'"

Mae then pointed to one of the famed pictures on the wall showing Mae, Paul, and a young girl during what appeared to be Christmas. "So we did. Her name is Sue, and she is all grown up now. I even have an adorable granddaughter named Luna," she added while pointing to another picture on the wall.

David's mood lightened upon seeing the photos. "What you did was wonderful."

And before he could think too much about it, the words slipped out. "I was adopted as well as an infant. I don't know anything about my birth parents other than they had died. My adoptive parents are amazing people; they live in California. They loved me and supported me, and I believe I owe them so much."

Mae had a huge smile. "What a wonderful part of who you are. Remember, child, God has a plan for all of us. You were supposed to meet Hannah, and she will always be in your heart. Remember, your future is not set, and your journey is still unfolding, so you should learn to cherish each day."

David smiled at Mae's words. "You're right, and I like what you said; you can't change your yesterdays, but you can change your tomorrows!"

Mae's smile widened even more and without hesitation, she pulled David into a big hug. "You're going to be okay," she whispered.

David closed his eyes for a brief second. He didn't know if that was true. Not yet. But for the first time in a long time, he thought maybe—just maybe—it could be.

CHAPTER 13

MR. OWL

David sat in his house, the sound of the refrigerator filling the otherwise quiet space. The weekend at the lake cottage had been exactly what he needed—a moment to breathe and step away from everything consuming his mind. He had spent hours looking out at the water, the gentle waves putting his mind at ease.

Mae had been there, her presence offering him much-needed comfort. He was glad that he'd been able to tell her about Hannah. Saying it out loud had been harder than he expected. It wasn't just the words—it was the way they made everything feel real again, as if speaking about Hannah's death gave it new life, fresh pain. But Mae had understood.

Still, he had kept other things to himself—the list, Nella, and the strange quest to uncover the mysteries before them. However, he was looking forward to the day he would eventually share the wild tale with Mae.

He also thought about showing Nella the lake cottage—the place that had become his retreat from everything. For a brief second, he could see it: Nella sitting on the dock, the water calm beneath her. The sun setting behind the trees, casting long shadows over the lake.

But the thought faded quickly. Everything was still very fresh, and his heart was still fragile. He wasn't ready to tell Mae about everything, and he also wasn't ready to take Nella to the lake cottage.

For now, there were more pressing things to focus on. The weekend had given him space to breathe, but it hadn't changed what was ahead. There was still the list and the questions that needed answers. And most importantly, there was still Dr. Walter Chadwick—the man who might finally be able to give them the truth they were searching for.

David exhaled and pushed himself up from the couch. He had a long week ahead of him.

•••

Monday morning came too soon. The alarm on David's phone buzzed against the nightstand, dragging him out of a restless sleep. He groaned, rubbing his eyes before sitting up. His body was awake, but his mind felt sluggish, weighed down by everything he was trying to push aside.

His week was filled with work deadlines and responsibilities he didn't have the energy for. He knew he had to focus, but his thoughts kept circling back to the mystery he and Nella were caught up in. No matter how much he tried to concentrate, there was always a nagging feeling of something unfinished, something waiting just beneath the surface.

At the office, David sat at his desk, staring at the open file on his computer. A half-finished floor plan filled the screen—lines and dimensions that refused to come together the way they should. He had been working on this project for weeks, but now, even the simplest adjustments felt impossible. His mind wasn't here. It was elsewhere, trapped in questions that had nothing to do with architecture.

He tried to force himself to focus, sketching out different variations, but the work felt slow and frustrating. Every time he made progress, his mind drifted. He thought about the list. Thought about the way things seemed to be pulling them deeper, step by step, with no clear end in sight.

It wasn't just him. Nella was feeling it too. She was buried in deadlines, trying to keep up with her workload at the *Boston Rag*. She had mentioned in passing how exhausting it was, and how the pressure from her editor was making things worse. She had also reached out and left Dr. Walter Chadwick a voicemail.

On Wednesday evening, as David sat on the couch at home, his phone lit up with a message from Nella.

Nella 8:24 PM
Finally heard back from Dr. Chadwick.
He agreed to meet us on Saturday

> **David 8:25 PM**
> What did he say?

> **Nella 8:26 PM**
> Didn't say much. Just that he'd be available to talk. Seemed hesitant at first but agreed in the end

David stared at the message, tapping his foot nervously. The anticipation in his chest tightened. There was always the possibility that Chadwick wouldn't have anything useful to tell them. But there was also the chance that he did. That he knew something about Dr. Friston's research—something that might help them finally understand what they had stumbled into. What he and Nella knew was that, according to the timeline when he was given the list, they were meant to find Leonard Friston. Now, they could only hope that Dr. Chadwick could offer them a second chance for the answers they sought.

After a moment, he texted her back.

> **David 8:29 PM**
> Saturday it is

•••

When Saturday arrived, David picked up Nella at the Alewife train terminal, ensuring they could get an early start. The sun was bright and the day clear and brisk. The forecast had mentioned possible snow, but things turned out fine as the clouds remained south of the city as they headed north toward the state of Maine.

For the first half hour, they made casual conversation—complaints about work, musings about what they might find in Maine, observations about the changing scenery. But as the miles passed, their conversation took a more personal turn.

"You ever think about fate?" David asked suddenly, his hands steady on the wheel.

Nella glanced at him. "What do you mean?"

He adjusted his grip, his fingers tightening slightly. "Like, how in life, certain choices and certain roads you take that don't really make much sense at the time, may later have a profound impact on your life?"

Nella nodded slowly. "Yeah. I think about that a lot, actually."

David let out a small breath, his hands steady on the wheel as the road stretched ahead of them. He glanced at Nella for a moment before speaking.

"You want to hear something crazy?" he asked quietly.

Nella's mouth tugged into a small smile as she replied. "Always."

David's fingers tightened slightly on the steering wheel as he thought back, pulling the memory forward. "When I was about ten years old... I used to spend almost every Saturday at this old arcade with my best friend, Shawn."

He paused, letting the images fill his mind again—the sound of machines, the smell of fried food mixed with sweat and cheap air conditioning.

"That day, it was summer. The air was sticky, humid. We'd been inside for hours, burning through tokens, trying to beat each other's high scores. And when we finally walked out, it was dark. Streetlights flickering. I remember how loud the night felt after all the noise inside."

Nella stayed quiet, listening closely.

"We had this stupid bet," David continued, shaking his head. "Whoever had the higher score at the end of the night got to choose the way home. There were two ways— one was the long, safe road, full of lights, houses, people. The other was shorter, but darker. Dark Alley we called it. No lights. No people. Just a long stretch of broken pavement between empty lots and chain-link fences."

He let out a short laugh, but there was no humor in it.

"I beat him that night. By one point. Literally one point." David glanced at her. "9872 to 9871. He was pissed, but we laughed about it. A bet is a bet, and I'd won."

He took a breath, the memory tightening in his chest, and he rubbed his hands together, as if he was remembering the feel of the bike handles under his palms that day.

"We stood there, right at the intersection. I tried to call it off, told him, 'Let's just call it a tie.' I could see it in his face. He didn't want to go down that alley. Neither of us ever did. But Shawn... he shook his head and said, 'No. A bet's a bet.'"

David's voice grew quieter. "I watched him ride off. His bike had this little red reflector on the back. I stood there and watched until I couldn't see it anymore. Then I took the long, safe road."

The hum of the car engine filled the silence between

them. David's eyes stayed on the road, but his mind was far away.

"When I got to the other end, he wasn't there. I waited. I kept looking back, expecting to see his bike coming out of the dark. But minutes passed. Then a car came down the road. An old, rusty Ford sedan. It rattled when it moved, like something was broken inside."

He swallowed; his throat dry.

"As the car passed under a streetlight, I saw him. Shawn. He was in the front seat. His face was pale. His eyes wide. He looked right at me. It was only a second, but I knew. Something was wrong. He looked scared. Like he was trying to say something without moving his mouth."

David's fingers drummed lightly against the wheel, the memory pressing heavier now.

"I didn't stop to think. I pedaled home as fast as I could. I burst through the front door, yelling for my parents, trying to explain what I saw. The next few days… they were a blur. Cops coming to the house. Questions. I told them everything I remembered. The car. The color. The shape of the man driving. Part of the license plate. I kept seeing Shawn's face over and over."

David shook his head. "They found his bike abandoned in the middle of Dark Alley. Two days later, they found the man's house. His name was Carl Trippet."

His voice dropped lower, like the name itself tasted bitter.

"They found a locked room in his basement. Chains. Locks. A little wooden box filled with stuff they wouldn't even talk about on the news. They said Trippet had done it before—at least four other boys."

David's grip tightened on the steering wheel again. "Shawn was gone. Asphyxiated, they said. It was all over the news. My parents stopped letting me watch it, but I still heard enough."

For a long moment, neither of them spoke. The sound of the tires on the road filled the space.

David's eyes stayed ahead, but his voice cracked slightly when he finally added, "I always thought about that night. About how one stupid point in a video game decided who took the safe road and who didn't." He clenched his jaw. "One point saved me. One point killed Shawn."

"I am sorry, David," Nella whispered when he finished. "What a horrible story. The fate of one point decided the road you took and saved your life. I am so sorry for your friend."

Nella studied him for a moment before looking out the window. "It's weird, isn't it?" she said. "How the smallest things can change everything?" Nella was quiet for a moment, as if weighing something in her mind. Then, she continued. "You know? I actually have a similar story about fate... it was life changing for me too."

David glanced at her briefly before returning his focus to the road. "Tell me about it."

Nella took a deep breath then began telling David how she had always cherished the summers she and her brother spent on Cape Cod with her cousin, Emily. She talked about the salty air, the sound of the waves crashing against the shore, and the endless days filled with laughter, which were a welcome escape from her everyday life.

David listened intently without interrupting her. She kept silent for a moment before continuing.

"There was this one time I went to visit my cousin in the middle of winter. It was a crisp winter day and my parents had gone on a ski trip. Emily and I decided to go ice skating on a small pond situated along their property line. The sun shimmered on the smooth ice as we slid effortlessly across it, and our laughter could be heard through the quiet landscape. We spent hours twirling and spinning, our joy contagious.

"As dusk settled and the stars began to twinkle in the sky, we reluctantly headed back to the house, our cheeks rosy from the cold and our hearts full of warmth. However, as I prepared for bed, I realized with a sinking feeling that I had left my beanie down by the pond.

"It wasn't just any hat. It was a gift from my grandmother, a keepsake that held memories of cozy afternoons spent knitting by the fireplace and stories whispered in the soft glow of the lamp light. I cherished it dearly, and the thought of losing it filled me with dread.

"Determined to retrieve it, I decided to sneak out of the house after everyone had gone to sleep. I remember how the moon shone softly on the snow-covered grounds as I quietly made my way down to the pond. But when I arrived, I couldn't find the hat anywhere.

"Heart pounding with anxiety, I scanned the large stretch of ice-covered water, my gaze finally settling on a dark shape at the far end of the pond. It was my hat, blown away by the wind. Without hesitation, I cautiously walked out onto the ice, my footsteps muffled by the soft soles of my boots.

"As I reached for the hat, a sickening crack echoed through the night."

David could already see where this was going. "The ice…"

"It cracked…" Nella confirmed, "plunging me into the frigid water. The shock of the cold took my breath away, and I instinctively screamed for help before sinking.

"The darkness seemed to swallow me whole as I struggled to find my way back to the surface. The freezing water numbed my limbs, and my cries grew weaker with each passing second. Just as I was about to give up hope, a strong hand grasped my arm and pulled me out of the icy depths.

"Gasping for air, I found myself face to face with my brother Marcus. In a low and soothing voice, he whispered: 'You're okay, I got you.' I was freezing and shivering so much that I wasn't able to properly thank him then. He wrapped me in his warm arms and carried me back to the house. I remember hearing the sounds of my aunt and cousin's frantic calls in the distance. And well, the rest is history."

David shook his head, exhaling sharply. "That's terrifying."

Nella gave a small smile, but there was something distant in her eyes, as if she were still trapped in that moment. "Yeah. It was. If Marcus hadn't been there…" She trailed off, letting the words hang in the air.

David didn't say anything right away. He was thinking about how close she had come to dying, how easily that moment could have ended differently. And then, without meaning to, his mind drifted back to Hannah.

"Do you ever wonder," he said quietly, "if someone is actually watching over you? Like a guardian angel or something?"

Nella turned her head toward him, studying his profile. "Yeah. I do. I like to believe that when Marcus saved me that day it was a part of his purpose in life."

David swallowed. "This might sound stupid, but I used to think that, too. But then, if that were true… why didn't someone save Hannah from the accident."

Nella didn't answer right away. Instead, she reached out and took his hand, her grip firm and reassuring. "Some things are out of our control," she admitted. "But I like to believe that the people we lose don't really leave us. Maybe they still watch over us in their own way."

David kept his eyes on the road, but he felt the warmth of her hand against his. He let her words settle, let himself believe them—if only for a moment.

"Yeah," he murmured. "Maybe."

They fell into a comfortable silence as they continued north, the open road stretching ahead, leading them toward whatever answers waited in Maine.

•••

The drive stretched longer than David had expected. The main highway had been straightforward enough, but now they were driving through narrow, tree-lined roads that twisted and bent. David glanced at Nella. She had been quiet for the last few minutes, her eyes fixed on the road ahead.

A curve in the road opened up to a sudden, breath-taking view of the bay—a sign that they were getting close. The water was wide, calm, and a deep shade of blue under the cloudy sky. Small islands could be seen in the distance, forming dark shapes against the horizon.

"Wow," Nella murmured.

David slowed the car, taking in the sight. "Not bad, huh?"

She shook her head. "No. It's beautiful. By the way, Dr. Chadwick said to look for a white-and-black wood sign on a pine tree, number 380."

They continued along the road, and soon, they came upon the wood sign carved between a cluster of pine trees, directing them onto a narrow dirt driveway. David turned in, the tires crunching over gravel. The trees grew even closer here, the branches arching overhead to form a sort of tunnel. The driveway stretched on longer than expected, bending out of sight.

David's grip tightened on the wheel. "This guy really doesn't want to be found, does he?"

Nella let out a small laugh. "No kidding."

Then, just ahead, the trees parted, revealing a white clapboard house situated atop a hillside. Above the garage door, a wooden sign read: *The Owl's Nest.*

Before David could pull up to the house, movement caught his eye. Two white huskies came running up to the car, jumping and playing in excitement.

"This must be it," Nella said, and David nodded in agreement, slowing the car to a stop.

Before they could open their car doors, the front door

of the house opened, and out came a heavy-set man, his round glasses perched on his nose. He had a big round belly, a white beard, and a receding hairline.

Suddenly the sound of a sharp whistle cut through the air, triggering both dogs to turn and trot back toward the man. David and Nella then stepped out of the car, the cold biting at them instantly. After locking the car, they both walked toward the door, where the man was no longer in sight. However, as they approached, he returned.

"I put the dogs in the back room for ya," the man said. "Long drive?" he asked, turning to David and extending his hand.

"Not too bad," David replied as he shook the man's outstretched hand.

"Hello, Dr. Walter Chadwick, I am Nella Allen with the *Boston Rag*, and this is my friend David Bishop," she said, shaking the man's outstretched hand and gesturing to David.

Dr. Chadwick smiled at her. "Good grief, I haven't been called that in a while. Just call me Walt; some of the residents call me Doc, but Walt is fine," Walt said, gesturing for them to enter the house. "Come on in, it's chilly out here."

They followed him inside, and Walt offered them a seat in the living room. The house had a lodge feel, with a touch of seaside Maine. David's eyes then landed on the coffee table in the middle of the living room.

It was made from a lobster trap. The wood was, new, never having been used and the ropes neatly coiled around its edges. At first glance, it was just a table, but the more he looked, the more he saw the intricate details—the careful craftsmanship, the way it had been repurposed into something functional.

"Cool coffee table," he said to Walt.

"You like it? There is this guy in West Bath, about fifteen minutes from here. He spends all winter building these things. It's a wood lobster trap, you know. Anyway, I happened to drive by his place sometime in October— this was a couple years ago—and he had about a half- dozen lobster traps stacked outside his barn. Then sometime in April I drove by again, and I see that his whole yard is full of them. So, I stop and introduce myself.

"After exchanging a few pleasantries, I find out he builds these all winter, and by May, they are all sold off. So, I bought a couple. I used this one for a coffee table but drop the other one in Sagadahoc Bay in the summer."

Walt then pointed out toward the driveway. "The strip of water you see along the road, that's Sagadahoc Bay. I catch a few lobsters a week, right off the shoreline."

David just stared in amazement, while Nella took a second look at the lobster trap coffee table, having never seen one before.

Walt then got up and offered them a drink. "What's your poison?" he asked with a smirk.

"Poison?" David said under his breath, not sure he had heard Walt correctly.

Nella, seeing that David hadn't caught the meaning, chimed in. "Water… water is our poison," she replied, understanding what Walt had meant by the word.

Walt nodded, turning and mumbling to himself as he

headed to the kitchen. "Water it is."

After a few minutes, he returned, handing two bottles of water to David and Nella. "If you don't mind... and if you do, I don't give a shit," he added jokingly, "I'm gonna pour myself a small glass of Scotch."

David and Nella were taken aback a bit, but they neither reacted nor replied. Walt sat back down in his lazy boy chair, then began, "So you are here to do a story of some kind on my old friend Dr. Leo Friston, is that right?"

"Yes, that's right. First, I just want to thank you for agreeing to meet us. And for allowing us into your home. Now, a little bit of context, I am doing a tribute of former professors in the Boston area, and Dr. Friston's name came up," Nella explained.

"We met with his daughter, Roslyn, and she was the one who actually gave us your information. She thought you might be able to help," David added.

Nella then continued. "We wanted to know if you could fill in the timeline on some of his accomplishments. For example, his research at MIT's Building 20."

Suddenly Walt's eyes widened. He took a deep breath and leaned forward in his seat. "Building 20? That's an interesting place to begin," Walt said, getting up and going to the kitchen to retrieve the bottle of Scotch.

David and Nella exchanged a quick glance, both of them anxious about what Walt would reveal. He returned to his chair a moment later, filled his glass once again, then took a long swig. Finally, he sighed and leaned back against the chair, his eyes never leaving the glass in hand.

"I always knew someone would come along and ask

questions one day," he said quietly, his voice turning serious. "I didn't know who, but I knew it would happen. Surprisingly, it never did. Now, what did happen was that my old friend Leo was pushed down a flight of stairs to keep him from talking. You know why I left the city and built this house on ten acres of land in Maine?"

David and Nella shook their heads to show they didn't.

"To lie low," he said, then paused, his eyes moving between the both of them as if weighing whether he should continue. Then with a slow nod, he did.

"When Leo wrote that book, *Induction Theory and Cognitive Sciences,* he put a target on his head. And not just a target, he opened Pandora's box. Sometimes, when you mess with the past, the past messes right back," Walt narrated, taking another swig of his Scotch.

"So, you don't think it was an accident either?" Nella asked.

"Friston was silenced Nella. Besides, accident or not, it doesn't matter anymore. Once he published that book, the cat was out of the bag. I don't think he was pushed down a flight of stairs for what he exposed in his book. I think it was for what he was going to do next."

David and Nella listened intently, their attention fixed on Walt. David then asked, "What was he going to do?"

"He was going to stop something that was already happening," Walt answered.

The silence that followed felt suffocating. David's mind raced, trying to understand what Walt meant. *What had Dr. Friston been trying to stop? What had already started?*

"Are you afraid for your life as well?" Nella questioned

after a while.

Walt laughed and poured himself another drink.

"Afraid, no. Whatever it was that Leo planned to do, I wasn't a part of it. Do you ever watch those crime shows on TV? Well, I was watching this crime show one time and this guy was being interviewed. He was some old-time mafia guy. Apparently, he ratted out his whole gang—the captains, the mob boss, everyone. They all got pinched... tried and locked up. Yet there he was thirty years later doing an interview on national TV. He wasn't hiding, he wasn't in disguise, and he wasn't in the witness protection program anymore. You know why? Because the guys that he had wronged, and the shit that he knew didn't matter anymore. All the guys that gave two shits were dead, long gone. He was the last man standing, and nobody cared about his secrets anymore."

David and Nella looked at each other and then back at Walt sitting in his chair and acting as if he had nothing more to hide. "We think our roads were meant to cross and that you might be able to fill in some of the puzzle pieces we seek," Nella confessed.

"You have no idea how many puzzle pieces I can fill in," Walt said with a slight grin. "You want to know what was going on in Building 20? It was called the *Athena Project*."

CHAPTER 14
ATHENA PROJECT

W alt leaned forward, putting his glass on the side table, then resting his forearms on his knees. His eyes flickered with something hard to define: Was it regret? Caution? Maybe both. He exhaled through his nose and ran a hand through his hair before speaking.

"They called it the Athena Project. You know that Athena, the Greek goddess of wisdom, has an owl on her shoulder. Anyway, the Athena Project was funded and approved by the Central Intelligence Agency (CIA) in 1988. It was a legal and approved alternative to a similar program called Project MKUltra. MKUltra was exposed and shut down in 1973 for its role in illegal human experimentation. The program was accused of using drugs, brainwashing, and psychological torture as a method to manipulate a subject's brain function."

David and Nella exchanged a glance.

"I mean, some of this shit goes back to what the Nazi's were doing at Auschwitz," Walt added.

"You're saying they shut it down in '73?" David asked.

"Yeah, that's exactly what I said. They shut down MKUltra in '73. But that program dates back to 1953, meaning they were fucking up people's brains for decades. Look at that guy who shot Reagan in '81. Hinckley. He became so obsessed that he tried to kill the president. They say he attended Texas Tech in the early '70s. I bet if you could get your hands on those classified files, you would find the truth. MKUltra was known to recruit subjects at several universities. For all we know, they dropped a manipulated thought in his brain, then when the program ended, he went rogue."

"Like brainwashing him to kill the president?" David asked, his tone full of disbelief.

"It could have been any trigger word. Kill the president, Jodie Foster, or the movie Taxi Driver; they say he was obsessed with all of them;" Walt said.

David and Nella listened carefully, their interest fully piqued. They were both wondering if all this was leading them to the answers they sought. However, neither of them voiced their thoughts.

Walt then continued with the story. "Well, like I was saying, the Athena Project was legal and sanctioned by the CIA and run out of MIT. Leo recruited me to join his team in '88, and we set up shop in Building 20. Leo had been working on the *induction theory of the brain* for some time. Through the use of radio induction implantation frequency, we called it RIF, he believed he could put an idea directly into someone's head. Make them believe it was their own thought, and make them act on it."

Nella frowned. "Like brainwashing?"

Walt shook his head. "Brainwashing makes you think of prisoners of war being broken down, turned into something else. This was more subtle. This was about planting a seed. You put an idea in someone's head, and if you do it right, they nurture it all on their own. It grows like a cancer; they obsess over it. They believe it's their purpose. And they follow through."

Nella felt like retching. The idea of someone being manipulated like that, without even knowing it, made her stomach twist.

David swallowed. "Are you suggesting they could safely do such a thing?"

"Don't be naïve, kid. It was an approved program, but like anything the government does, they did it in secret for a reason. To ensure maximum success, Leo created an intensive qualifications process for subject recruitment. They had to be volunteers, willing and able, and they were given money to participate. But they also needed to score extremely high on the pre-qualification questionnaire. Leo had established three elements in the pre-qualification questionnaire process.

"The first one was *Current Cognitive Status*. This element was used to determine the current career path and area of higher education. The second element was *Asch Conformity*, which helped with determining the subject's tolerance to suggestible content. The last element was the *Rorschach Test*.

Through the use of inkblot images, the test was used to assess an individual's response to ambiguous stimuli, to uncover unconscious thoughts and also to help determine how the prefrontal cortex processes stimuli. Three elements... three subjects."

"Do you recall the subjects' names?" Nella asked.

"Names? No, it was all confidential. Other than the screening process, the subjects were separated. Leo describes the process of the experiment in his book in more detail. Basically, the subjects are placed on a special chair in a room. During phase one, they are bombarded with images and words that are designed to unlock parts of the brain. Some of the words are perceived as neutral, some positive, and some negative. It's like a combination lock; the viewing order of the images and words were designed in a way unique to each subject based on their pre-qualification questionnaire and three-element test results. We called it the variables of induction phase.

"Phase two was called the variant of induction phase. During this part of the experiment, a radio frequency was tuned on, targeting the memory functions of the temporal lobe. During this time, a word or phrase was implanted into the brain, basically an implanted thought. It was also followed up with a tangent or trigger phase."

David looked confused. "I don't understand. What do you mean by implanted?"

"Implanted! You know it is like subliminal implantation! Advertisers do it all the time in commercials. But this was way more advanced...I mean Leo did most of the research on Induction Theory, and this was nothing close to the shit they did in MKUltra. I mean he was obsessed with this…he had no doubt it would work. Leo even had a nickname for it, for the implantation process…he called it the metal worm. It had to do with all the algorithms used for both phases of the experiment."

Nella's eyes opened wide, and her jaw fell in surprise, hearing a familiar word, "I don't understand, why would he call it the metal worm?"

David saw her reaction and offered a suggestion. "Perhaps he felt that it was similar to an artificial worm deep in the brain."

"No, no, no… Leo had a reason for everything. He talks about it in his book," Walt said, getting up abruptly and walking into another room. The sound of shuffling and cabinets being opened and closed echoed through the house. He then returned with a copy of Dr. Leonard Friston's book, *Induction Theory and Cognitive Sciences*. He sat back down and began flipping through the pages.

As he was doing that, he continued with the story. "Leo had this entire process nailed down. If metal worm was the nickname he used for the variant of induction phrase or the key that opened the implanted thought, then it was also directly related to a tangent phrase used to trigger the implanted thought."

He then found the page he was looking for. "Here it is," he said, holding up the book. "*Chapter 19: Mr. Owl Ate My Metal Worm.*"

Nella gasped and turned to look at David. "Oh my God, it's a palindrome, the same palindrome that was written on my father's desk calendar the day he did… well, you know."

Walt raised his eyebrows out of curiosity. "That's right, not everyone knows that. During the variables of induction phase, which I said is phase one; palindrome words were mixed in with regular words, images, and even semordnilaps."

David furrowed his brows. "Semordnilaps?"

"Palindromes in reverse," Walt clarified. "Words that mean something different when flipped backward. Like 'stressed' and 'desserts.' The brain tries to make sense of it, but it can't. It forces the subject to think differently, to see patterns where there weren't any before. It makes them more... vulnerable."

David inhaled deeply, his heart racing.

"Moving forward, it was part of that unlocking or re-keying the mind that I was telling you about. Getting the brain to process words and images both forward and backward. Leo was ahead of his time; his induction theory was formulated around the basic idea that you implant the metal worm, then through the use of the trigger or the tangent phrase the subject will manifest, obsess, and become so driven with their implanted directive they will make it come to fruition," Walt said.

"A self-fulfilling prophecy," David mumbled.

"Kinda like that. You guys look confused as hell! Okay, let me put this in layman's terms: phase one, rekey the brain; phase two, cut a new key, and phase three, when the key is used, the implanted thought is released, and the subject acts on it. Well, if it actually works," Walt clarified.

Nella looked over at David, her eyes filled with deep

concern about what they were learning.

David whispered to her, "You need to tell him."

It seemed like Walt had caught that because he leaned forward in his chair and then looked at both of them. "Tell me what? Listen, I don't mind giving you all this information... most of the secrets are already out anyway. But don't go sharing something with me that will result in a team of assassins at my door in the morning. I may look like one of those crazy antigovernmental doomsday conspiracists, but I'm not. This isn't a movie, and I'm not Gene Hackman. I like my simple life, my dogs, and my little lady friend down at the library."

David smiled, short of bursting into laughter at Walt's last words. "No, it's like that. It's about Nella's father."

"I want to be clear with you both. The minute you asked me about Building 20, I knew you weren't here to do a story on the life and times of my old friend Leo. And like I said earlier, most of all this shit was published long ago in Leo's book. As you can tell, I don't mind helping you out. Don't think I didn't see your face change three shades," he said, pointing a finger at Nella, "when I mentioned the metal worm. So, if you have something you want to share with me, I suggest you do so. Because there is no way it's a coincidence that you knew the inducted phrase was a palindrome, and there is no way something like that would be written on your father's calendar if something wasn't amiss."

Nella's hands clenched together in her lap. She took a deep breath then began to tell Walt the story about her father, about how he had changed, his obsession, and what she had found in his office.

Walt listened as she spoke, and when she finished her bit, he replied, "I can't say for sure if one of the subjects was your father, but my guess would be he was. One of the subjects was African American and was in medical school at Boston University, if my memory serves me right. As far as the variant of the induction words, the metal worms, I never knew what they were. Maybe they are in Leo's book." Walt then began flipping through the pages again.

"I know the metal worms, the implanted thoughts, were meant to be plausible, possible, or impossible in nature. Every subject was required to conduct a follow-up evaluation over a period of two years; however, the program was defunded and closed less than a year later with no follow-up," Walt said as he continued with this task.

He stopped at one page in the book and said, "Here they are. These are the variant of induction words the metal worms." He then held up the book for the both of them to read.

Nella's fingers tightened around the edges of the book as her eyes scanned the list Walt had pointed to. The words blurred slightly, her brain refusing to process them all at once.

Piano Symphony
Time Travel
Cure Cancer
Skyscraper
Fusion Energy

Lake House
Neurosurgery
Mandarin

Once she had gone over the list, one word stood out, burning into her vision. *Neurosurgery.*

Her breath hitched, and a sharp, painful gasp escaped her lips. "Neurosurgery is one of the words! That's what they implanted in my father's brain. What the fuck were they thinking? They drove him crazy! It's their fault he killed that woman... what kind of monster would do that to someone?"

"Her father was Robert Allen, that guy who took over an operating room and killed a 47-year-old mother in Boston a few years ago," David explained to Walt while placing a steadying hand on Nella's back in comfort.

Walt nodded, his fingers idly tracing the edges of his seat's armrests. His face was unreadable, but there was something distant in his eyes, like he was somewhere else—somewhere in the past, reliving the choices that had led to this moment.

Then, he cleared his throat, and in a quiet, almost detached voice, he began to speak:

"As the memory of past misfortunes pressed upon me, I began to reflect upon their cause—the monster whom I had created, the miserable daemon whom I had sent abroad into the world."

His words hung in the air, settling between them like a heavy fog. Nella's breath came in shallow bursts, her chest rising and falling unevenly. She didn't need to ask where the quote was from. She knew. Everyone knew.

Victor Frankenstein.

A story about a man who played god. Who built something he thought he could control—something he believed would serve a greater purpose. But in the end, his creation became a nightmare, an uncontrollable force with its own will.

David continued to rub Nella's back as she cried, her tears wetting his shirt. He was silent for a minute. Suddenly, he realized something important. The words *lake house* were in the book, one of the metal worms. And though at the moment, his mind was not able to connect all the pieces, his instincts could tell that something was amiss. The list, John Doe, Hermit Lake, and the lake house… they all circled back to this moment. He couldn't help but wonder what it all meant.

David and Nella had been concerned about not finding the answers they sought when they went to Owl's Nest; however, all that concern had faded. Walt had been as forthcoming as ever, offering them new light on thoughts that had been battling around in their heads. Seeing that Nella's sobs had come to a stop, Walt got up and went to get her a tissue. As he left, David and Nella both agreed that they had gotten everything they needed.

Once Walt came back into the room, he handed Nella a packet of tissues, and they stood up and thanked him for all the information he provided. "Thank you for filling in so many pieces of the puzzle for us," Nella said to him.

"Yes, we can't thank you enough for being so forth-coming," David added, holding his hand out for Walt to shake.

"I knew this day would come sooner or later; I had things to answer for. I know it doesn't change things, but I am sorry about your father," Walt said, shaking David's hand and turning to Nella.

"Wait a second, I think I might have something that can help," Walt said suddenly, rushing to another room, where the sound of shuffling and cabinets being opened and closed echoed through the house once again. When he returned, he handed over an old VHS video tape.

"Here, take this, and whatever you do, don't tell anyone where you got this from!" His eyes expressed his serious tone. "It may still have some video on it... I believe it dates back to the days of the Athena Project."

David felt a chill run down his spine, but he took the tape from Walt's hands.

"You guys be careful out there. You know what happens when you pull a thread: The whole sweater unravels. With winter upon us, you're going to need your sweater," Walt said with a soft smile.

They both smiled back, and as they walked to their car, David remembered that he had forgotten to ask Walt a final question. He immediately turned and yelled back at Walt, who was still standing at the open door.

"Hey, Doc! I forgot to ask, do the initials M.F. mean anything to you?"

"M.F.?" Walt said slowly. "Doesn't ring a bell. Nope! Never heard of it."

David turned back and continued walking to the car.

Suddenly, he stopped and turned again. "What about

the name Emmitt Poole?"

Walt smiled, taking a pause, and then hollered back. "Those are semordnilap words. When spelled backward, they read as time and loop."

David turned toward Nella, an expression of shock covering their faces. "Holy shit, did you hear that? Time loop."

•••

David gripped the wheel with both hands, his knuckles white as they drove down the empty highway back home. Nella sat beside him, her eyes fixed on the road ahead but seeing little of it. Outside, the night had settled in, wrapping everything in a blanket of darkness. The only light came from the streetlamps flickering by and the occasional passing car. They both had so many questions, yet each answer only seemed to bring more confusion. David broke the silence, his voice quiet but filled with tension.

"What could it all mean? Time loop, I mean..."

Nella shifted uncomfortably in her seat. "I don't know. Perhaps it has something to do with the Athena Project. But it doesn't sound like a coincidence. It's like all the other items on the list that John Doe gave you; he must be trying to tell us something. Maybe there's something about time they were experimenting with."

She swallowed, her throat dry. "Maybe they were trying to control time, not just minds."

Suddenly, David took notice. The headlights in his rearview mirror had been with them for miles. He had first noticed them when a car on one of the back roads near

Walt's house pulled in behind him. He and Nella had been talking, going over all the new details they had learned, and in that time, David hadn't realized until that very moment they were being followed.

David, confirming his suspicions, "Don't look back, but we are being followed."

Nella glanced in the side mirror. "Are you sure?"

David nodded. "Since before the highway, I'm sure. It's the same type of headlights for the last twenty minutes."

David began speeding up as Nella told him not to panic. Behind him, the following car sped up as well. Suddenly, a mutual feeling of discovery took place.

"Whoever it is knows we know…they sped up." David cries out.

Nella suggested, "Maybe we should just call 911."

David responded, "Let me try something, maybe I can lose them."

David sped up and began passing other cars.

Nella grew more concerned. "No, David, this is crazy. We don't know what they want or what they are willing to do."

David's hands gripped the steering wheel as he swerved between cars at sixty-five miles per hour. As he approached an upcoming exit ramp, he veered right and got onto the exit ramp. The following car tried to follow but missed the turn-off. David raced to the end of the exit ramp. In his mirror, he could see the following car stop and back down the highway, attempting to get on the exit ramp.

David and Nella confirmed their fear... they were definitely being followed. David pressed the gas and raced down the dark road, noticing a small turn-off. He abruptly turned the steering wheel, the car skidded, and he entered the dark wooded turn-off, killing his lights. David and Nella sat in darkness, looking out their rearview window, watching for the following car. Their hearts raced, their breath fogging the windows. In the darkness, headlights approached.

"I hope they don't see us," Nella whispered.

David readied his hands and feet in case he had to race off and find an escape route. The headlights closed in, then the dark sedan quickly passed them. As the car faded, David and Nella pulled back out onto the road and quickly returned to the highway, heading south toward the city. David remained quiet and focused, taking a deep breath, trying to rid himself of the lump that had lodged in his throat. Suddenly Walts wild claims of government conspiracies, assassins and the mystery person who wanted to keep Dr. Friston from talking had became all too real. The possibilities seemed endless, and yet none of them made sense. They had uncovered so much, but the answers still felt so far away. And now a new twist, had they been followed.

"Look," David said, his voice more determined now, "If that car was actually following us, we need to figure this out. I'm setting up a whiteboard when we get home. We need to visualize everything—every connection, every theory. Maybe when we can see it all laid out, it'll make more sense."

Nella nodded, though her mind was still swirling. "I agree and let's not forget about the video tape," she said. "What do we do with that? We don't even have a way to watch it."

David's eyes narrowed. "We'll figure that out. I believe I have something that can help."

"Okay then, I'll come by your house during the weekends to help with solving the clues," Nella said.

The hours ticked forward and the city was coming into view now, the streetlights ahead flickering faintly in the distance. The car rolled slowly through the dark streets, the familiar sights of home not offering the comfort they once did. Everything felt different. Scary.

The world outside the car was still and quiet. But inside, both of them could feel the storm waiting to break.

CHAPTER 15
EMMITT POOLE

David stood at the bottom of the basement stairs, an old, dust-covered VCR cradled in his arms. The device was heavier than he'd expected, its metal casing cold against his fingertips. He could feel the layer of grime clinging to its surface, sticking to his hands as he adjusted his grip. The basement had been dark and musty, the air thick with the scent of aged wood and forgotten things. It had taken him nearly fifteen minutes to find the VCR, buried under a pile of old electronics, tangled cords, and discarded boxes. Now, as he climbed the stairs, he felt his heart pounding in his chest—not just from the weight of the machine, but from the anticipation of what they were about to uncover.

At the top of the stairs, Nella stood waiting in the dimly lit living room. She had her arms crossed, her fingers drumming lightly against her forearm. Her expression was a mix of curiosity and apprehension, her brows slightly furrowed as she watched David set the VCR down on the coffee table.

"I can't believe we're actually doing this," she said, her voice quiet but filled with nervous energy.

David wiped his hands on his jeans, smearing the dust across the fabric. "Me neither," he admitted. "Hopefully, this should still work," he said, running his fingers over the buttons on the VCR and feeling the raised plastic under his fingertips. It had been years since he last used one of these—probably back when he was a kid at his grandmother's house, watching old cartoons on VHS tapes. The thought made him pause for a moment. Those were simpler times. Now, this old piece of technology wasn't about nostalgia. It was about finding answers.

He crouched beside the television, plugging in the red, white, and yellow RCA cables, carefully matching them to the corresponding ports. The TV screen flickered as he switched the input, a blue screen appearing with faint static humming in the background.

Nella stepped closer, holding the VHS tape in both hands. The plastic casing was scratched and scuffed, the label on its spine faded and peeling at the edges. The only thing still legible was the date: *November 11, 1988.*

David took the tape from her, feeling its weight in his palm. "You ready?"

Nella exhaled sharply. "As I'll ever be."

David slid the tape into the VCR, pressed play, then settled on the living room sofa beside Nella. The machine let out a mechanical whir, swallowing the cassette with a soft clunk. The reels inside began to spin, and the static on the television screen briefly intensified before fading into darkness.

For a moment, nothing happened. Then, the screen flickered to life. A grainy timestamp appeared in the bottom right corner: *Nov 11, 1988, 9:14 A.M.* The image sharpened, revealing a dimly lit sterile and clinical room. The camera, positioned on a tripod, faced a large chair that resembled something from a dentist's office. The upholstery was cracked and worn, the armrests fitted with thick leather straps. A man sat in the chair, young, college-aged, his wrists bound to the armrests. His breathing was uneven, and his fingers were twitching against the restraints.

A second man moved into the frame, adjusting the camera slightly before stepping back. He was older, maybe in his fifties, with sharp features and piercing eyes. He wore a lab coat over a white shirt and tie, his posture upright and deliberate.

The man spoke, his voice clear despite the distortion of the old recording.

"Athena Project, November 11, 1988. Rif Phase 2—Variant of Induction of Subject 1."

David felt his stomach tighten. He turned to Nella, whose face had gone pale.

"That has to be Dr. Friston," David whispered.

Nella swallowed hard, nodding. "It looks just like his pictures, but younger."

"But who's Subject 1?" David's asked, his voice barely above a breath.

Nella shook her head. "I don't know, but at least it's not my dad." The thought of her father subjected to whatever was happening on the screen sent a shiver down her spine.

David reached for her hand, a gesture that silently reassured her. His attention snapped back to the screen. Dr. Friston moved to the side, wheeling a small machine into view. The device had a built-in monitor and peculiar headgear attached by several coiled wires. It looked primitive but unsettling, like something designed for experiments rather than medical treatment.

Dr. Friston gently placed the headgear onto the young man's head, adjusting the straps with practiced movements. The subject flinched slightly but remained silent.

"This will only take a moment," Dr. Friston said, his tone disturbingly calm. "Try to keep your breathing steady."

The subject's hands clenched into fists. Once the headgear was secured, Dr. Friston reached up and pulled down a dual-screen apparatus, positioning it directly in front of the young man's face. He then rolled a screen made of some kind of sequin, reflective material into view, surrounding the subjects' chairs on three sides. After that, Dr. Friston retreated and activated the device, and the screens flickered to life, displaying waves of data scrolling rapidly across them. The subject's gaze locked onto the moving symbols.

A low hum filled the room, mechanical and rhythmic. The screens began to pulse, emitting a slow, steady glow that illuminated the subject's face in brief flashes.

The young man's breathing grew uneven. His fingers dug into the armrests, knuckles whitening. The pulsing light on the screens began to speed up, the data shifting at a dizzying pace. The humming sound grew louder. The reflective curtain grew bright... reflecting a glimmering wall of gold petals, and then blackness erupted over the surface of the curtain.

Nella inhaled sharply, clutching the edge of the couch's armrest. "This is—this is doing something to him."

David nodded, unable to tear his eyes away. The subject's body tensed. His face twisted in confusion, then fear. His lips moved, barely forming words.

Dr. Friston leaned closer, over the back of the chair, his face just inches from the subject's. He spoke two words, barely audible over the hum of the machine.

"*Time travel.*"

David felt his breath catch in his throat.

Nella's hand shot up to cover her mouth.

"Did you hear that?" David's voice was hoarse. "He said time travel. His metal worm was time travel!"

"I heard it." Nella's eyes were wide, her expression a mix of horror and realization. "This—this could be our M.F. Oh my God! Subject 1 could be M.F.!"

Before they could say anything else, the subject on the screen let out a sudden, gut-wrenching scream. His body thrashed against the restraints, muscles straining as if he were trying to escape something unseen. His voice was filled with terror.

"Stop!" he shrieked. "Please stop! Make the upside-down man go away!"

Dr. Friston's face tensed. He quickly reached for the device, adjusting its settings. The flashing slowed. The humming softened. The subject sagged in the chair, his breaths coming in harsh, uneven gasps.

On the dual screens, the image shifted. The scrolling data vanished, replaced by a stark, white emblem: shaped like a bird, its wings outstretched, its piercing eyes staring forward. Below it, a single word appeared in block letters.

ATHENA

David's skin prickled with unease.

A moment later, as Dr. Friston removed the headgear, the door in the background opened and another figure stepped into the room. He was younger than Dr. Friston, with dark hair, a beard and an intense gaze.

David squinted. His heart nearly stopped.

"Nella," he whispered. "That—that looks like Walt."

On the screen, the young Walt moved toward the camera. His expression was unreadable. He reached out, his fingers brushing the edge of the lens—

The image dissolved into static.

David and Nella sat frozen, the room around them silent except for the faint hiss of the VCR.

David swallowed hard. "Holy shit! We have proof." His voice was barely above a whisper. "We know Dr. Friston implanted the idea of time travel into Subject 1's mind."

"My father wasn't crazy," Nella murmured. "This is

proof. They turned him into a monster." Her eyes glistened with tears as she said this.

David met her gaze, his own filled with sadness and the burden of their discovery. He reached for the VHS tape, pulling it from the machine and placing it in Nella's hand.

"Take it. Maybe it can help," he said. "Maybe it can fix what they did."

Nella nodded slowly, her fingers tightening around the cassette. "Thank you," she whispered, her voice thick with emotion. "We have to find out what happened to Subject 1. I strongly believe he's our M.F., and I think he's somehow connected to Item 6 on the list, Emit Pool, or time loop, whatever it is. I think he's probably suffering the same madness my father did. The same cognitive meltdown, obsessed with time travel."

David nodded as a heavy silence settled over them. It was all too much. He couldn't believe that the truth was out there, captured on an old VHS tape.

•••

The weeks passed quickly and the seasons changed— from winter to spring. David and Nella spent most of their free time together, poring over everything they had discovered. The walls of David's den had transformed into a huge web of notes, photographs, and theories. The list was pinned in the center of the largest board, surrounded by strings connecting each item to their possible meanings.

At first, their research was frantic. Every new discovery felt like a breakthrough, every small detail like a missing puzzle piece. But as the days stretched into weeks, they settled into a routine.

Most evenings, Nella would show up at David's house, sometimes with takeout, sometimes with coffee. They would sit side by side, combing through articles, books, and old documents. They had learned how to challenge each other's ideas without frustration, how to push one another toward new conclusions.

It was easy. Comfortable.

But there was something else, too.

A sizzling tension between them—unspoken, just beneath the surface. Neither of them brought it up. Neither of them dared to. Nella had often wondered if David felt the same underlying desire for more between them. But then she'd quickly remind herself that he might not be ready, or worse, he might not see her in that kind of way.

One evening, the door buzzer rang, and David practically jumped off the couch to answer it. When he opened the door, Nella stood there with two cups in her hands, her cheeks slightly flushed from the cold.

"A mocha frappe for you," she said with a grin, holding out one of the cups. "And a hot caramel macchiato for me."

David took the drink, shaking his head with a small smile. "Thank you, Nell! You know, you really don't have to keep bribing me with coffee to let you in."

Nella smirked. "Maybe I just enjoy watching you get all excited over caffeine."

David stepped aside, letting her in. As she walked past him, she glanced over her shoulder. "You know, you should just get me a key at this point."

David raised an eyebrow. "You think so?"

"Yeah," Nella teased, nudging him playfully. "Big step though. Are you sure you're ready for that level of commitment?"

David chuckled, shaking his head as he followed her to the den. Their teasing had become natural. Effortless. But underneath it, something lingered—something unspoken. Neither of them acknowledged it. For now, the mystery they were unraveling took priority.

As they moved, Nella suddenly spoke out. "I have some good news for you!"

"Let me guess, you solved the last two items on the list," David said with a smirk on his lips.

Nella giggled before letting out full-blown laughter and hitting David playfully on his shoulder. "No, you oaf! I heard back from my dad's lawyers. The video tape... it's a big deal. They think it will help their appeal, being new evidence and all..."

David smiled and gave her a big hug. "Wow, Nells, that is great news!"

Once they reached the den, they began their usual work, spending most of the time running over the theories and notes. Time passed by quickly and they were getting tired. David sat in a chair and rubbed his temples. Nella stood by the board, arms crossed, scanning it with a frustrated expression.

"Alright," David said. "It's getting late, so let's run down these different theories again. It seems like when we finally make sense of one possible solution, we either find a hole or we are still missing a key piece, and the whole thing falls apart."

Nella sighed and nodded.

David continued. "What we know is that the list was given to me by a John Doe seven years ago, one year before I met Hannah. Then, seven years after I was given the list, I discovered the Hermit Lake and the lake house, and soon after that, I met you, the Ladybug tattoo."

They looked at the list again, on the whiteboard in the middle of the room.

Hannah
Hermit Lake
Ladybug tattoo
18 Vassar Street
Leonard Friston
Emmitt Poole
Cathedral Rock
Kill him

"We have since found out that 18 Vassar Street is the old home of Building 20, where Dr. Leonard Friston, as well as our buddy Walt in Maine, conducted the Athena Project in 1988," David continued.

"After watching that video of what they did, it was more like Frankenstein's workshop! We now know that my father, Robert Allen, was implanted with the inducted phrase: neurosurgery. Then, sometime after my brother's death in '07 but before 2018, he was exposed to the palindrome tangent phrase, *Mr. Owl Ate My Metal Worm*, causing him to snap," Nella added.

David looked at her and said, "We also know that in 1999, someone going by the initials M.F. met with Dr. Friston at his book signing and perhaps was also exposed to the tangent phrase, making that person one of the two other subjects in the Athena Project in '88, most likely Subject 1. I think M.F. pushed Dr. Friston down the stairs to prevent him from stopping whatever he was going to do. Or prevent me from talking to him. And that same person also left the note with the name Emit Pool."

"Which we now know means time loop," Nella injected.

"Right, I always assumed it was a name when I heard it, and wrote it down as Emmitt Poole, I assumed that is how you spell it. I never realized it wasn't a person's name," David explained.

"Clearly the Athena Project played on the use of palindrome and semordnilap words, something that would not be easily noticed by the average person yet had become an inedible part of the subjects' psyches," Nella said. "I mean, we both saw what that device was doing to the guy on the table!"

"According to Dr. Leonard Friston's book, *Induction Theory and Cognitive Sciences*, he listed eight variants of induction words or as he called them, 'metal worms.' And as you said, we now know your father must have been implanted with the phrase: neurosurgery. But I also suspect M.F. was implanted with the phrase: time travel, which makes sense for a person using time loop in their note at Dr. Friston house," David said.

They looked at the list of metal worms they had acquired:

Piano Symphony
Time Travel
Cure Cancer
Skyscraper
Fusion Energy
Lake House
Neurosurgery
Mandarin

There was a small moment of silence before Nella spoke out. "David, I know you haven't brought this up yet, but we can't ignore that the *Lake House* is also on the list of metal worms. I mean, you told me you only discovered the lake house because item 2 on the list was Hermit Lake. I know you are concerned about your relationship with Mae, but maybe she knows more than we realize. If her late husband Paul was one of the subjects, if Paul was triggered at some point, then she should know the truth."

"I'm not afraid to tell her what I know. I'm afraid she may tell me what I don't want to know," David replied in a somber voice.

Nella walked over to him and gave him a hug, holding him tightly and whispering, "I know David. Just remember, there are no consequences."

"I agree. I am also afraid of what will come of number 8. *Kill him.* I don't want to assume, but it seems all the clues and predictions are leading us to stopping someone, or should I say, to killing someone," David said, feeling like the walls of the den were closing in.

"I know, and I am afraid as well," Nella added. "We keep ending up in this same place. We have no clear direction on how to move past item 6. There is a reason *Time Loop* is listed after Dr. Friston; could M.F. have also been given a list, which is why he killed him? And if so, why is *Kill him* now number 8 on the list? I think if this M.F. did murder Dr. Friston, maybe Dr. Friston was trying to stop M.F. Perhaps he was afraid M.F. would succeed and build a time machine, thus the time loop. Similar to what happened to my father, perhaps Dr. Frankenstein was trying to stop his monster."

Hearing Nella say this, David perked up. "That could be what we have been missing. We never considered the fact that someone else may have the list and is trying to prevent us from following the clues and finding the truth."

"What if someone saw the list, have you shared it with anyone but Hannah and I?" Nella continues.

David eyes widen, "That's it, I never told you what happened after Hannah and I began investigating the list, item 2, Hermit Lake. Soon after we visited Hermit Lake we arrived home to find our house ransacked. Nothing was taken but someone was looking for something and the list was hung to the refrigerator."

"Do you think someone broke in and saw the list?" Nella adds.

"It's possible, what if M.F. got wind of our visit to Hermit Lake, then ransacked the house looking to see what we knew. If M.F. saw the list he would have more reason to kill Dr. Friston, to tie up loose ends and prevent us from learning more. It could the same reason someone was following us that night after we went to see Walt.

Hearing David say this, Nella jumped up. "It makes so much sense. And what if Dr. Friston saw what had happened to my father on the news, and realized that the publishing of his book, which included the tangent phrase, must have triggered one of the other subjects—M.F. specifically—to try and build a time machine."

"Everyone knows that building a time machine is like *Oppenheimer and the Atomic bomb*." David continues. "That kind of endeavor could destroy the fabric of time. I mean, there are endless books and movies on this shit. Paradoxes, butterfly effect, and grandfather theory."

"Time loops?" Nella added.

"That's right. It would make sense that a guy like Dr. Friston would risk his life to stop something like that. And let's remember, seven years ago a man I never met, with no name called on me by name and gave me the list. Clearly, he knew something we didn't and needed us to try and stop it. I was given the list for a reason, and finding you was a part of that journey. The questions now are who, where, when, and how?" David said.

"The who is M.F and the how is Kill him," Nella simply stated. "We should have done this weeks ago. Let's look up number 7, Cathedral Rock on the web... it could be the where."

David took out his phone and did a quick web search for Cathedral Rock. He discovered that it was a natural red sandstone butte near Sedona, Arizona. He related his findings to Nella, and together, they came to the realization that the rock formation must be related to the "where" in their theory. David noticed that it was too late for Nella to leave so he suggested that she spend the night.

Nella agreed without hesitation, and as David entered the living room, he offered to give her his bed, saying he will sleep on the sofa. She agreed and as they sat, talking about the idea, Nella suddenly went silent, and David immediately noticed the shift.

"Nell, what's wrong?" he asked. However, she offered no response; rather, she simply stared at the wall, the one with the abstract art piece.

After a moment of silence the words slipped from her lips, her face void of expression, "Malik Farnsworth is M.F."

David looked over at the art piece. *Geometric Tangent... oh my God, all this time it had been right under my very nose,* he thought, amazed and excited. He opened his phone again and began a new web search for Malik Farnsworth.

"Oh shit! It says that he was a mathematics professor with a PhD from MIT. Apparently, he lost his wife and daughter in a car accident and began doing abstract art as therapy. This must be the guy! As an artist, he is huge, he is very well known, I mean, his stuff is world famous." David pierced two and two together.

"Jackpot! I found a recent bio. Listen to this: Malik Farnsworth is an American contemporary artist specializing in mathematical formulations, geometry, and mass to extract abstract equations within a multicolored canvas. Over the past few years, Malik Farnsworth has been sculpturing and erecting a large-scale land art project for the State of Arizona. Commissioned by the City of Sedona, the project is located at the base of Cathedral Rock's natural red sandstone butte. The Alcubierre Vortex, as it's been named, consists of subterranean negative forms in relation with protruding levitated masses of sculptured boulders. The structure is designed to enhance the natural production and energy of the up-flow vortex found in the area. The project is expected to be completed by March 20th, this year," David read.

Nella jumped out of her seat. "That's it! Malik Farnsworth is the *who*, Cathedral Rock in Sedona is the *where*, and March 20th is the *when*. Oh my gosh, David! That's only a few weeks away. We need to get there before that date!"

The urgency in her voice matched the racing thoughts in David's head. They had no more time to waste. The answers they needed, the truth they had been searching for—it was all going to be revealed in Sedona.

CHAPTER 16
CATHEDRAL ROCK

T he plane rattled as it dipped lower, slicing through the dry Arizona air, and every few seconds, a sudden tremor ran through the cabin as the aircraft hit pockets of turbulence. Nella sucked in a breath and gripped the armrest, her fingers pressing hard into the worn fabric. The seat belt across her waist felt too tight, almost suffocating, but she didn't dare loosen it.

The descent was rougher than she'd expected. The plane shuddered again, making her stomach twist, and for a brief moment, it felt like they were dropping. She reached out without thinking and grabbed David's hand. His skin was warm against her cold fingers, but she could feel the tension in his grip. He was trying to stay calm, but she knew he wasn't as relaxed as he pretended to be.

She had never liked flying. It wasn't a fear of heights or

even the idea of crashing that got to her—it was the feeling of helplessness. Being trapped in a metal shell, thousands of feet above the ground, completely at the mercy of forces she couldn't control. Every time the plane jolted, her mind went straight to worst-case scenarios: malfunctioning engines, failing landing gear, a miscalculation by the pilot. She squeezed her eyes shut for a second, forcing the thoughts away.

David gave her hand a reassuring squeeze. "Almost there," he said, his voice calm, but there was an edge to it, like he was trying to convince himself as much as her.

The runway came into view, a long stretch of concrete surrounded by flat desert land. The city sprawled in the distance, clusters of buildings softened by a thin haze. The plane lowered steadily, but just before touchdown, it lurched slightly to one side before correcting itself.

The wheels hit the ground with a hard thump. A loud screech filled the cabin as the rubber tires skidded against the tarmac, the force jerking them forward against their seat belts. The engines roared as the reverse thrust kicked in, slowing the plane down with a deep, mechanical growl. Nella felt her body push forward, the strap of her seat belt digging into her stomach. The force of the deceleration finally eased, and the plane settled into a smoother roll as it taxied toward the terminal.

A crackle sounded over the intercom, and the pilot's voice filled the cabin. "Ladies and gentlemen, Southwestern Airlines welcomes you to Phoenix, Arizona. The local time is 3:52 p.m., and the current temperature is a comfortable 74 degrees. For your safety and the safety of those around you, please remain in your seats as we taxi to the terminal. On behalf of our crew, we'd like to thank you for flying with us, and we hope you enjoy your stay."

Nella exhaled and slowly released David's hand, flexing her fingers to get the blood flowing again. "Thanks," she muttered, glancing at him. "I always get a little tense during landings."

David stretched his fingers and gave her a small smile. "We made it. No fiery crash." He leaned back in his seat, rolling his shoulders as if shaking off the stress. Then, in a lighter tone, he added, "Did you hear the pilot? It's seventy-four degrees outside."

Nella let out a short laugh, finally allowing herself to relax. "Yeah, way better than the forties we left behind in Boston." She reached down and adjusted her seat belt, rubbing at her arms, which were still tense from gripping the armrest.

Nella took another deep breath and leaned back in her seat, finally letting the tension drain from her body. She glanced out the window, watching as the airport buildings came into sharper view. The landscape was so different from what she was used to—no dense city streets, no clusters of tall buildings. Just open space, flat land stretching toward the horizon, with jagged mountains rising in the distance.

David nudged her lightly. "Still thinking about the landing?"

"No," she said, shaking her head. "Just... everything feels different here. The air even looks different."

David chuckled. "It's nothing like Boston, that's for

sure!'"

Nella smiled slightly but didn't say anything. She wasn't sure if it was just the dry desert air or the fact that they were now this close to finding Malik Farnsworth, but something about being here made her feel... uneasy.

David and Nella then checked out their rental car and got on the road to Sedona. The highway stretched ahead of them, long and empty, cutting through the huge Arizona desert. The rental car moved steadily as David kept a firm grip on the wheel, his eyes focused on the road ahead. The sun hung low in the sky, casting an orange glow over the horizon.

Nella stared out the window, watching the landscape shift as they moved farther from Phoenix. At first, everything was flat—wide stretches of sand and rock with occasional patches of dull green vegetation and cactus. But as they drove north, the scenery began to change. The land became rugged, and distant mountains rose from the earth, their outlines growing sharper as they approached.

After about an hour, the first red rock formations appeared. Tall cliffs of deep red and burnt orange stood against the fading sky. The colors seemed to glow in the evening light, as if the rocks themselves were alive. The road curved through the rising landscape, curving between canyons and hills. It was nothing like Boston—no buildings, no city noise, just endless open land and the tall stone giants watching over them.

David glanced at Nella. She had been quiet for a while, her arms crossed as she stared outside. He knew she was thinking about tomorrow. He was thinking about it too.

He decided to break the silence.

"We have a big day tomorrow. I printed a map of the Cathedral Rock trail; we can park at the trail head, but it's about a half mile to the Alcubierre Vortex construction site."

Nella looked at him, a serious expression on her face. "David, we really need to talk this through. Assuming Malik Farnsworth is there... I mean, he must be there, it's March 18th; he is supposed to finish the project in two days. So, assuming we see him, what are we going to say… what are we going to do? I mean, we really can't just walk up and kill the man."

David laughed, unable to hold it in. "Maybe I shouldn't be laughing, but we obviously can't kill him. I mean, we are not murderers. I already thought about this, and I think we should just come clean. We should tell him the whole story and see what happens next. I mean, what other options do we have?"

Nella nodded in agreement. "Okay, let's do that, but I just want you to remember three things. And you need to be ready for anything, I mean anything. First, he very well may have killed Dr. Friston; he could be a murderer. He could be so obsessed by the shit they implanted into his head that he will kill to prevent anyone from stopping him. Second, this is most likely the guy that has been following you, following us, he very well may have broken into your house. And third, everything on the list, items 1 through 7, have all been proven true. So don't be naïve about this. John Doe put item 8, *Kill him*, on that list for a reason," Nella explained, concern clouding her eyes.

David's throat tightened, and he tried to assure Nella that he had things under control, although he knew that was far from the truth. He calmly stated, "It's okay, Nell. We are going to just try talking to him first; we will just tell him everything."

Nella sighed and leaned back into her seat, and David turned up the volume on the radio, needing something to fill the uncomfortable silence in the car. A slow country song played through the speakers, the kind that felt right for a drive through the desert. He wasn't trying to ignore her, but he also didn't want to talk about it anymore. Not right now. They expected to arrive within the hour. And it was a good thing they had already booked a room at a local hotel.

By the time they reached Sedona, the sun had set, leaving behind a dark blue sky sprinkled with stars. The town was small and quiet, and streetlights cast a warm golden glow over the sidewalks, illuminating small shops and restaurants with rustic wooden signs. The air smelled different here—clean and dry, with a faint hint of pine from the nearby forests.

David slowed the car as they entered the main street. The buildings had a southwestern charm, their walls painted in earthy tones that blended with the landscape. Some storefronts had hanging lanterns, their soft yellow light flickering against the deep red cliffs in the background. It was peaceful.

Their hotel was a small, boutique-style inn with a southwestern design. The exterior was made of smooth stucco, with wooden beams and terracotta tiles giving it a warm, rustic feel. A few desert plants lined the entrance, their spiky leaves casting sharp shadows under the lights.

Inside, the lobby smelled of leather and cedarwood. The front desk was made of polished wood, and a small fireplace crackled softly in the corner, adding to the cozy atmosphere. The receptionist, an older woman with silver hair, greeted them with a friendly smile as she handed over their room keys.

Their room was on the second floor, with a small balcony overlooking the dark silhouettes of the surrounding cliffs. Nella stepped outside for a moment, resting her hands on the wooden railing. The night was quiet, except for the occasional chirp of crickets and the distant sound of a car passing on the main road. She looked up at the sky—it was clearer than in the city, the stars brighter and more numerous.

David set their bags down and stretched. "Hungry?"

Nella nodded. "Yeah. Let's find something close by."

•••

They found a small restaurant just down the street, a quiet place with dim lighting and wooden tables. A waitress brought them menus and two glasses of water. David flipped through the options, but his mind wasn't really on the food.

Nella was the first to order. "I'll have the green chile enchiladas," she said.

David glanced at the menu and picked something randomly. "Same for me."

After a while, their food was ready and the waitress set their plates in front of them. The enchiladas smelled good, the smell of roasted chilies and melted cheese filling the air. But she barely touched her fork.

David took a bite, the spicy flavor warming his mouth. But the food did nothing to ease the heaviness in his chest.

"We need to be ready for anything," Nella said finally. "You know that, right?"

David met her eyes. "Yeah," he said quietly. "I know."

•••

Back at the hotel, David fell asleep quickly, his breathing steady and even. But Nella lay awake, staring at the ceiling. After a while, she got up and stepped onto the balcony. The night air was cool against her skin. She looked out at the dark silhouette of Cathedral Rock in the distance, its jagged form rising against the starry sky.

Tomorrow, they would be there. Tomorrow, they would face Malik Farnsworth. And she had no idea what would happen next.

•••

The morning air was crisp and cool when David and Nella stepped out of the hotel. The sky was a deep shade of blue, untouched by clouds, and the rock formations in the distance glowed with the first light of day. The sun had just started to rise, its golden light stretching across the landscape.

Nella pulled her jacket tighter around her shoulders. The temperature was still low, but she knew that within a few hours, the desert heat would take over. David locked the car and stretched, rolling his shoulders as he looked around.

"You hungry?" he asked.

Nella nodded. "Yeah. Let's grab something quick."

They found a small café near the edge of town. The place wasn't crowded—just a few early risers, some of them in hiking gear like David and Nella, others looking like locals reading the morning paper.

David ordered black coffee and a breakfast burrito, while Nella went for iced coffee and a bagel with cream cheese. They took a seat by the window, where they could see the red rock formations standing in the distance, and ate their food in silence.

•••

The drive to the trailhead took about fifteen minutes. Upon reaching the parking lot, they noticed a large sign displaying the upcoming project. The sign read:

ALCUBIERRE VORTEX LAND ART – COMING SOON
DESIGNED BY MALIK FARNSWORTH

David and Nella took a moment to acknowledge their efforts of having made it this far. Their attention then shifted to the breathtaking views, a true visual transformation from their usual scenery of Boston and life in an urban environment.

The scarce green vegetation, primarily made up of cactus and desert trees, grew out of a truly breathtaking sea of red rock in all the directions they looked at. The landscape and views stretched for miles, creating a huge horizon of red rock hills, formations, and mesas.

"This place is beautiful. I could never imaged such a vast landscape of natural red rocks and formations,"

Nella said, as her eyes took in the openness around her.

"It's incredible; you can see for miles in all directions, and the sky is so blue and huge," David agreed.

David and Nella walked uphill, following the stacks of rocks used to mark the trail. They trekked up steep, unshaded slopes of rocks, crossed runoff washes carved in the low areas, and moved through the irregular route that led them to the base of Cathedral Rock. As they approached a clearing, they noticed a large mobile generator. Just beyond the generator they saw a utility task vehicle parked and a service trail leading down the slope toward the main road. Yellow construction tape surrounded the area, fluttering slightly in the breeze. A sign was posted nearby:

RESTRICTED–CONSTRUCTION AREA

David and Nella exchanged a look.

"This is it," Nella whispered.

David swallowed hard. His heartbeat was steady, but his stomach felt tight. There was absolutely no turning back now. Seeing no one around, they crossed the tape line and entered the construction site.

As they followed the area of work up the hillside, they found the most unusual formation. The area was carved out like an ellipse—at the low end, a massive depression and at the high end, an equally massive, raised arc. Directly in line with the ellipse was a towering needle-shaped rock, the natural form known as Cathedral Rock.

Suddenly a voice called out with a distinctive accent,

"You shouldn't be here!"

David and Nella quickly turned around and were met with a dark-skinned man of Native American decent.

"This area is off limits due to construction," the man continued.

"Hello, my name is David, and this is Nella. We are actually here to meet Malik Farnsworth," David responded.

"Oh, okay. Then you can be here." The man giggled. "Malik is down by the road, but he will be back soon," the man replied. "My name is Chitto, I work for Malik," he added.

David's and Nella's faces broke into welcoming smiles. "Hey Chitto, is that Cathedral Rock?" David asked, pointing up toward the towering needle-shaped rock.

"Yes, that is Cathedral Rock. It is a very special place, lots of energy," Chitto replied.

"Nella and I have never been here. Can you please tell us what makes this place so special, and what kind of energy are you talking about?" David asked.

Chitto gestured for them to walk with him up the hill a bit. He then stopped and had them turn around, using his hands to show them a shadow being cast down the hillside. The shadow was in the shape of a spire, like the point on top of a cathedral. David and Nella noticed that the point was in line with the ellipse formation on the hillside.

"See, the shadow of the needle points to the center of an up-flow vortex, one of only four vortexes in Sedona. Some say the most powerful of the four," Chitto explained, waving his arms around. He then continued with his lesson. "The energy of the earth that aligns here allows for introspective power to connect memories of past lives. *Mañana*, tomorrow is the Spring equinox; the sun will be directly above the equator, and the Cathedral Rock vortex will be at its greatest up-flow. See, this is a special place. Many tribes in the area believe Sedona to be the center of the universe. And whatever happens here tomorrow… it will not be like any other day."

David exchanged a look with Nella. The list. March 20th. The deadline for Malik's project. It wasn't a coincidence.

Chitto studied their expressions. "You came here for a reason," he said. "And you will find what you're looking for. Just be ready. The vortex does not care what you want. Its energy source is of sacred and spiritual origin, acting as an amplifier for change, and bringing with it the potential for intense revelation."

Nella shifted uncomfortably. "That sounds… ominous."

Chitto let out a short laugh. "Maybe." He gave them one last look, his dark eyes steady. "Or maybe it's just the truth."

A distant sound of an engine reached their ears. Chitto headed back down the hill, and David and Nella followed along. Up ahead, a rugged bearded man rolled up on an ATV and climbed off the four-wheeler. Chitto called out to David and Nella, "Malik is here."

Malik stoically stood in the distance as Chitto, David, and Nella walked back down the hill in his direction. His eyes were hidden in the shadow of his brow, the skin on his face creased with age, and a dark complexion had set in from years of sun exposure. His body was stiff and thin, yet he projected a stature of toughness in his uneven posture. Red dust coated his clothes, a sign of his time spent sculpting Sedona's red rock.

Chitto immediately approached Malik, gesturing back at David and Nella, "Hey, boss, this is David and Nella; they said they came to see you."

Malik's eyes, still in the shadows, gave no indication of movement, but his lips did. "Thanks, Chitto. Start setting up the primers. I brought up the last of the copper cable."

CHAPTER 17

KILL HIM

They were close now. Malik stood several yards ahead of them. The moment felt heavier than David had anticipated. He had imagined this meeting a hundred times over, played out conversations in his head, and prepared arguments and counterarguments. But now, as he stood just feet away from Malik, all of that preparation felt useless.

His chest tightened, and his palms grew damp. He clenched his fists, forcing himself to breathe evenly. His heart pounded, but he didn't know if it was from fear, anticipation, or something else entirely.

Beside him, Nella walked with steady steps, her posture rigid but controlled. Her face betrayed no fear, though David knew her well enough to recognize the tension in the way she held her shoulders. She didn't speak, didn't look at him, but her fingers moved absentmindedly to the back of her hand, tracing the outline of the ladybug tattoo inked there. It was something she did when she was anxious.

David knew what she was thinking about. Her father. Robert Allen. The man who had once been kind, brilliant even, before Dr. Friston's experiment changed him. Before the obsession took hold. The same obsession that had consumed others. The same obsession that now held Malik in its grip.

They were now in front of Malik, and David was the first to speak. "Malik Farnsworth, my name is—"

"I know who you are!" Malik interrupted David mid-sentence.

Malik's words stopped him cold and caught both he and Nella off guard. They weren't expecting that.

David hesitated. "You do?"

Malik didn't answer right away. Instead, he brushed off his right hand as if dusting away dirt and extended it toward Nella. "However, you—I don't know."

Nella took a moment before stepping forward, her expression unreadable. She reached out and grasped his hand, her grip firm and unwavering. As their hands met, Malik's gaze flicked downward, noticing the ladybug tattoo on the back of her hand. He lingered on it for just a second, his brows furrowing slightly before a small, almost amused smile touched his lips. Nella didn't react to his curiosity, nor did she offer an explanation. She simply pulled her hand back and let her arms fall to her sides.

Malik turned then, gesturing toward the hillside,

toward the ellipse formation. "Walk with me," he said, already moving forward without waiting for their response.

David and Nella exchanged a glance. This wasn't how they had imagined things going. They had expected confrontation, maybe even resistance. They had expected to be the ones controlling the conversation, pressing Malik for answers. Instead, they were following his lead.

David didn't like it.

Still, he moved forward, falling into step beside Malik as Nella walked just behind them. The wind picked up again, sending another swirl of dust into the air. David swallowed hard. This was not going to be as simple as they had hoped.

As they followed Malik up the hillside, he began sharing details of his project. "You know... they said it couldn't be done. But Einstein knew better. His theory of relativity is over a hundred years old, yet people still don't fully grasp its potential. For Einstein's theory to work, he needed an energy source and exotic matter."

David and Nella listened in silence as Malik spoke. His arms moved as he explained, and his eyes held fire and an energy that was almost hypnotic.

"Everyone assumed that to harness these two elements, one must be in outer space. In space, it would be the fundamentals of warp-drive, also known as Alcubierre Drive. Quantum physicists have long proposed models of dynamical warp-drive in which a warp bubble is formed in a previously flat space. This would allow a bending of time and space, the movement of an object at faster-than-light speed."

Though David and Nella were impressed by Malik's intellect and display of passion over his achievement, David couldn't help but shift uncomfortably. "Malik, this is all theoretical. You're talking about bending space-time like it's something you can just... turn on and off."

Malik turned to face him fully now, his eyes narrowing slightly. "No," he said firmly. "Not theoretical. I've done the calculations. I ran the numbers; the mathematical equations check out. The effects of time dilation would apply to any object moving at near-light speeds. The Alcubierre metric would result in the formation of a warp bubble in which time inside the bubble would slow... even reverse."

David hesitated. He understood the theory—at least in principle. But understanding the theory and believing it could actually be applied in reality were two very different things. Malik's voice had risen slightly, not in anger, but in pure, unfiltered passion. He truly believed what he was saying. David felt Nella shift beside him. He knew she was thinking the same thing he was. Malik wasn't lying. He wasn't trying to deceive them. He genuinely believed he had unlocked the secret to time travel.

Malik took a slow breath, calming himself before continuing. "I was able to solve the equation for the slowing of time, as well as how to bring it to a standstill. However, I needed to find a way to go back, not hours but years. I also needed to find a way to do it on Earth, not in space. Then it came to me, using the ADM formalism of general relativity to go backward, I would need to slide the bubble through the initial space, essentially pushing space aside, moving backward within the exotic matter of space and time."

David's stomach twisted. "Whoa, listen, Malik... you said you know who I am, and I appreciate you telling me how all this works, but there is something you don't know."

Malik held up his hand to stop David from continuing. "I understand... I will explain everything... just listen to me for a moment."

Nella couldn't help but throw in her own words. "Is that what all this is? Are you saying you built some kind of time machine?"

Malik smiled then continued. "Actually, that is exactly what I did. The ellipse is a giant Alcubierre Drive, and tomorrow the primers will be in place around the perimeter. They will be used like an electromagnetic field, creating a faster-than-light speed gyro event within the ellipse. The generator will produce an energy condition of 66,000 volts. At 5:39 p.m. tomorrow, the shadow of the Cathedral Rock needle will be aligned precisely at the center of the ellipse, generating an up-flow vortex of exotic matter. When the Alcubierre Drive is energized, I will be standing in its center, inside the formation of a warp bubble. The opposing regions of expanding and contracting spacetime will displace the region while the warp bubble remains fixed. Time dilation will occur, moving me backward in time."

David couldn't hold it in any longer. His chest was tight, his breath uneven, and his hands clenched into fists at his sides. His mind had been trying to process everything

Malik was saying, trying to find some way to make sense of it—but there was no sense in this.

"Do you understand how insane this all sounds?" he finally snapped, his voice sharp and unsteady.
Malik turned to him, calm and collected, as if David's frustration was nothing more than a minor inconvenience.

David stepped forward, his words coming fast now, driven by anger, by fear. "You're talking about hypothetical time travel, exotic matter, and 66,000 volts of electricity. Don't you see the risks? For all we know, this thing could implode in a burst of dark matter and create a black hole that destroys the world."

Malik exhaled slowly, shaking his head like a teacher disappointed in a student's lack of understanding. "David," he said, his voice almost condescending.

David raised his hand up, stopping him from continuing with what he was about to say. "No! Listen to me, Malik. I need to tell you something. I need to explain what they did to you!"

Malik shook his head frantically, circling around David and Nella while waving his hands in protest. His voice rose as he shouted, "They did nothing to me! And it's ridiculous to think this could destroy the world. I believe in what I am doing; this is my destiny. All this is going to change everything! Don't you see what I am trying to do? I don't have to resent the past anymore. I don't have to live in guilt and pain for the tragic loss of my family. I can change it all! You know it to be true. That's why you're here! Dr. Friston gave me a gift! He was afraid, but I wasn't. I couldn't let him stop me. He gave me a gift to change the past, to save my family."

Then Nella stepped forward. Her voice wasn't sharp like David's. It was softer, filled with something deeper—something real. "Malik, we do understand. We understand your pain. Believe me, among the three of us, we have all lost someone. David lost his wife Hannah a few months ago. I lost my brother in Iraq many years ago."

"Every day, we wake up with that same feeling. That same hole inside us, the same thoughts running through our heads: What if things had been different? What would we change if given the chance? What if we could have stopped it? But we can't, Malik. No one can. And one more thing, I know what Dr. Friston did to you... what he did to my father, Robert Allen."

"You're Robert Allen's daughter?" Malik questioned.

"Yes," Nella replied before continuing, "the metal worm Dr. Friston put in his head drove him to do something unthinkable. That is what he did to you too, don't you see? This obsession is eating at you like a cancer to build a time machine, to save your family, it's not real... you are engaged in a self-fulfilling prophecy based on your exposure to a horrible experiment."

Malik dismissed Nella's statement. "No, you're wrong! I ran the numbers... I spent years running the numbers. I am sorry about your father. He was a very good friend of mine. But if there is one thing I know, it's that this is going to work... it must work."

Malik turned away, his back to them now, breathing hard. He ran a hand through his hair, muttering something under his breath.

Then, slowly, he straightened. When he spoke again, his voice was calm. Too calm.

"You two need to go. I have a lot of work to do before tomorrow."

David felt a sinking sensation in his chest.

"No," he said, shaking his head. "We're not done."

Malik turned to him, eyes cold. "Yes, we are."

David clenched his jaw. He couldn't let this end like this. Neither he nor Nella knew what else to say or do. And David had one burning question he had wanted to ask Malik from the moment they first spoke.

"Before I go," he said, forcing his voice to stay steady, "I need to know something."

Malik raised an eyebrow.

"You said you knew who I was," David continued. "I believe I deserve to know how you knew that. Are you the one who ransacked my house, the one following us in your car?"

For a moment, Malik didn't answer. He just studied David, a strange expression flickering across his face—between amusement and something darker. Then, he walked over to David and looked him in the eyes and slightly smirked.

"You do deserve an answer," he finally said.

David's pulse skyrocketed.

"Meet me at the Chapel of the Holy Cross," Malik continued, his tone almost playful. "Tomorrow at noon."

Then his eyes flicked past David's shoulder, toward Nella standing behind him.

"And come alone."

A chill ran down David's spine.

Nella stiffened beside him, but she didn't say anything.

David swallowed hard. He wanted to press for more, to demand an explanation *now*, but the look on Malik's face told him that wasn't going to happen.

The conversation was over.

David and Nella turned away, walking back down the hill toward the trailhead in silence. The air was thick and heavy, pressing against them as they moved. When they reached the rental car, David climbed into the driver's seat, gripping the steering wheel tightly. He exhaled slowly, trying to steady himself.

Then, in the rearview mirror, he caught sight of the large sign standing near the entrance to the site.

It was the project announcement.

ALCUBIERRE VORTEX LAND ART – COMING SOON
DESIGNED BY MALIK FARNSWORTH

David's breath hitched. His mind processed the letters almost without thinking, his eyes shifting, refocusing. And then, suddenly, his entire body went cold.

The name in the mirror—backward.

ꓘI⅃AM

His lips parted slightly, the words slipping out before he could stop them.

"Oh my God."

Nella, startled, turned to him. "David, what is it?"

David could barely speak. He lifted a trembling hand and pointed to the rearview mirror.

"Look."

Nella frowned but followed his gaze. She stared at the reflection, her brows furrowing. At first, she didn't see it. Then—

Her eyes widened as realization struck.

She whispered, "No…"

The letters spelled something else in reverse.

KILAM

David couldn't breathe. "Malik's name in reverse reads *Kill him*, Nella. And that's the eighth and final item on the list."

A cold silence filled the car. Nella turned to David, her expression filled with something between fear and disbelief. For so long, they had been trying to decipher the meaning of the list. It had led them from one impossible clue to another. But now, here it was. Clear. Undeniable. This was the answer.

David's head spun. He forced himself to breathe, but that was turning out to be harder as the seconds went by.

"No," she whispered. "We can't."

David's grip tightened on the steering wheel, as if letting go would send him spiraling. He stared at the reflection, the words burning into his mind.

His voice was quiet, almost hollow when he finally spoke. "I don't know anymore."

Nella reached for him, her fingers lightly touching his

arm. "There has to be another way."

David shook his head slowly. "I don't know what to do."

Nella's voice was barely audible. "Are you really going to meet him tomorrow?"

David exhaled, closing his eyes for a moment. Then he nodded.

"Yes."

CHAPTER 18

CHAPEL OF THE HOLY CROSS

David lay on his back, staring at the ceiling of his hotel room. The dim glow from the streetlights outside seeped through the thin curtains, casting long shadows across the walls. The alarm clock on the nightstand read 2:37 a.m. The numbers glowed red, sharp against the darkness. He had been watching the time change for hours, waiting for exhaustion to take over, but his mind refused to rest.

The bed beneath him felt too soft, too unfamiliar. The blanket was tangled around his legs from his restless movements. He turned onto his side, pressing his head into the pillow, but the moment he closed his eyes, his thoughts flooded back—loud, intrusive, unstoppable.

He could still hear the beeping of the hospital machines from that night seven years ago. The shallow breaths of the dying man in the bed. The weight of the crumpled piece of paper as it was forced into his hand. The list. Eight items. Seven had already come true. The final one—the most terrifying one—remained.

David inhaled deeply, staring into the darkness of the room.

Am I really supposed to kill him?

The thought had been circling in his mind ever since he realized what the final words meant. David squeezed his eyes shut, pressing his knuckles into his temples as if that could stop the thoughts from coming. He felt like he was standing at the edge of a cliff, staring down into an endless void. If he let himself fall, would he ever stop falling?

What if this list—this strange prophecy—was real?

Had everything that happened to him been preordained? Had every step he had taken—every choice he had made—led him here, to this exact moment, to this exact night, staring at the ceiling, questioning whether his fate had been written for him all along?

Or had it all been coincidence?

David sat up suddenly, throwing the blanket off. His skin was clammy, and the air in the room felt stifling. He ran a hand through his hair, exhaling sharply.

Coincidences.

There had been too many of them. Too many strange encounters. Too many moments that had led him exactly where he needed to be—whether he had realized it at the time or not. He had been led here for a reason.

He glanced at the alarm clock again. 3:12 a.m. Only a few more hours until sunrise. Only a few more hours until he would face Malik again. Until he would have to decide what kind of man he really was. David lay down, staring at the ceiling once more. He knew sleep would not come.

•••

Despite the sleepless night that had stretched into a restless dawn, morning came anyway, indifferent to David's anxieties. The hours before noon ticked by in a disorienting blur, each minute feeling like it lasted forever. David's thoughts, fragmented and restless, circled endlessly around his impending rendezvous, the high-noon meeting that loomed like a dark storm cloud on the horizon. David gripped the steering wheel tightly as he navigated the narrow, winding road leading up to the Chapel of the Holy Cross. The black asphalt curved sharply, following the natural contours of the tall red rock cliffs. Each turn revealed a new stretch of rugged desert terrain, the kind of landscape that seemed untouched by time.

The morning air was warm but dry, carrying the smell of sandstone and desert sage. Every breath he took was filled with the earthy aroma, a reminder of just how different this place was from the world he had come from.

David kept his eyes on the road, but his mind was elsewhere. He didn't know what he was going to do when he saw Malik. He had followed the list, followed the clues, followed everything that had led him here—but now that he was at the final step, he had no idea what came next.

Another sharp turn. Then suddenly, there it was.

The Chapel of the Holy Cross.

David felt his breath catch in his throat.

The chapel rose from the red rock buttes like an

extension of the earth itself. Its angular walls and huge cross stood in sharp contrast to the rugged, uneven terrain around it. The structure was simple but powerful, a geometric masterpiece nestled into the natural world.

For a moment, he forgot why he was here. His architectural instincts took over. It felt like he had seen this before. Not in person, but perhaps in a classroom, years ago.

David forced himself to keep driving, following the road as it led him higher and higher. The chapel grew larger in his windshield, its cross standing tall against the cloudless sky. He didn't believe in fate. He never had. But as he approached the parking lot, as the weight of the past seven years settled onto his shoulders, he couldn't shake the feeling that he was exactly where he was meant to be.

•••

David stepped out of the car and into the silent heat of the Arizona day. The parking lot was nearly empty, save for a few other vehicles. The only sounds were the soft rustling of the wind against the rocks and the distant murmur of voices from tourists exploring the chapel grounds.

His heart pounded as he made his way toward the entrance. His shoes scuffed against the stone pathway, the sound almost too loud in the quiet. He forced himself to take deep, slow breaths, but no amount of calm thinking could prepare him for what was waiting inside.

As he stepped through the heavy doors, a hushed stillness settled over him. The interior of the chapel was simple yet overwhelming in its presence. A curator wandered past David toward a set of stairs that led to a souvenir shop on a lower level. A row of wooden benches stretched toward the altar, which was bathed in light from the massive windows behind it. The huge bronze crucifix stood at the center, Christ's figure sculpted in haunting detail, his arms outstretched in agony, his head tilted slightly downward.

And there, in the very first pew, sat the man he had come to see—Malik Farnsworth.

David stopped in his tracks.

Malik's head was bowed low, his hands clasped together in front of him. His shoulders were stiff, his posture that of a man who carried a weight too heavy to bear. For a moment, David hesitated. He had thought about this meeting for hours, rehearsed what he would say, tried to prepare himself for every possible scenario. But now that he was here, standing just feet away from the man who was possibly the end of it all, he didn't know what to do.

He took a slow step forward. Then another.

Malik didn't look up.

David moved down the aisle, his footsteps muffled by the smooth stone floor. When he reached the front pew, he carefully lowered himself onto the bench beside Malik.

A long silence stretched between them.

Then, in a whisper so soft it was almost lost in the still air, Malik spoke. "I am glad you came."

David felt a shiver run through him.

"I came to get the answers I seek," David replied. His voice was quiet, but firm.

Malik slowly lifted his head. His face was lined with exhaustion, deep shadows beneath his eyes. He didn't look at David right away. Instead, his gaze moved upward, toward the massive crucifix above the altar.

"Isn't that why everyone comes to a place like this," Malik murmured, "to sit before Jesus in search of the answers they seek?"

David followed his gaze, staring up at the bronze figure of Christ. The outstretched arms, the metal nails driven into his wrists. The pain frozen in time.

"I suppose," David said.

Malik let out a slow breath. "Are you happy, David?"

David blinked at the question. He hadn't expected it.

"Not as happy as I once was," he answered truthfully. Then, after a pause, he added, "But I am healing from the loss of my wife Hannah, each day is better than the last."

Malik nodded slightly, as if he already knew. "Nella seems like a nice gal," he said.

"She is," David said. "She is a good friend... more than a friend."

At this, Malik finally turned his head to look at David. His eyes studied him for a long moment before he turned back toward the crucifix.

"They say this crucifix was designed to symbolize humanity's journey from its fall in the Garden of Eden... to God's intended redemption," Malik said, gesturing at the massive sculpture.

David listened, unsure of where this was going. Malik's voice took on a different tone now—low, almost distant.

"Look at him," he said, his eyes never leaving the

crucifix. "Hanging from the nails in his wrists. Do you know what they did to him? Everyone looks up at him and sees the suffering, the nails, the crown of thorns, the cross. But do you know the whole story, how they described it in the Bible?"

David hesitated. "No," he admitted. "I never read the Bible."

Malik exhaled slowly. When he spoke again, his voice was quieter but carried something darker beneath it.

"They flogged him," he said. "From his shoulders to his legs. The whip they used consisted of several strips of leather. In the middle of the strips were metal balls that hit the skin, causing deep bruising. Sheep bone was attached to the tips of each strip so when the bone made contact with his skin, it dug into his muscles, tearing out chunks of flesh. By that point, he would have lost a great deal of blood and most likely would have succumbed to shock.

"Then the Roman soldiers placed a crown of thorns on his head. They hit him in the skull, and the thorns from the crown pushed into the skin causing him to bleed, damaging the nerve that supplies the face. He would have felt intense pain down his face and neck. They mocked and spat on him, and made him travel over two miles barefoot from Pilate to Herod."

David clenched his jaw. He didn't want to hear more. But at the same time, he couldn't look away.

"Then you have the crucifixion. He was nailed to the cross while lying down. When they nailed his wrists, it probably caused continuous agonizing pain in his arms. Once secured, the guards lifted the cross in place. And as he was lifted, his full weight pulled down on the nailed wrists and his shoulders and elbows dislocated. His feet were nailed through the tops as often pictured. And what did he say after all they did to him? Forgive them!"

David finally found his voice. "Why are you telling me this?"

"Because I want to ask you something important," Malik said.

David just stared at him, waiting for him to continue.

"Can you forgive me, David?" Malik asked.

"I don't understand," David said, his voice barely above a whisper.

"Can you forgive me," he said again, "for giving you up after I lost your mother and sister?"

David's breath hitched and his eyes began to water. His face was frozen in a mask of confusion. "Are you saying you are my real father?"

"Yes, my son. Now can you see why I must go back. I must stop the accident; I have to save our family," Malik explained.

David's mind began racing as images of his life flashed before his eyes. Moments of unusual circumstances began to reconcile in his brain. The occasional feelings of being watched over. *Could it be... could it have been my father watching over me in the shadows?* he wondered.

Then an old memory came to mind. That day in the rain, the figure that had jumped out in front of his car. The figure that had stood watching him in the rain under the blue awning in front of Newbury Studios.

"Many years ago, was that you in front of Newbury

Studios? The day I fell in love with that piece... your own *Geometric Tangent?*" David asked him.

"Yes, David," Malik replied. "When I found out you were attending MIT, I would come around and get a look at you occasionally from a distance. The accident broke me inside. I was supposed to be on that trip with your mother and sister. I wasn't the same after that. The guilt, the resentment... it ate me up. The police said it must have been a drunk driver who drove her off the road. Poor little, Bethany; she had just turned six and was the light of my life. She was killed instantly. But when they pulled your mother out of the wreckage, she was still alive... barely. They did all they could to save her, but she didn't make it. But you did. They performed an emergency cesarean; they were able to save you. See, David, she was eight months pregnant with you, my son. By some miracle, they were able to remove you from your mother's belly before she died."

David was shocked by the news. All that had happened to in his life had led him to this place. "I don't understand. Why was I adopted? Why did you give me up?"

"The accident happened here, in Arizona. It was your mother's dream to see the Grand Canyon. When I got the call, I lost it. I was so distraught, so alone. I couldn't take care of myself, let alone a newborn. The hospital in Flagstaff kept leaving me messages. Then one day, I received legal documents, so I just signed them and moved on. You have to understand, I was a wreck. I had not yet seen your face," Malik explained.

Malik's voice rose as he continued, "But it's okay now.

David, look at me, I can change the past. Today at 5:39 p.m., I promise you I am going back to 1996, back to Route 64. I'm doing this for you, for your mother and for Bethany."

David's thoughts cleared. He reminded himself that he was led to this place, to this time, perhaps to stop his father. For whatever reason, he knew he had to stop his father. "Wait, I need to tell you something."

David pulled a folded piece of paper from his pocket. He unfolded it, revealing the list. "I have been following these clues, these predictions, and they led me to this place, to you. I believe I am supposed to stop you."

Malik looked down at the paper, reading the eight items on the list. He then asked David, "Where did this list come from?"

David looked up and began explaining. "Seven years ago, it was given to me by a man with no name, a John Doe in a hospital who died in my presence. The eighth item is a semordnilap, a word that spells a different word backward. At the time, I thought it read *Kill him*, but now I know it reads Kill am, in reverse it reads *Malik*."

Malik looked at David in anger. "It's just another attempt to stop me! Is that really what you came here to do? Kill me? You're not a killer, David. You're my son. Think about what I have accomplished. I can take away all your pain as well. By going back in time, I can bring back Hannah. I understand your loss, David. I was there that day at the chapel. I heard your eulogy."

David stood, growing angry as well. "You were the man who fled out the exit door! I remember you now.

Don't you understand? This is all in your head! They fucked you up with their *Mr. Owl ate my metal worm* bullshit! You can't change what has already been done. And going back in time wouldn't have stopped Hannah from being struck by that car. You have got to let go of your resentment, your guilt... you need to leave the past in the past."

Malik stood up as well. "I know now how Jesus could take all that pain... all that suffering and still, in the end, love and forgive us. I can, because I would do the same thing for my own family... for those I love. Since the day they died in that accident, I have been nailed to a cross. Look up at him hanging there, do you think he will forgive me for what I am about to do?"

A bitter laugh escaped Malik's lips.

"God sacrificed his only son to atone for the sins of humanity. Where was God when Molly died, Bethany... Hannah? God will not save us. I used science and the powers of the universe and found my own way to get them back... to resurrect the past. Remember what happened after they killed him." Malik pointed up at Jesus on the cross. "Remember... the earth shook, the rocks split apart, the graves broke open, and God's people who had died were risen to life. When the Roman soldiers saw the earthquake and everything else that happened, they were terrified and said, 'He really was the Son of God!'"

David's heart pounded as Malik continued his speech. "When I make the earth shake, and the rocks to split apart... when I raise the dead and save your mother, your sister... what will they call me? Will they call me a God?"

"You asked me if I can forgive you... I can, I do forgive you!" David cried out, his voice raw with a desperate plea.

Malik took a step back, his expression unreadable. "David, it was me. It was always me. I saw you at Hermit Lake. I couldn't understand how you knew to go there. Then I broke into your house and saw the list. Don't you see, David? Someone gave you those clues to stop me, and I had to find a way to stop you from stopping me. But I could tell nothing was going to stop you, so I had to try something else."

"I don't understand. What did you do?" David whispered, his voice barely audible.

"I don't want your forgiveness. I want your resurrection. I want you to be born again in a world without pain and the sins of your father. So, like me, I gave you an intolerable pain. Something you cannot forgive," Malik continued, his voice taking on a chilling intensity. "I killed Hannah... I was the man behind the wheel."

David's breath hitched, a strangled sound in his throat, and his eyes flooded with a molten rage. His face contorted, frozen in a mask of fury.

"Nooo!" he roared, lunging at Malik, his fist connecting with brutal force, sending Malik staggering backward. Malik recovered, stepping back and raising a hand to ward off David's advance.

"Redemption, David," Malik insisted, his tone disturbingly calm. "God sacrificed his only son to atone for the sins of humanity. I did all of this for you, for our family. You can hate this life as I do and embrace the gift I am offering you, the gift to change the past."

David simply stared, his body trembling, an inferno of rage and pain consuming him.

"Can you forgive me, David?" Malik asked, his eyes searching David's.

"No, never!," David cried out, his voice a broken whisper.

Malik retreated further, his gaze unwavering. "Now you are ready for what I am about to do. I love you, son, but don't try and stop me." He then turned abruptly and bolted out of the chapel, leaving David alone in the echoing silence.

David sat frozen for half a second. His mind was still trying to process everything—the confessions, the plan, the madness in Malik's eyes. David couldn't help but realize that his father had gone mad, and that his mind was truly lost.

•••

The hotel room was quiet when David stepped inside. Nella was sitting on the edge of the bed, staring at the floor. When she saw him, she sprang up.

"David!"

Before he could react, she threw her arms around him, holding him tight.

"What happened?" she whispered.

David didn't move. His body felt heavy, his mind still racing from everything that had happened.

"I need to figure out what do next," David mumbled.

"I hope you're not considering killing him," Nella said softly.

David looked at her. "I think I was meant too, but he is my father."

Nella's eyes widened. "Your father?" she cried out in shock.

"Yes, Malik is my father; he told me himself., David said sorrowfully. "He also told me that he was the one who killed Hannah. He was the hit and run driver. You know what, come to think of it, it makes so much sense now. All these years, he has been watching, waiting, and building his time machine. Plotting how he will go back in time and stop the accident that killed my mother and sister. An accident that almost killed me. Trying to figure out how he will change the past. He also somehow thinks it will change the present, bringing back our family. And when he discovered I was on to him, the list and the clues he killed Hannah in hopes that I would accept his diabolical plan and join him on his quest to change the past."

Nella studied him for a long time. Then she said, "David, think about how insane this is. This Alcubierre Drive he built, it has the potential to destroy everything. It's just another one of Frankenstein's monsters. And if it did work, if he could travel to the past, then what? You and I would no longer exist, and everything we know would be different."

"You know, now I wonder if it wouldn't be for the better," David muttered. "What would you change if given the chance?"

Nella knelt down by David and held both his hands, looking deeply into his eyes. "David, listen to me. I wish we could change what happened to Hannah, my father, my brother, your best friend Shawn, but that would also change me and you. Maybe this time you don't survive the accident. Maybe my brother doesn't pull me from the broken ice. Maybe I die and he lives, never going to Iraq. Maybe it is you who takes the dark alley that day from the arcade. Think about it, do you really think if you could time travel... that you would be able to save Hannah? Change what happened? What's done is done."

David stared back at her. "I would be lying if I told you I had not thought about it, I have. I thought to myself, *If I could go back, if I could time travel, what would I do?* And you know what I realized? I realized that if I had the power to go back, the power to change my past..." David began, tears running down his cheeks.

"I know this will probably sound horrible, but if I could go back, I would never have accepted those Red Sox tickets. I would never have entered that pub that night. Knowing what I know now... knowing the horrible pain I endured from her loss... I would never have wanted to feel that way, to feel that gut-wrenching pain that left me feeling hollow and broken inside."

Silence stretched between them. Then Nella took David's hands in hers and pulled him closer.

"Oh, I know, David. I know. I felt that way when Marcus was killed. Even if we had that kind of power, it isn't natural; we aren't supposed to change the past. We are meant to heal. My mother always told me... we're meant to feel pain for the people we lost. How else would we know how important they are to us?"

David rubbed the tears from his eyes. "I see that now.

We can't change the past."

"That's right, we can't take the risk, and don't forget we are still missing one big piece of the puzzle," Nella said.

"Missing one big piece?" David questioned, puzzled.

"Yes. Who was John Doe seven years ago? We know that his list, the one he gave you, was full of clues and predictions of all that has happened. We also know his eighth item was *Kill am...* Malik. Clearly, he wanted you to stop him. Clearly, Malik is the final item on the list!" Nella said excitedly, as if she had finally cracked a huge case.

Hearing Nella say this, David jumped up.

"What is it?" Nella asked, startled.

"It was something he said... something my father said at the chapel when I told him about the list, about item eight. He said, 'It's just another attempt to stop me!' He didn't know who gave me the list, he doesn't know who my John Doe is."

Nella and David both exclaimed in sync, "There are no coincidences, John Doe gave you the list for a reason!"

They stood up quickly, with newfound determination. David's hands trembled as he said, "The list was meant for me to stop him. We must stop him!"

CHAPTER 19
THE ALCUBIERRE DRIVE

David and Nella readied themselves and drove to the Cathedral Rock trailhead. During the drive, David exhaled sharply and glanced at Nella, who sat beside him in the passenger seat. She had been quiet for most of the drive, but he could tell by the way she was gripping the door handle that she was just as tense as he was.

"We're really doing this," David said, his voice low.

Nella turned her head to look at him, her dark eyes filled with a mix of determination and concern. "Yeah," she said. "We are."

"You know... he thinks he's doing the right thing," David murmured, gripping the wheel tighter.

Nella shifted in her seat, pulling her legs up slightly and turning toward him. "David..."

David let out a slow breath and focused on the road

ahead. The turnoff to the Cathedral Rock trailhead was just a few minutes away. Once they got there, they would have to hike up to the construction site where Malik had set up the Alcubierre Drive.

"What is the plan, David?" Nella asked, pulling him out of his thoughts.

"Knowing what he did to Hannah makes me want to kill him, but I have another idea, I think we should sneak into the construction site and find a way to disable the generator. If we can prevent the flow of electricity, then my father won't be able to energize the Alcubierre Drive," David explained. "We don't have to kill him; we just need to stop him from turning on that device."

Nella's voice softened. "Then let's stop him before it's too late."

David swallowed past the lump in his throat and gave her a small nod.

For a moment, silence filled the car. The road stretched ahead, empty and quiet.

Then, in a clear attempt to break the tension, Nella smirked and said, "Who would have known that day you showed up in my lobby, acting a bit shy and uncertain, that we would both end up here? Racing to stop a deranged scientist from using a time machine."

David gave a short, breathy laugh. It wasn't much, but it was enough to lighten the suffocating weight in his chest.

Nella grinned. "I swear, after this, we need a vacation. Somewhere quiet. No chasing clues on a list, no time travel, just beaches and naps."

"I'll hold you to that," David said, shaking his head.

They fell into another brief silence as they approached the turnoff to the Cathedral Rock trailhead. David slowed the car as they pulled into the trailhead parking lot and turned off the engine. Then David exhaled sharply, squared his shoulders, and reached for the door handle. "Let's do this."

Nella nodded, her expression serious once more. "Yeah. Let's go."

They stepped out of the car, the dry desert air hitting them immediately, and with one final glance at each other, they began their hike up the trail toward the Alcubierre Drive. As they approached, they saw Malik working at the generator, the heavy black wires connected from the generator to the ellipse. Around the ellipse were dozens of primers. Suddenly the generator powered to life with a loud rumble, the sound filling the whole area. David and Nella could barely hear each other's voice as they tried to coordinate their plan.

David swallowed hard. This was real. This was happening. Then, his eyes locked onto a figure moving near the generator.

Malik.

His father stood with his back to them, adjusting something on the machine. Even from a distance, David could see how calm he looked—focused, methodical. There was no hesitation in his movements, no second-guessing. He was ready.

David's stomach twisted. His father wasn't acting like a madman. He wasn't ranting or rushing. He was simply doing what he believed had to be done. And that scared David more than anything.

Beside him, Nella leaned in slightly, raising her voice to be heard above the sound but low enough that Malik couldn't hear them. "This is it. We just need to get to the generator."

David and Nella then saw Malik walk up the hill toward the ellipse. David looked at his watch, and noticed the time—5:29 p.m. Speaking over the thunderous sound of the generator, David told Nella to stay hidden, then he tried to move closer.

He made his way to the side of the mobile generator and looked for a way to cut off the fuel supply. He suddenly realized that he would need to open an access panel to see the fuel tank. He pushed against the panel, but it wouldn't budge—it was locked in place by fasteners. David cursed under his breath. He needed a tool, something to pry them open.

His eyes darted around the site, searching for anything useful. The seconds felt like they were slipping away too fast. He could feel his pulse hammering in his chest. David moved frantically, scanning the scattered equipment. There! A small toolbox lay a few feet away, half buried in the dirt. He rushed over, dropping to his knees and flipping it open.

Screwdriver.

Grabbing it, he sprinted back to the generator, wedged the tip under the panel's fasteners, and forced them loose. One by one, they popped free. Finally, the panel swung open with a metallic creak, revealing the resin fuel tank inside. A thick rubber fuel line ran from the base of the tank into the engine. That was it. If he could cut that, the generator would lose its fuel, and the whole thing would shut down.

David reached inside, stretching his fingers toward the fuel line. Too far. He adjusted, leaning in closer, his arm disappearing into the opening. His fingertips brushed against the rubber hose. Almost. But it wasn't enough. He couldn't grip it. Frustration bubbled up inside him. He tried again, straining, but the angle was wrong. His fingers kept slipping off the rubber surface.

He stepped back to see if there was another way to turn off the generator. The small control panel displayed gauges and on and off switches with a timer for energizing the output, but the controls used a toggle key for access. David realized that his only option was to somehow sever the fuel line and hope the fuel drained out before his father energized the Alcubierre Drive.

The noise of the generator's engine was deafening. Suddenly Nella approached him from behind, startling him.

"David! I was trying to get your attention. Your father is coming back down the hill," Nella frantically whisper-shouted.

David's head snapped up. Malik had stopped walking toward the ellipse. Instead, he had turned and was heading back down the hill—toward them. David clenched his jaw. They were out of time. Gritting his teeth, he pointed down through the access panel and told Nella that they needed to cut the fuel line, but he was having trouble reaching it.

"See what you can do. I will go and distract my father," he shouted urgently.

Nella's eyes widened. She wasn't expecting that.

"Are you sure?" she yelled back.

David didn't hesitate. He had to trust her.

"Just do it!"

Then, without another word, he stood and took a deep breath. His heart pounded in his chest, but he forced himself to move. This was it. No more hiding. No more running.

He stepped out from behind the generator, stepping directly into Malik's path. Malik, who had been walking briskly down the hill, stopped in his tracks. For a moment, he looked surprised to see David standing there. His eyes flickered with recognition, then concern. But just as quickly, his face hardened.

"David," Malik said, his voice firm but not unkind. He lifted his wrist and glanced at his watch. "You shouldn't have come. In less than ten minutes, I will be standing inside the ellipse when the Alcubierre Drive energizes and the warp bubble is created. I have no idea what could happen to you if you're too close." He lowered his arm and looked at David with urgency. "You need to leave. Now."

"That's my point, Father. If you turn this thing on, nobody knows what will become of all of us. I came to ask you... to beg you. The list, the clues lead me to this place for a reason; perhaps all of this was meant to simply bring us together, to help you see the pain you have caused," David said. His voice was firm, but his hands were clenched into fists.

Malik took a step forward, closing the distance between David and him, and placed his hands on David's shoulders. "Son, please go… there is no more time to debate this. I must stop what happened and make it right. Tomorrow, when you wake, you will wake in a world where you have your mother, your sister, your father, and Hannah. A world where you will have your family again."

David shook his head. "No. No, Father, you don't understand. All of this has helped me realize I am happy. I have had a good life. The father and mother who raised me, who loved me like a son, have given me so much to be thankful for, to appreciate. If you go back, if you are able to change things, you do it at the cost of the wonderful life I have lived."

Malik paused for a moment, and his expression changed. For the first time, he looked uncertain. His fingers tightened around the watch on his wrist, but he didn't check the time. Instead, he looked at David, really looked at him.

•••

Nella's hands shook as she reached into the open panel of the generator. The metal edges of the opening pressed against her arms, but she ignored the discomfort. The fuel line. It was right there, but no matter how much she stretched, she couldn't reach it. Her fingers brushed against the rubber tube, but it was just out of her grasp.

She gritted her teeth. "Come on, come on…" she muttered under her breath.

Her arms ached as she tried again, forcing herself deeper into the panel. The resin fuel tank sat above the line, smooth and solid, while the black rubber hose snaked down below it. If she could just grab it—pull it, twist it, anything—she could cut off the fuel and stop the generator.

But it was too far.

Frustration bubbled inside her. She pulled her arm out and looked around desperately. *Think. There has to be something,* she thought to herself.

Her eyes darted across the construction site, searching for anything she could use. That was when she spotted it— a shovel—half buried in the dirt a few feet away.

Without hesitation, she lunged for it, wrapping her hands around the wooden handle. It was heavier than she'd expected, but she ignored the weight and hurried back to the generator.

Her breath was quick and uneven as she forced the head of the shovel into the opening. Carefully, she angled it downward, sliding it into the tight space near the fuel line. The smooth metal edge pressed against the rubber tube.

Nella gripped the handle tightly.

And slammed it down.

The impact sent a sharp vibration up her arms, the force jarring her shoulders. The fuel line held.

She cursed under her breath and struck it again. And again.

Each hit echoed through the machine, but the rubber refused to break. The sweat on her hands made the wooden handle slick, but she adjusted her grip and slammed it down harder.

Crack.

The rubber split.

For half a second, there was silence. Then—gasoline burst out of the broken line.

Nella stumbled back as the liquid poured from the fuel tank, gushing out in a thick stream. The smell was overpowering, sharp and pungent. The fuel spread quickly, soaking into the dirt and running downhill away from the generator.

Her heart pounded in her chest. She had done it.

•••

Malik's moment of deep thought was interrupted by the smell of the gasoline. He looked up and realized what Nella had done. David turned and took notice as well.

"Damn it!" Malik's voice cut through the roar of the generator. Frustrated, he once again looked down at his watch, and saw that the time was now 5:35 p.m. He turned back to David, his face twisted in rage as he took in the sight of the spilling fuel.

"You are not going to stop me!" He shouted.

With that, Malik began hurrying back up the hill toward the ellipse. Seeing this, David quickly chased after his father, intent on stopping him. Upon reaching him, and with all the force he could gather, David threw himself forward, colliding into his father's back. The impact sent both men crashing to the ground, their bodies twisting as they tumbled down the rocky hillside. Dust exploded around them as they rolled, jagged stones scraping against their skin.

Malik grunted in pain but fought to regain control. He twisted his body, trying to throw David off, but David held on, his arms locked around his father's torso. "Stop! Just stop!" David yelled, his voice raw with desperation.

Malik didn't answer. He only fought harder.

They rolled over a sharp rock, and David let out a pained gasp as the impact sent a shock through his ribs. His grip loosened for a split second—enough for Malik to shove him off.

David hit the ground hard, the breath knocked from his lungs. He barely had time to react before Malik was on top of him, his hands grabbing at David's shoulders, trying to push him aside so he could stand.

David refused to let go.

He tightened his grip, wrapping his arms around Malik's waist and pulling him back down. They struggled in the dirt, both gasping for air. Malik fought with all his strength, pushing, clawing, kicking. David held on, gritting his teeth through the pain.

Then—a sudden blow.

Malik's fist slammed into David's ribs, forcing a sharp cry from his lips. David's body curled inward from the impact, but he still didn't let go. He clenched his jaw, ignoring the pain, and tried to wrestle his father back to the ground.

"You're not doing this!" David yelled, his voice hoarse.

"David, stop! I must do this!" Malik cried out.

"No, Father, I must stop you!" David yelled back.

Malik thrashed beneath him. He was running out of time. He knew it. David could see the panic flicker across his face. He needed to reach the ellipse, but David couldn't let him. Malik's breathing was heavy, his chest rising and falling in sharp bursts. Then, for a brief second, he hesitated—his gaze darting to his watch.

5:38 p.m.

Malik's eyes widened and a look of cold determination crossed his face. He did the only thing he thought was best for a man obsessed with the need to change the past.

He raised his fist, shooting forward.

The punch landed hard against David's face. A blinding pain ripped through his skull and the world spun. David's grip weakened as his arms went slack.

Malik pulled free.

David's body slumped against the ground. His vision blurred, the sounds around him fading. He tried to move— to stop his father—but his body refused to listen. Through the haze, he heard Malik's voice.

Low. Breathless. Almost a whisper.

"I will see you on the other side, my son."

Then—footsteps.

Malik was gone.

•••

Malik stumbled forward, breathing heavily, his body aching from the struggle. His legs felt unsteady, but he forced himself to move. He had no time to hesitate. The ellipse was just ahead. The moment he stepped inside, everything would change.

His watch read 5:39 p.m.

With a final push, Malik crossed the threshold. At that exact moment, the generator's timer reached zero. A deep, mechanical click echoed through the air. Then—the surge. 66,000 volts of raw electricity shot through the thick black cables. A deafening crack split the sky as sparks exploded from the generator. The energy surged up the hillside, racing toward the primers surrounding the ellipse.

•••

David felt a sharp pressure on his shoulder. A hand was gripping him tightly, shaking him.

"David, get up... get up!"

His eyes fluttered open. His head throbbed. The world around him blurred and spun. He barely registered what was happening before he heard Nella's voice again, more urgent this time.

"We need to get out of here! He has activated the Alcubierre Drive."

Her panicked face came into view, her eyes wide with fear. She pulled at his arm, trying to drag him up. She succeeded and pulled him forward, their feet pounding against the rocky ground as they ran down the hill.

As they neared the generator, David's heart stopped. A river of spilled fuel ran down the hill, and at its source— flames. Sparks from the overloaded generator had ignited the gasoline. The fire raced across the ground, crawling toward the generator's base.

David's body tensed. This wasn't just a malfunction anymore. It was about to explode.

He tightly grabbed Nella's hand, now fully aware of the situation.

"Run! This thing is gonna blow!" he yelled.

As they tried to get as far away from the area as possible, a bright light began glowing from the Alcubierre Drive, and a strong wind current began as well. The humming grew louder and louder as the Alcubierre Drive spun faster and faster. The inside of the ellipse distorted in color, and a ball of energy began forming in its center—a bubble, with Malik inside. Both the Alcubierre Drive and the warp bubble grew brighter and brighter, turning into a storm of energy. Lightning bolts radiated outward, and the color of the sky and hillside became distorted, the hum sound becoming more deafening.

"There!" Nella shouted, pointing ahead.

David followed her gaze. A massive rock formation rose up from the hillside, jagged and uneven. Between two boulders, a narrow crevice cut through the stone.

A place to hide.

David didn't hesitate. He pulled Nella with him as they ran toward the opening. The wind was howling now, whipping dirt and debris across their skin. The light from the Alcubierre Drive had become blinding, flickering like a storm of electricity.

David reached the rock crevice first, pressing Nella inside. The stone was cold, rough, barely wide enough for them both. David then squeezed in beside her, their bodies pressed tightly together.

David wrapped his arms around her, trying to shield her from whatever was about to happen. The wind screamed past the rocks. The light flashed wildly and the ground rumbled beneath them.

Then—the sound of an explosion.

The blast ripped through the air, sending metal and debris flying in all directions. Shattered pieces of the machine tumbled down the hill, crashing into the rocks. Then came the final moment. A sound like tearing fabric.

A flash of white light so bright it burned into David's vision.

Then—silence.

Everything stopped.

No hum. No fire. No wind.

Just silence.

David's breath was shaky. His arms were still locked around Nella, her face pressed against his chest.

Slowly, he opened his eyes, Nella following suit. They could no longer see the brightness from the Alcubierre Drive.

"David…" Nella's voice was barely a whisper.

He turned to her. Her eyes were wide, her face streaked with dirt. She looked afraid to move, afraid to step out and see what was left.

David swallowed hard. "Come on." His voice was hoarse.

Carefully, they untangled themselves from the rock crevice and stepped out. The ground beneath them was coated in ash and scattered debris. Pieces of metal from the generator lay twisted and broken, half buried in the dirt.

David's eyes slowly traveled up the hill.

His breath caught in his throat.

The ellipse was gone.

Not just destroyed—gone.

There was no wreckage, no frame, no remnants of the Alcubierre Drive. The space where it had been was now just empty ground, disturbed only by the explosion's aftermath.

Malik was gone too. No body. No sign of him at all.

David and Nella stood frozen, staring at the empty space. The only sound was the soft crackling of dying embers around them.

"Do you think that it actually worked?" Nella finally asked, her voice barely more than a breath.

David couldn't answer. His mind was spinning. Malik was gone. The Alcubierre Drive was gone. *But did that mean the timeline had changed? Or had something else happened?*

He shook his head slowly. "I don't know."

Nella turned to him, searching his face for answers he didn't have.

David let out a long, unsteady breath. "But at least... we're still here."

For the first time since the chaos started, David felt the weight of everything hit him at once. His body sagged with exhaustion. His chest felt tight. Did he stop his father—and if so, at what cost?

Nella stepped closer, wrapping her arms around him. David didn't hesitate. He held her tightly, feeling the warmth of her presence, the reassurance that they had made it through.

Neither of them spoke.

They just stood there, holding onto each other, knowing that after everything they had seen, everything they had done—nothing would ever be the same.

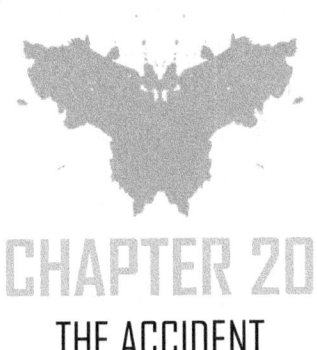

CHAPTER 20

THE ACCIDENT

A soft glow filled the small bedroom, creating warm, pink hues across the walls. The light came from a small lamp shaped like a rabbit, its ears stretching toward the ceiling. The room was neat but filled with signs of a child's world—stuffed animals resting against pillows, a collection of dolls lined up on a white wooden shelf, and a few stray crayons left on a tiny desk near the window.

The air smelled of lavender, a lingering scent from the bubble bath taken just before bedtime. It mixed with the faint aroma of fabric softener from the fresh sheets, creating a comforting sense of warmth. A slow, rhythmic ticking filled the quiet room—the sound of a small, round clock sitting on the nightstand beside the bed. Underneath it, a music box sat half open, releasing a soft, delicate tune that drifted through the air like a lullaby.

Near the bookcase, a little girl aged six stood, her small fingers brushing along the edges of colorful book spines. She was barefoot, her pink nightgown reaching just below her knees. Her dark brown curls were still damp from her bath, clinging slightly to the sides of her face.

"This one, Daddy!" The girl's voice was bright and filled with excitement as she pulled a book from the shelf. She turned, holding it up for her father to see. The cover was slightly worn, its corners softened by years of being held in small hands.

The man sat in a plush pink armchair near the bed, his legs stretched out in front of him. He smiled as the little girl ran to him, her tiny feet barely making a sound against the soft carpet. As she climbed onto his lap, he caught the scent of her lavender-scented shampoo. She curled against him, pressing her warm body into his chest as she handed him the book.

"This is one of my favorite stories," the girl said, flipping through the pages with small, eager hands.

The man ran his palm over the cover, feeling the slightly raised letters beneath his fingertips. *Alice in Wonderland.* He knew this book well. They had read it countless times, but the little girl always asked for the same part.

He watched her for a moment, taking in every detail—the way her fingers twisted a loose curl of her hair, the way she tucked her legs up, pressing her tiny toes against his thigh. She was so content, so safe, so unaware of anything outside this little world they had created together.

From the doorway, a voice interrupted the moment.

"It's bedtime, Bethany."

The man glanced up to see a woman standing there. She leaned against the doorframe, one hand resting on her round belly. She was glowing, her pregnancy nearly full-term. The soft fabric of her nightgown draped over her form, and her free hand smoothed over the curve of her stomach in an unconscious, gentle motion.

"I know, Mommy," Bethany replied, her voice filled with the casual certainty of a child who believed bedtime could be delayed just a little longer. "Daddy is almost done with the story."

The woman smiled faintly but didn't argue. She gave the man a knowing look before stepping away, leaving them in the warm cocoon of the bedroom once again.

Bethany turned the pages with purpose, stopping at Chapter 6.

"A Mad Tea Party," the man read aloud, his voice soft and firm.

Bethany rested her head against his chest, her small fingers still twisting her hair. The man began reading, his voice moving through the words, bringing them to life.

"If I had a world of my own, everything would be nonsense. Nothing would be what it is because everything would be what it isn't. And contrary wise, what is, it wouldn't be. And what it wouldn't be, it would."

Bethany giggled, the kind of giggle that only came from pure happiness. She lifted her head, her wide eyes shining as she looked up at her father.

"If I had a world of my own," she whispered, her voice soft but filled with certainty, "I would always be six years old."

The man felt something tighten in his chest. He swallowed, holding the little girl, Bethany, a little closer.

Then, something shifted.

The warmth around him began to fade.

Bethany's voice, still so close, seemed to stretch, slowing into something distant and distorted. Her face blurred, her features dissolving into soft, fading colors. The pink walls darkened, the soft glow of the rabbit lamp dimming until it flickered out completely. The music box slowed, its melody warping into a deep hum before vanishing entirely.

Malik tried to hold onto the moment, to pull Bethany back into focus, but she was slipping away. The book in his hands became unreadable—the letters on the page twisting and shifting before melting into darkness.

The warmth of Bethany's body against him disappeared.

The armchair beneath him vanished.

The scent of lavender, of home—gone.

Everything was gone.

Malik's eyes shot open.

Above him, the dark sky stretched out, filled with stars. The air was sharp against his skin, and beneath him, rough gravel dug into his palms. He was no longer in a warm, pink bedroom.

He was outside.

Alone.

He lifted himself up and noticed that he was standing on the edge of a hillside surrounded by red rocks. He turned in a slow circle, scanning the landscape, searching for something—anything—that would confirm what he was seeing. His breathing grew heavier, his hands trembling.

Then his eyes landed on the place where the ellipse had been. There was no sign of his work. It was as if it had never existed.

Did I make it? Am I in the past? he wondered.

He looked down at his wrist, his fingers fumbling to check his watch. The screen was frozen.

5:39 p.m.

Malik stared at the unmoving numbers, his breath coming in short bursts. His mind raced. *Was the watch broken? Had it stopped because of the time travel?*

His throat felt dry.

He needed to be sure.

Malik turned toward the trail leading down the hillside. His muscles tensed as he pushed forward, breaking into a run. The uneven dirt path was familiar beneath his feet— he had walked this way many times before. But this time was different. This time, every second mattered.

The cold air stung his face as he ran. His breath came in sharp bursts, his lungs burning. His feet pounded against the earth, kicking up dust with every step. When he finally reached the trailhead, the parking lot stretched out before him, empty except for a single car parked near the edge.

Near the car, an older woman walked her dog along the gravel shoulder of the lot. She was bundled in a light jacket, her posture relaxed as she slowly moved along the edge of the desert. The small dog trotted beside her, its leash hanging loosely in her grip.

Malik's stomach tightened.

He had to know.

The pounding in his chest grew heavier as he stumbled forward. His throat was dry, his voice raw from exhaustion, but he forced the words out anyway.

"Excuse me!"

The woman flinched. She turned, her grip tightening on the leash as she took in the sight of him. Malik saw the fear in her eyes immediately. He knew what he looked like—his clothes were wrinkled and filthy, his hair and beard unkempt. He had the look of someone who had been lost in the wilderness for days, a man out of place and desperate.

The woman didn't respond right away. Her hand gripped the leash tighter, pulling her small dog closer to her side. She glanced toward her car, a clear sign that she was already thinking of leaving.

Malik raised his hands slightly, trying to show he meant no harm.

"Please," he said, his voice shaky from both exhaustion and urgency. "I—I got lost in the desert. I just need to know the time... and the date. Please."

The woman hesitated. Her expression was cautious, but she answered, keeping her distance.

"It's around 6:45 p.m.," she said, her voice uncertain.

It wasn't enough. Malik needed more. His pulse quickened as he took a step closer.

"No, I mean the date," he said, his voice rising with desperation. "What's the date today?"

The woman stiffened. She took a step back.

"I think you should sit down," she said carefully. "I can get someone to help you."

Panic gripped Malik's chest. He could feel time slipping away. He didn't have time for this—he needed answers, and he needed to move.

"Please," he said again, more forcefully this time. His breathing was unsteady. "Just tell me the date. I swear I won't hurt you. I just need to know the date."

The woman's face paled. She took another step back, reaching for the car door.

Malik's heart pounded. She was going to leave. She was going to get in that car, drive away, and take with her the time he didn't have.

Without thinking, he lunged forward and grabbed her wrist before she could open the door, snatching the car keys from her hands.

The woman screamed.

Her dog barked wildly, straining against the leash as she struggled to pull away.

"Please!" Malik begged, gripping her wrist just tight enough to keep her from escaping. "Just tell me what date it is!"

Terror filled the woman's wide eyes. Her breathing was quick and shallow, her free hand shaking as she tried to pull away.

"October 13th!" she blurted out, her voice high with fear. "Sunday, October 13th!"

But he needed more.

"The year," he rasped. "What year is it?"

The woman's lips trembled. She was shaking. Malik could feel her pulse racing beneath his grip.

"1996," she whispered.

Malik's grip loosened. The words hit him like a shock wave, and he swallowed hard. His chest ached from the rapid beating of his heart.

He had made it. He was in the past.

Malik then let go of her, and the woman stumbled back, clutching her wrist as she gasped for breath.

"I'm sorry," he said quickly, his voice barely above a whisper. "I'm so sorry."

But he had no time to explain. His eyes flicked to the car. Without thinking, rushed to the driver's side.

"No!" she screamed.

Malik hesitated. He knew what he was doing was wrong. But he also knew what was at stake.

His family.

His wife.

His daughter.

He clenched his jaw, pushed down the guilt, and threw himself into the car. The woman's screams filled the air as he turned the key. The engine roared to life.

"I'm sorry," he muttered again, but he didn't look back.

He slammed his foot down on the gas pedal. The tires screeched against the pavement as he tore out of the parking lot and onto the open road, moving north, toward the Grand Canyon. All that mattered now was getting to Route 64 before 9:20 p.m.

•••

The road stretched endlessly before him, a ribbon of

asphalt cutting through the dark expanse of the Arizona desert. Malik's hands gripped the steering wheel so tightly his knuckles turned white. His heart pounded against his ribs, the adrenaline coursing through his veins as he pressed his foot harder against the gas pedal. The speedometer crept past 80 miles per hour.

The car rumbled beneath him, the engine straining as it tore through the open highway. The world outside was huge and empty, the desert stretching out in all directions, its sharp-edged cliffs and scattered rock formations barely visible in the dim glow of the moon. The only other lights came from his headlights, cutting through the darkness like a knife. The isolation was suffocating.

Malik's thoughts swirled in his head, a chaotic storm of fear, hope, and desperation.

What if I'm too late?

He clenched his jaw. He couldn't afford to think like that. He had made it back. That had to mean something. But doubt clawed at the edges of his mind, whispering that he might have miscalculated, that time had already sealed their fate.

No. I won't accept that. I can fix this. I have to.

He knew that the accident that had killed his wife and daughter had occurred at the Dead Indian Canyon bridge on Route 64 at approximately 9:20 p.m. He had calculated that he'd arrive somewhere around 9:00 p.m. And he knew he was already cutting it close as it was.

As the hours past, the road signs blurred past him in the night, each one a marker, a reminder of how close he was getting.

Cameron—15 Miles

His fingers tightened around the wheel.

Route 64—Grand Canyon—10 Miles

His stomach twisted into a knot. The turnoff was coming. He was getting closer.

For the first time, a flicker of hope sparked in his chest. Maybe—just maybe—he was going to make it.

His foot pressed harder against the accelerator. Then, up ahead, he saw some bright lights, not those from an incoming car, but rather, a gas station mini mart. He slowed a bit, giving himself the chance to survey the parking lot. It had been miles since he had seen much of anything, besides the occasional passing of a car going in the opposite direction.

As he cruised past the gas station, his eyes widened in utter shock. There, at the gas pump stood his wife, Molly. His vision blurred at the edges as his body reacted before his mind could catch up. His foot slammed against the brake pedal, the tires screeching in protest as the car swerved. His whole body jerked forward as he fought to control the wheel.

He did a sharp U-turn and went back to the gas station. The car flew into the parking lot and came to an abrupt stop, then Malik jumped out. He saw Molly, as beautiful as ever, her belly showing her nearly full-term pregnancy. She had just finished pumping gas and had already begun climbing back in the driver's seat of the car.
Malik ran to the side of the vehicle and began banging on the window.

"Molly, Molly!" he hollered, his voice coming out

desperate and raw.

Molly's face snapped up and panic set in. She had no clue who the man screaming and banging on her window was, and he looked nothing like the 30-year-old husband waiting for her in Boston. Even little Bethany whimpered in the backseat, curling up against the door, her wide eyes darting between her mother and the strange man.

Suddenly, the engine roared to life. Before he could react, the car lurched forward, tires screeching against the pavement. Malik stumbled backward, barely avoiding getting hit as Molly's car sped toward the road.

His heart pounded.

No, no, no! This wasn't how it was supposed to happen!

Out the rearview window, he could see his beautiful Bethany looking back with fear in her eyes. Malik raced back to his car, his hands fumbling to yank open the door. His body was running on instinct. There was no time to think. No time to question. He had to stop her.

He threw himself into the driver's seat and turned the key. The engine growled, and he slammed his foot onto the gas pedal. The tires spun for a second before catching the pavement, launching the car forward and chasing Molly down the road.

Molly, scared and determined to escape the strange man chasing her and her daughter, drove faster. Malik, equally determined to get Molly's attention and stop the impending accident, floored it too. Neither of them were aware of the impending fate they were both barreling toward.

Malik pushed harder on the gas, inching closer until he

was side by side with her. He rolled down the window, the night air slamming into his face.

"Molly!" he shouted, his voice ripping through the wind. "Pull over! Please, just stop!"

Inside the car, Molly's hands were clenched around the wheel, her body stiff with panic. She drove faster. Malik waved his hands frantically. "Please, just pull over! I just want to talk! It's okay! I swear, it's okay! It's me, Malik!"

For a split second, Molly turned her head and their eyes met. Malik saw the fear in his wife's and daughter's eyes. And all she saw was a madman. A filthy, desperate stranger chasing her in the middle of nowhere. She didn't know that he was trying to save them, that he wanted them to be reunited as a family again. She wasn't aware of the permanent consequences of what was about to happen.

Just then, she gasped and yanked the wheel.

The car veered too hard to the right. A cloud of dust exploded into the air as her tires hit loose gravel. The back end of the car skidded sideways. Her taillights swung wildly, red streaks flashing in Malik's vision. Then—

The guardrail.

Molly's tires clipped the edge of the pavement. The car jolted violently. For a moment, it looked like she might regain control—

But then the front wheels went over.

Time seemed to freeze. The car tipped forward, the headlights suddenly pointing downward. Then, in an instant, it disappeared.

Gone. Vanished into the darkness below.

Malik slammed his foot onto the brakes. His car

skidded sideways, the tires screeching against the asphalt. A thick cloud of dust swallowed everything, making it impossible to see.

His heart pounded against his ribs.

"No, no, no, no—"

He flung the door open and stumbled onto the road, his legs almost giving out beneath him. He ran to the edge of the canyon, barely able to see through the swirling dust. Far below, the glow of headlights flickered weakly in the darkness. The shape of the car was barely visible, crumpled against the rocky slope.

"No, no, what have I done?" he howled, falling to his knees. Suddenly, memories and flashbacks crashed over him all at once as he began making sense of what he had previously been ignoring in his obsession to go back and change the past.

The flashback of the Chapel of the Holy Cross loomed in his mind, a stark, red silhouette against the bruised desert sky. David's voice, a ghost in the echoing silence, resonated with chilling clarity. "Seven years ago, it was given to me by a man with no name, a John Doe in a hospital who died in my presence. The eighth item is a semordnilap, a word that spells a different word backward. At the time, I thought it read *Kill him*, but now I know it reads *Kill am*, and in reverse, it reads *Malik*." The word, a venomous whisper, coiled in his gut, a cold, hard truth he'd tried to bury. *When did I become the monster?*

Another memory surfaced, of the moment on the hillside, David's face illuminated by the fading sun. "Father, you don't understand, all of this has helped me realize I am happy, I have had a good life. The father and mother who raised me, who loved me like a son, gave me so much to be thankful for, to appreciate. If you go back, if you are able to change things, you do it at the cost of the wonderful life I have lived." The plea, a desperate, fragile thing, now felt like a curse.

He reminded himself of the words he had been told over the years, how the past was the past, and how one must let go of the pain and resentment. How one couldn't change what had already been done. Malik's mind filled with the mathematical equations he once thought he had solved, realizing that his time machine was nothing more than an invariant loop, never changing.

Finally, the flashbacks ended and he concluded that everything must end right there and then. Malik stood at the edge of the canyon, stepping over the guard rail and readying himself. His eyes lifted from the wreckage, looking out at the empty road, east. In the distance, a set of headlights was approaching, cutting through the darkness.

Help was coming. It was most likely the good Samaritan who had called first responders, the same responders who had ended up saving his son David. The wind was colder here, stronger, pushing against him as if trying to hold him back. He looked down one last time, and murmured, "A man looks into the abyss... in that moment, the man finds his character." Then he remembered his daughter's words the last time he saw her, the last time he read her a bedtime story.

He closed his eye s as he remembered the moment,

Bethany in her pink room, looking up at him from where she sat in his lap, smiling and content. He remembered the words she had once whispered.

"If I had a world of my own, I would always be six years old!"

His lips parted, his voice barely more than a whisper.

"If I had a world of my own, I would always want you to be in it."

And then—

He jumped off the edge, falling to his death below.

CHAPTER 21
THERE ARE NO COINCIDENCES

David and Nella returned from Arizona, stepping back into the familiar world they had always known. The streets looked the same. The buildings stood where they had always been. Nothing seemed out of place. Yet both of them carried the weight of something invisible, something the world around them could never understand.

As soon as they got home, they made their phone calls. Nella dialed her mother, listening carefully to her voice, searching for any sign that things had changed. There was none. Her mother spoke as she always did, unaware of the strange journey her daughter had just taken. David called his adoptive parents. They sounded exactly the same. No shifts in their words, no hesitation in their memories.

The timeline had not changed.

And yet, Malik was gone.

They had watched him disappear. The machine had roared to life, its deafening hum filling the air. Then came the blinding flash of light, swallowing him whole. And then… nothing. No sign of where he had gone. No proof of whether he had succeeded or failed. Only the silence that followed.

The rest of the day passed in a strange, quiet tension. David and Nella didn't talk much about what had happened, but every glance they exchanged carried the weight of it. They had seen something that defied reason, something that had once seemed impossible. But now, they were back in their normal world, where things like time travel were supposed to be fiction.

David tried to accept what that meant. If their world was unchanged, then Malik must not have been able to alter the past. If he had, wouldn't something feel different? Wouldn't something be missing or added? But everything was exactly as it had been.

He had to face the truth: His father had failed. His mother, Hannah, his sister, they were still gone. They had never come back. Nella's brother was still dead, and her father remained in prison. The people they had lost were still lost.

•••

That evening, David lay on his bed, staring at the ceiling, but his mind refused to rest. His thoughts kept circling back to the list. The eight clues. Each one had led him somewhere—Hermit Lake, Mae, the strange trail of secrets he had followed. There were so many possibilities, and so many unanswered questions. *Who was John Doe? Was there more to Paul Miller, with their shared love of architecture, lake houses, and MIT?*

There are no coincidences. The phrase echoed in his thoughts.

David closed his eyes, the memory of John Doe burning in his mind. Thin, hollow cheeks. Yellowed skin stretched over fragile bones, A hairless head and age spots marking his frail body. The way his breath rattled in his chest. The way his weak voice had spoken those final words, listing the eight items as if they meant everything.

David tried to recall every detail. The fleeting glance into those eyes. Had he seen those eyes before? Something about them felt familiar. Not just in the way all people sometimes resembled each other, but in a deeper way. A way that made his stomach tighten with unease.

Then a thought struck him.

Paul Miller.

Could it be? Were those perhaps Paul Miller's eyes? Had Paul been the one to send him on this path? To Hermit Lake? To Mae? To the truth? The thought made his heart pound.

But then, an even more unsettling idea formed.

What if it wasn't Paul? What if the dying man had been someone even closer?

The realization sent a shiver down his spine. The resemblance, the way the clues had been left for him to find... could it be possible? Could those fading eyes have been his own? Had he, somehow, in another timeline, sent himself on this mission? Had he tried to stop his father before?

It was impossible. And yet, the idea wouldn't leave him.

David sat up, running a hand over his face. His thoughts were spiraling. He needed answers. And there was only one person who might have them.

Mae.

If anyone could help him figure out the truth, it was her. He needed to see Mae. He needed to look into her eyes and find out, once and for all—

Who was John Doe?

•••

David had wanted to bring Nella to the lake house for a long time. He realized that he was now ready to introduce her to Mae. Through everything they had been through together—the fear, the danger, the heartbreak—this place had remained separate, untouched by all of it. But now, the time felt right. Their bond had grown strong, built on trust, on shared struggles, on understanding. He was ready for her to see this part of his life.

They arrived late on a Friday evening, just as the last light of the day faded behind the trees. The cottage sat quietly by the water, its windows glowing faintly in the dusk. It looked exactly as David remembered—calm, and unchanged.

Mae was nowhere in sight. The main house was dark, its windows reflecting only the stillness of the lake. She had likely already gone to bed.

Inside the cottage, Nella glanced around, taking in the small but cozy space. Her eyes landed on the single bed.

"I can take the sofa," she said, her voice light but

unsure.

David met her gaze, something quiet and certain in his expression. He stepped closer, his voice barely above a whisper.

"I'd rather we share."

Nella's hesitation melted away, her breath hitching as his fingers traced the curve of her jaw. She had waited for this—for the certainty in his eyes, for the way his body pressed against hers, leaving no room for doubt. He wanted her, needed her, just as fiercely as she ached for him. With a slow, deliberate nod, she parted her lips, a knowing smile curling at the edges before their mouths finally crashed together.

The first touch was electric—soft at first, testing, then deeper, hungrier. His tongue slid against hers, coaxing a moan from her throat as her hands tangled in his hair, pulling him closer. Words were useless now; the scrape of his teeth on her lower lip, the way his hands gripped her hips, told her everything.

What began as a gentle kiss became something desperate, consuming. His fingers found the edge of her shirt, dragging it up as she arched into his touch, skin burning where he explored. She felt the wetness form between her legs, the touch of his fingers as they followed the heat of her growing passion. Then his fingers found her…there was no hiding what he was doing to her as they slipped inside. Clothes fell away in impatient tugs, fabric pooling at their feet until there was nothing left between them but heat and want.

His mouth fell open when her hand found his erection,

taking it firmly in her grip, a clear desire for him to be inside her. She gasped as his hands gripped her thighs, lifting her, pressing her back against the bed. His mouth trailed down her neck, teeth grazing her collarbone before closing over a peaked nipple, drawing a shuddering cry from her. Every touch was a promise—no more hesitation, no more waiting.

She opened her legs, and he lay on top of her, a moment of longing she had almost forgotten. He slid inside her, slow and easy. Nella wrapped her feet around his back, drawing her arms outward above her head, stretching them across the bed. She wanted it as badly as he did, and she wanted it to last—letting her body and mind absorb the intense pleasure of his dominance.

Their bodies moved together in a rhythm as old as time, skin slick with sweat, breaths ragged. He filled her completely, each thrust drawing them deeper into the fire between them. Her nails scored his back as pleasure coiled tight in her core, his name a broken chant on her lips.

That night, they loved each other with the raw, unfiltered hunger of two people who had fought for the right to take, to give, to lose themselves in each other without restraint. And when the world finally shattered around them, they clung to one another, breathless, knowing nothing had ever felt more right.

CHAPTER 22

INVARIANT

Morning came softly. Sunlight slipped through the thin curtains, casting golden lines across the bed. The air smelled of fresh earth and lake water. Birds chirped somewhere nearby, their calls blending with the soft rustling of leaves.

David stretched, his arm still wrapped around Nella. He turned his head to look at her, finding her already awake, smiling to herself.

He smirked. "What's so funny?"

Nella giggled, pulling the blanket over her face for a moment before peeking out. "Just happy."

David raised an eyebrow. "I bet."

Nella rolled her eyes and grinned. She leaned in and kissed him again, pressing quick, playful pecks all over his face.

"Smart ass," she teased. "I mean it. I'm happy to be here. Happy that things stayed the same."

David's fingers traced lazy circles against her arm. "Me too, beautiful."

They stayed in bed a little longer, letting the morning pass slowly, unhurried. But eventually, they got out of bed for coffee, and with warm mugs in hand, they stepped out onto the deck.

The lake stretched wide before them, calm and glassy. It reflected the trees, the sky, the rising sun—an unbroken mirror of the world above.

David exhaled, steadying himself.

"It's time, are you ready?" he murmured.

Nella turned to him, her expression gentle but certain. She reached for his hand, squeezing it. "Go talk to her alone," she said. "I've found my answers." She placed her other hand over his chest, feeling his heartbeat beneath her palm. "This is your moment to get the final answer you seek. I'll be here when you're done."

David studied her for a moment, then nodded. He pulled her into a brief but strong embrace before turning toward the main house.

He knocked on the patio door. The kitchen lights were on, but the room was empty.

"Mae?" he called, stepping inside. His footsteps echoed in the quiet as he moved toward the kitchen. No answer.

Then, outside, the faint sound of a car rolling to a stop drew his attention. As he tuned back,, his eyes were drawn to the framed piece of abstract art hung on the wall. He had seen it before—a single ink blot, dark and shapeless, a mess of random patterns. Except now... it wasn't just a mess.

It was an owl. Wings spread wide.

David's breath caught.

It had been there all along. Hidden in plain sight. And in the corner of the painting, a signature. *Malik Farnsworth.*

David's chest tightened. The whisper of a sliding door pulled him from his thoughts. Cool air brushed against his skin as the patio door eased open.

David turned.

A woman stepped into the room, her dark hair framing a face nearing fifty, a quiet intensity radiated from her. Her presence filling the space like a quiet storm. He looked at her, and something inside him jolted—like a memory trying to surface, like déjà vu gripping him in its invisible hands.

He knew this face. But at the same time... he didn't.

David blinked, trying to shake the feeling, but it clung to him. His mind scrambled for an explanation, for context, for reason. But the familiarity faded just as quickly as it had come.

He was standing in front of a stranger.

"Excuse me," he said, clearing his throat. "I'm sorry, I was just looking for Mae."

The woman smiled, gentle but knowing.

"David," she said softly.

He froze.

Then, she spoke again.

"It's me, Mae."

The words hit David like a physical blow, leaving him momentarily stunned. His gaze dropped, and he felt a wave of heat and then cold washing over him. Mae's fingers curled around his, grounding him.

"You're not alone," she murmured, pulling him toward a chair. "I understand more than you think what a shock this must be. Let's sit. I believe we have much to talk about."

David sank into the chair, the worn fabric cool against his skin. Mae's gaze held his, unwavering.

"April 21st, 2013," she began in a low voice, recalling a date imprinted in her memory. "The Sunday after the Boston Marathon bombing. We'd just come home from church. Paul, Sue, and I." She paused, her eyes flickering toward a distant point.

"Wakefield. The house where we lost Mable," Mae continued.

A tremor ran through David.

"Sue was eleven then. We'd adopted her seven years earlier." She paused again and the air grew thick with unspoken meaning. "A man waited on the porch. Malik Farnsworth, your father."

David's breath caught, his eyes snapping to hers. "You knew?" he asked. The question hung between them, raw and disbelieving.

"Yes," Mae said, her voice firm, "more than you realize. Paul and Malik's story goes way back, to their college days. They were friends, of some sort. Shared drinks, fleeting encounters..." She paused again, taking a deep breath and allowing the information to sink in for

David.

"Then, nothing. After... after everything you lost, after the accident, Malik disappeared. He walked away from his life, his career. A clean slate," she continued. "He found another canvas... art... a therapeutic hobby at first. Paul saw him in Boston, his art drawing attention as people gathered to view his collection of work."

Mae's gaze drifted to the framed piece on the wall, her eyes lingering on the intricate details. "In 2004," she murmured, "after we lost Mable, Malik came by. He brought that." She said, gesturing toward the artwork.

"He called it 'Mr. Owl.'" A sigh escaped her lips. "It wasn't until that Sunday, after the bombings, that I understood," Mae said, shifting in her chair, her expression hardening.

"He was agitated... frantic. He paced, his words tumbling over each other. He kept circling back to the bombing, how easily it could have been us. Then, he started talking about 'what ifs.' What if time could bend? What if we could erase the pain, undo the past? What if he could bring back his family? What if Mable..." Her voice trailed off, the unspoken name hanging heavy in the air. "'What would you change if given the chance?' he said."

"So, you knew he was trying to build the Alcubierre Drive, a time machine?" David asked.

"Not until then," Mae said, her voice barely a whisper, as a shadow crossed her face.

She paused, as if gathering the strength to continue with the story. "He started with the Athena Project. The name alone sent a chill through Paul and I." She looked at

David, her eyes filled with knowledge. "Malik, Paul, Robert... they were all participants. Recruited, like lab rats. They had no idea what was being done to them, not then. They went on with their lives, blind to the truth. Until 1999." She paused again, the silence between them stretching.

"Three years after... after everything. He went to a book signing. Dr. Leonard Friston. *Induction Theory and Cognitive Sciences*." Mae's voice dropped an octave. "The phrase was buried within the pages: *Mr. Owl Ate My Metal Worm*. Malik read it, and something... shifted. A darkness settled over him. Time travel became his obsession, fueled by grief, a relentless, consuming fire."

She paused again. "It wasn't just a theory; it was a compulsion. He recited the phrase to Paul, perhaps as a desperate plea for understanding. He sought out Robert, offering the same cryptic words, perhaps in a shared burden." She shuddered slightly. "He saw a chance, a twisted logic. Three fathers, three losses. Mable, Marcus... your sister. He believed they could build it, a machine to erase their pain, to rewrite time."

David's voice was flat and lacking emotion as he stated, "They didn't join him. They couldn't." He paused, a bitter understanding settling over him. "What my father didn't know... was that they weren't all given the same induction words. Different directives, different instructions. Each man steered in a separate direction."

Mae's head dipped, silently acknowledging David's words.

"Yes. Each man followed a different path... a different

directive." She paused, her voice heavy. "Paul was lucky... his obsession took root in the blueprints for a lake house. Robert..." She trailed off, a flicker of pain in her eyes. "His story is a tragedy we both know too well." She shuddered slightly. "Then, the dreams began. Paul would wake, his skin clammy, his eyes wide with fear. He'd describe the owl, its white feathers stark against the darkness, those yellow eyes burning into him. Then, the man in white, distorted, inverted, a phantom of Dr. Friston. The lingering remains of the Athena Project."

David unfolded a worn piece of paper and placed it on the table between them.

"Seven years," he began, his voice low, "a hospital room, a dying man. No name, just a *John Doe.*"

He tapped the paper, the sound sharp in the quiet room. "He knew my name. Knew things he shouldn't. He gave me this." He paused, letting the weight of the moment settle. "This list led me to Hannah. To you. To the lake house. It led me to Nella. And it led me..." His voice trailed off, the unspoken words hanging in the air.

Mae's voice cut through the silence. "The list. I know it." She paused, a hint of finality in her tone. "And I know the answers you're searching for."

David's eyes flickered down to the folded paper, then back to Mae. "The puzzle is nearly complete," he said, his voice low and firm. "Everything you've told me... it fits. Almost. Just two pieces remain."

Mae's gaze held David's, unwavering. "You want to know how it is that I appear so young?" she asked, the question hanging in the air.

David's eyes narrowed, a flicker of suspicion in their depths. "And?" he prompted, his voice low.

"And you also want to know who was the man who gave you the list," Mae said, her tone flat. "Your 'John Doe.'"

David nodded, his jaw tightening. "Was it Paul?" he pressed, posing the question as a challenge.

Mae's lips curved into a thin, almost unsettling smile. "Paul dismissed your father's obsession as madness. But I..." She paused, her eyes glinting. "I saw an opportunity."

David's breath hitched, his eyes widening. "You?" he breathed, the single word full of disbelief.

Mae's voice cracked, full of raw pain. "Inside," she whispered, her eyes glistening with unshed tears, "I was consumed by guilt. Mable... I never forgave myself."

She clenched her hands, her knuckles turning white. "I didn't need some implanted directive to crave a second chance. When your father offered a sliver of hope, I seized it. If I could rewrite one moment, just one... it would be that day, by the swing set."

David's voice trembled in a mix of desperation and confusion. "Five days ago," he said, his words rushed, "Nella and I... we stopped him. At Cathedral Rock. The Alcubierre Drive. We stopped my father, I think. Because nothing's changed. Except you!" He gestured wildly. "You weren't there. You weren't caught in the machine. You weren't sent back."

"I was there, David," she said, her voice low. "Not in this timeline, not the one you see now." She paused, her eyes searching his. "The Mae consumed by grief, the one who would have given anything to rewrite the past, to save Mable. The older woman you and Hannah met at the lake. The one you came to know."

David shook his head, trying to clear the fog from his mind, to fully and clearly understand what she was telling him.

"That trip five days ago," Mae said, "it wasn't the first time he'd done it."

David's mouth fell open in utter shock. He rose abruptly, his feet carrying him to the patio door. He stared out at the landscape, his mind conflicted.

Not the first time? The words replayed in his head.

Mae rose, her footsteps silent as she joined David at the patio door. "The older me," she began, her voice low, "chose a different path. She went with your father." She paused, her gaze distant. "They entered the drive together. When they emerged, the world was different. He was frantic, raw terror in his eyes. He stole a car, a hasty, desperate act. They sped toward Route 64, near the Canyon." She shuddered slightly. "At a gas station, they saw her. Your mother. He tried to reach her, to stop her, but she recoiled. He was a stranger to her, aged, bearded, disheveled. Panic seized her. She fled, and they pursued."

A single tear fell from David's cheek. Mae's hand settled on his shoulder in a gesture of comfort.

"It was him, David," she said softly. "Your father, in his desperate attempt to change the past, caused the very tragedy he sought to prevent. When he realized what he had done, he fled. He spent the next two decades haunted, trying to undo his own actions."

She paused, her voice heavy with sorrow. "He was your 'John Doe.' The list... it was his confession, his atonement. A way to guide you, to give you the means to stop him, without shattering the fragile balance of time."

David turned to face Mae, his gaze searching hers, his expression a mixture of understanding and lingering doubt.

"It all clicks into place now," he said, his voice low. "His knowledge, the way he anticipated my every move, the breadcrumbs... it was him, guiding me." He paused, his eyes narrowing slightly. "But what about you? Did you succeed? Did the older you change Mable's fate?"

"The moment your father left our house in 2013... the day he asked Paul to join him," Mae said, her voice heavy with the weight of the decision, "I knew. I would join his obsession. I would give up my life with Paul and Sue. I would have done anything to change the past..." She paused, her expression shifting. "But then, the impossible happened. A knock at the door. And there she stood... me. The older me, the one from the future."

David's eyes widened. "No paradox?" he blurted out.

Mae's lips curved into a soft smile. "No," she said. "The universe didn't implode. No cosmic catastrophe. Though.." She chuckled softly. "I nearly collapsed on the porch. Seeing myself... it was a shock. We talked, for hours. Once the initial shock wore off and I could convince myself I wasn't hallucinating, she told me everything."

Mae took a deep breath before continuing. "She told me that she'd returned to speak to the younger me, the one consumed by regret, the one who blamed herself for Mable. She shared her journey, revealing that everything I sought, everything I yearned for, was here, in this moment." As she said this, a gentle smile touched her lips. "So, a few weeks ago, when the machine was ready and your father called, his voice filled with desperate hope, I said no. I stayed. I didn't repeat the mistake she once made. I closed my loop."

David was stunned. He couldn't help but ask, "But what happened with Mable? Didn't the older you try to stop her death?"

Mae remained silent.

At this, David was suddenly hit by a startling realization. "Mable," he said, the name hanging heavy in the air. "Wait... The older you, she couldn't change the past, could she?"

Mae's head dipped, a shadow falling across her face. "She recounted her journey," Mae began, her voice heavy with the weight of the past. "Her arrival in Boston, the solitary job, the gnawing loneliness." She paused, her gaze distant. "Eight years... eight years she waited for that single moment, to save Mable."

A sigh escaped her lips.

"She witnessed history unfold all over again, the events we all remember—9/11, the Red Sox World Series victory. She even observed our dying mother, concealed behind scrubs and a mask, a secret, painful goodbye." Her voice dropped to a whisper.

"She was cautious... terrified of the consequences. She knew the risks, the potential for erasure, the destruction of everything she held dear." She paused, her voice laced with sorrow. "And in those years, she ached for Paul and Sue.

The price of her choice... the stolen moments, the lost memories."

Mae drew a deep, shuddering breath, her shoulders rising and falling.

"The day came," she continued. "She tied a scarf around her head, as a disguise, and walked the familiar road. She saw us, the younger me and Mable, walking down the sidewalk. Mable went to the swings. She walked up the driveway, toward the gate. It felt like an eternity, a lifetime of yearning for this single moment to change."

She paused, her voice trembling. "Mable climbed the monkey bars. She called out, a desperate plea for her to come down. Mable looked up. Fear flashed in her eyes, a child's terror at the sight of her mother... aged, altered. Their eyes met, and Mable slipped, her small body falling through the bars, the rope ladder tangling around her neck."

David's breath hitched, a sharp intake of air. Mae's gaze met his, her eyes filled with sorrow. "She turned and walked away," Mae said, her voice a low, painful recounting. "By the time she reached the sidewalk, the sound of my screams pierced the air. She understood then, just as your father had. She was the catalyst, the cause of Mable's death."

David's voice was barely a whisper, a resigned acceptance. "No matter how many times he may try," he said, his gaze fixed on a distant point, "the Alcubierre Drive... it was an invariant loop. An unchangeable cycle."

Mae's lips curved into a gentle smile, her eyes reflecting a deep understanding. "It was a fixed point," she said, her voice soft, "a gateway to a single moment, but not a tool for alteration. The past remained immutable." She paused, her gaze meeting David's. "I'll never forget her words, the older me. 'You can't change your yesterdays, but you can change your tomorrows!'"

David's gaze shifted, his curiosity piqued. "Where is she now?" he asked, his voice laced with a hint of longing.

Mae's gaze softened, a hint of melancholy in her eyes. "The Mae you knew," she said, "the one we both knew... we understood, that if your father's journey ended, if I never repeated her steps, this day would arrive." She paused, her voice tinged with a quiet sadness. "She would simply... cease to be."

Mae's arm slid around David in a warm, reassuring embrace. "I miss her too," she murmured, her voice soft against his ear. "We were fortunate to know her, to see the woman I aspire to be." She paused, her grip tightening slightly. "She was a grandmother to Sue and Luna, a guiding presence." She gently squeezed his arm. "And remember, I'm still here. Still Mae. Perhaps not as seasoned, but still me."

She rubbed his shoulder soothingly. "Your father taught us something valuable, something that doesn't require time travel. Resentment chains us to the past, a place beyond our reach. Forgiveness, however, opens the door to the future, a future we can shape."

David's fingers held up the worn paper he'd carried for years. He turned to Mae, the list before them. "You've explained your path," he said, his voice low and steady, "but a question remains. How do I know he succeeded?

How do I know he closed his own loop?"

He paused, his brow furrowed. "When we met in Sedona, at the chapel, I showed him this." He gestured toward the list. "He looked at it... like a stranger, confused. He spoke of his grief, of losing my mother and sister. Of giving me up. Of killing Hannah."

"The answer," Mae said, her voice gentle, "lies within the very question you ask. It's been with you all along."

A look of confusion clouded David's features. "I don't see it," he admitted, his voice laced with frustration.

"Think back," Mae prompted, her gaze unwavering. "You lost both your parents... the accident. That's the story you've always known. In this reality."

David's eyes widened as he finally understood. "He did it," he breathed, a sense of relief washing over him. "He closed the loop."

David looked down at the unfolded the paper, his gaze sweeping over the list, from number one to number eight. He looked up at Mae, dawning understanding in his eyes.

"Kill am, Malik," he said, his voice low, "item number 8... it was always his burden. That's why he looked at it with such confusion in Sedona, the list was by him and for him as a way of redemption."

He paused as a sense of finality settled over him. "Alone on that road, confronted by the consequences of his actions, he chose the only path left. He joined his family at the bottom of the canyon...he ended his own life, closing the loop, ending the cycle of tragedy."

"There's something else," Mae said. She rose and left the room, returning moments later with a sealed envelope.

She extended it to David. "She wanted you to have this. She said... the man you met at the hospital, your father, gave it to her to give to you. This is the father you should remember, not the twisted monster you met in Sedona."

David's fingers closed around the envelope, his name boldly written in black ink. He hesitated, then slid a finger beneath the seal, breaking it. He inhaled deeply, the scent of aged paper filling his nostrils, and unfolded the letter.

David's eyes scanned the paper, reading the words that seemed to be a raw, unfiltered confession.

My Dearest David,

The letter went on to speak of a journey, a path David had been forced to walk. It went on to acknowledge David's strength, a quality the father had only witnessed from a distance. Then the father's own pain, which had become a constant companion, mirroring David's own. It detailed a descent, an obsession with rewriting the unchangeable. A grief-fueled delusion. The list had not been a solution, but a path to a truth the father couldn't confront. An attempt at redemption, a desperate plea for understanding.

The words were a confession of desperate love, turned to despair. A final act, closing the loop, ending the pain. They resonated a painful honesty, a plea, an instruction. A final, heartbreaking truth.

David's breath hitched, the words echoing the feelings he had struggled with for years. His hand shook slightly as he finished the final line. He folded the letter with meticulous care, returning it to the envelope. A single tear traced a path down his cheek; a silent release of years of pain; a quiet acceptance of the forgiveness offered, and the finality of his father's journey.

He looked up at Mae, his eyes clear and calm. "He found his peace," he said, his voice a soft murmur, a confirmation of the truth he'd sought.

Mae nodded, her eyes reflecting the depths of David's journey. "They both did," she affirmed, her voice soft, "and so have you."

A wave of tranquility washed over David, and the accumulated heaviness he'd felt for years dissolved like mist in the morning sun. The relentless pursuit, the haunting grief, and the unanswered questions all lifted, leaving him unburdened. He was free, untethered from the past, and released from the futile desire to rewrite what was.

He scanned his surroundings, the familiar furniture offering comfort, the warm light a gentle embrace, and the woman before him a beacon of guidance and friendship. A sense of belonging settled within him.

"Thank you," he said, his voice filled with a quiet gratitude, "for everything, Mae."

"You were always meant to find this path, David." Mae's smile was warm and knowing.

"Remember," she said, her eyes filled with gentle wisdom, "the past is a closed book. Today is the canvas upon which you paint your life. And tomorrow... tomorrow is a blank page, waiting to be written." She paused, her gaze steady. "Forgiveness is the brush that allows you to move forward."

Just then, a ball struck the patio doors with a resounding rattle, then rolled away. David and Mae looked out through the glass, their attention drawn to the scene beyond. Luna, Lucy, Mae's Shih Tzu, and Nella were playing in the lush green grass, their laughter and excited shouts filling the air. Nearby, a middle-aged man and a younger woman stood watching, their faces filled with pure joy.

A familiar image, a ghost of a childhood dream, danced at the edge of David's vision. A woman, a little girl, and a dog, their laughter echoing across a still lake.

Dream or vision?

Hannah's voice, a gentle promise, resonated in his memory. "Someday, my love, I promise."

Recognition struck David like a physical blow. This was the moment foretold, the moment fate had delivered. A sense of family washed over him as his gaze settled on Nella; love and hope had returned to his heart.

Mae's smile widened, a playful glint in her eyes. "Looks like Nella has a new friend," she observed, nodding toward the scene outside. "I think some introductions are in order. Sue's eager to meet you, and Paul's full of excitement to meet the architect who restored his old barn."

"Paul?" David's eyebrows shot up, a surprised laugh escaping his lips.

Mae chuckled, a light, airy sound. "Time to wake up, David. We're not in Wonderland anymore!"

"God, I hope not. I don't know how much more I can take," David retorted, a wry smile playing on his lips.

"I think I've had my fill of the impossible."

A wave of laughter erupted from both of them, the sound filling the room, as a testament to their shared journey.

THE ABYSS

A sharp knock on the door cut through the silence of Dr. Friston's home. The sound was firm, insistent—demanding attention.

Dr. Leonard Friston exhaled heavily, placing his pen down beside the stack of notes he had been reviewing. The soft glow of the desk lamp flickered slightly as he pushed back his chair, the worn Persian rug beneath him muting his footsteps. He crossed the dimly lit room and reached for the brass knob of the kitchen door.

When he pulled it open, he already knew who would be standing there.

Malik.

Dr. Friston studied him for a moment. The man before him looked tense, eyes dark with something unreadable. There was a nervous energy in the way he stood, his hands curled into fists at his sides, his chest rising and falling with quick, shallow breaths.

"Ah, Malik," Dr. Friston said, his voice carrying a strange mix of weariness and expectation. "I've been expecting you. Come in."

Malik stepped inside without hesitation, moving straight to the kitchen counter. He placed a thick, hardcover book down with a dull thud.

"I came to return your book," Malik said, his voice tight, controlled. He ran a hand over the worn cover, his fingers pressing into the title: *Induction Theory and Cognitive Sciences*. He swallowed hard before continuing. "And I have something important to tell you."

Dr. Friston nodded, his expression unreadable. "Let's sit."

They moved to the living room, where two armchairs faced each other. The furniture was old, softened by years of use. The room smelled faintly of aged books and burning wood, the embers in the fireplace still glowing.

A long silence settled between them before Malik finally spoke.

"I did it, Dr. Friston," he said. His hands gripped the arms of his chair. "I discovered the equation for time travel. Your experiment worked. I executed the induction phase." He leaned forward, his voice sharpening. "I plan to go back and change the past."

Dr. Friston didn't react. He only studied Malik, his fingers tapping lightly against the arm of his chair. Then, finally, he spoke.

"I know," he said simply. "And you won't find what

you're looking for." His voice was quiet but firm. "It's an invariant…a time loop, Malik. A closed equation that never changes."

Malik's expression darkened. "That's not true," he snapped. His hands clenched into fists. "You don't understand!"

Dr. Friston glanced at the antique clock on the mantelpiece, watching the pendulum swing in steady rhythm. Tick. Tock. Tick. Tock.

Then, he turned back to Malik, his gaze steady.

"Do you remember the first time we met?" he asked.

Malik frowned, confused by the question. "Of course," he said. "MIT, 1988. I was a participant in your experiment."

Dr. Friston leaned forward, his voice softer now. "No, Malik. The first time we met was in 1982. A crisp fall day. Cambridge Research Institute. Long before the Athena Project was ever conceived."

Malik's body stiffened.

"You came to me," Dr. Friston continued, his eyes locked onto Malik's. "You were as old as you are now. Mid-fifties. You told me the most incredible story I had ever heard. You told me about the Athena Project, about how it worked—the induction words, the trigger phase, the implanted directives. You told me that you had traveled from the future and that that I had to carry out the experiment to ensure it happened." He exhaled slowly. "You said it worked…except for a slight miscalculation. You arrived fourteen years too early."

Malik's mind reeled. His breathing became uneven, his

heart pounding in his chest.

"I don't understand," he whispered. "I haven't even built the machine yet."

Dr. Friston shook his head. "Don't you see? You already traveled back in time. You couldn't change the past then, and you can't change it now. Yet here you are... repeating the same implanted directive."

Malik pressed his hands against his temples. His head ached, his thoughts spinning like a whirlwind.

"If what you're saying is true," he muttered, his voice trembling, "then you gave me the answer I was looking for. You confirmed that time travel works. And that means I can go back and fix it." His eyes flashed with desperation. "Do you know what you did to me? To all of us?" His voice rose. "You scrambled our brains, left us with dreams we couldn't explain! No follow-ups, no warnings— nothing! But it's all crystal clear now. The owl that sits on my chest in my dreams... the logo for the Athena Project, the feathers of gold and then walls of mold, the reflective curtain you used to surround my body, and the upside-down man... it was you. It was always you."

"Malik, I am sorry." Dr. Friston's face darkened with regret. "No one could have stopped me either," he admitted. "Like you, I was blinded by the idea that it could work. I too was driven by your visit from the future, my experiment being possible. You convinced me and I never considered the consequences." He sighed. "But you can. Yes, it works, but it's nothing more than an invariant loop. You have done all this before, and you are trying again." Dr. Friston leaned closer, his voice urgent now.

"Think about your life. Has anything changed? Is Molly alive? Is Bethany safe? Did you stop the accident?" His voice softened. "No. And you never will."

The words struck Malik like a physical blow. His breath came shallow and quick, his mind screaming for a way out.

"Please, Malik," Dr. Friston pleaded. "You can't change what's already happened. But you can change what happens next. End this cycle and let go of this madness before you destroy yourself... don't end up like Robert."

Malik stood abruptly. His entire body was tense, vibrating with rage and desperation.

"No," he said. "I don't believe you." His voice was sharp, final. "You're just trying to stop me. Are you the one giving the boy the clues, the list of items to help him stop me."

He turned toward the kitchen, but Dr. Friston followed, his voice growing urgent.

"Malik, I don't know anything about a boy or clues, but don't do this!" he warned. "If you continue down this path, I'll have no choice but to report this to the authorities."

Malik stopped. Slowly, he turned back, his expression unreadable.

"Stop me?" he repeated, his voice eerily calm. "I'm here to stop you."

In one swift motion, he lunged forward, grabbing Dr. Friston by the collar and shoving him backward. The old man's back slammed against the basement door.

"Malik!" Dr. Friston gasped, struggling. "Listen to me—it doesn't matter what you do to me. The past will never change. What has happened before will happen again. You are trapped in an unchanging loop. Do you even know which version of yourself you really are?"

Malik hesitated for half a second. Then, his grip tightened.

"I know one thing," he said, voice raw. "My love for what I lost—Molly, Bethany, my son—transcends all time." His eyes burned with conviction. "What would you change if given the chance?"

Dr. Friston's breathing was labored. He met Malik's gaze, his own eyes filled with something Malik couldn't quite name.

"I would change the future," he said. "Because that's the only thing I can change. And so can you. Find the strength to end this. You must open your eyes and see it for yourself... only you can bring an end to the time loop!"

Malik said nothing. His fingers twitched.

Then, slowly, he pulled open the basement door. A dark stairwell stretched downward, disappearing into shadows.

Dr. Friston swallowed hard. He looked down, then back at Malik. His voice was barely a whisper.

"A man looks into the abyss," he murmured. "And there, he sees nothing staring back at him. In that moment, the man finds his character. And that is what keeps him out of the abyss."

Malik's gaze flickered to the darkness below. Then, back to Friston.

"Sorry, Doctor," he said coldly. "I already live in the abyss, and I can't let you stop me from finding a way out."

Then, with one final push, he sent Dr. Friston tumbling

down the stairs. The sickening *thud* echoed through the house.

Malik turned and walked toward the door. He passed the book on the counter, hesitated, then picked up a sticky note. He scribbled something, pressed the note onto the counter, and walked out.

As the door swung shut behind him, the sticky note fluttered slightly in the draft.

Thank you for giving me
the answers I seek.
—Emit Pool

ABOUT THE AUTHOR

A.G. SULLIVAN

Award winning author A.G. Sullivan grew up on Cape Cod in the small town of Dennis Port, Massachusetts. Since his youth he loved the art of story-telling. He studied at the Boston Architectural Center and later at the University of Phoenix, earning his degree in 1999. He lives in Arizona and enjoys spending time with his blended family.

Known for his young adult *Katzenstein Kids Trilogy* as well as his adult thrillers *Trypophobia* and *Invariant*. His work has earned him 5-STARS from READERS' FAVORITE, as well as a FIREBIRD BOOK AWARD.